ST. CHARLES PUBLIC LIBRARY

3 0053 003

W9-BNP-615

FIC O'MARIE

O'Marie, Carol Anne
        Death goes on retreat

14N95

OT 12/95
LM

56 x 2/11

ST. CHARLES PUBLIC LIBRARY
ONE SOUTH SIXTH AVENUE
ST. CHARLES, ILLINOIS 60174

DEMCO

DEATH GOES ON RETREAT

Also by Sister Carol Anne O'Marie:

A NOVENA FOR MURDER
ADVENT OF DYING
THE MISSING MADONNA
MURDER IN ORDINARY TIME
MURDER MAKES A PILGRIMAGE

⊰❖DEATH❖⊱ GOES ON RETREAT

SISTER CAROL ANNE O'MARIE

ST. CHARLES PUBLIC LIBRARY DISTRICT
ONE SOUTH SIXTH AVENUE
ST. CHARLES, ILLINOIS 60174

Delacorte Press

PUBLISHED BY
DELACORTE PRESS
BANTAM DOUBLEDAY DELL PUBLISHING GROUP, INC.
1540 BROADWAY
NEW YORK, NEW YORK 10036

COPYRIGHT © 1995 BY SISTER CAROL ANNE O'MARIE

ALL RIGHTS RESERVED. NO PART OF THIS BOOK MAY BE REPRODUCED OR
TRANSMITTED IN ANY FORM OR BY ANY MEANS, ELECTRONIC OR MECHANICAL,
INCLUDING PHOTOCOPYING, RECORDING, OR BY ANY INFORMATION STORAGE AND
RETRIEVAL SYSTEM, WITHOUT THE WRITTEN PERMISSION OF THE PUBLISHER, EXCEPT
WHERE PERMITTED BY LAW.

THE TRADEMARK DELACORTE PRESS® IS REGISTERED IN THE U.S. PATENT AND
TRADEMARK OFFICE.

LIBRARY OF CONGRESS CATALOGING IN PUBLICATION DATA

O'MARIE, CAROL ANNE.
    DEATH GOES ON RETREAT / SISTER CAROL ANNE O'MARIE.
        P.   CM.
    ISBN 0-385-31047-1
    I. TITLE.
    PS3565.M347D43   1995
    813'.54—DC20   95-8458
                                                                     CIP

BOOK DESIGN BY NANCY FIELD

MANUFACTURED IN THE UNITED STATES OF AMERICA

PUBLISHED SIMULTANEOUSLY IN CANADA

DECEMBER 1995

10 9 8 7 6 5 4 3 2 1

BVG

DEDICATION

In memory of "the real Sister Mary Helen,"
Sister Mary Helen Pettid,
a dear friend and mentor,
who went home to her God on May 17, 1993,
after ninety-two years of selfless living.

May He be enjoying her wit, her charm,
and her unconditional and uncompromising love.
And may she be resting in His eternal peace.

3 0053 00371 5466

Sunday, June 20

Father's Day

Day One

"We'll be there in a jiffy!" Sister Anne took one hand off the steering wheel and pointed to the mud-spattered road sign. "Santa Cruz County. Elevation eighteen hundred feet."

Just get us there alive, Mary Helen thought with a frozen smile. When Anne whizzed past the lonely Summit Inn, she heard Sister Eileen suck in her breath. Mary Helen was surprised. Eileen, sitting stiffly in the backseat, was always a bit of a daredevil; the sort who loved a roller-coaster ride. Apparently Anne's driving was too much even for her.

Mary Helen tried to distract herself. Shoving her glasses up the bridge of her nose, she stared out the car window at the trees and underbrush that grew alongside the twisting Highway 17. Hoping Anne didn't notice, she closed her eyes at the precise moment the young nun leaned the convent Nova into yet another series of turns for the descent.

This stretch of road, through the Santa Cruz Mountains from the Santa Clara Valley to the coast, was considered so dangerous that Cal-Trans had constructed a low cement divider along most of it to prevent head-on collisions.

Despite its treacherousness, the three nuns breezed along.

All the traffic seemed to be on the other side of the highway, coming back from the beach. Any cars ahead of them, Anne simply passed.

"Isn't Vine Hill Road the turnoff?" she asked her two numb passengers. Before either could answer, a brown and gold sign proclaimed in large, bold print, ST. COLETTE'S RETREAT HOUSE, 3 MILES. The arrow pointed into the hills.

Signaling, Anne made what Mary Helen considered a death-defying left-hand turn. She glanced behind her. Eileen, her soft, broad face wrinkled into a frown and her eyes squeezed shut, fingered her Rosary beads.

Vine Hill Road, which might more aptly be named "Pothole Lane," had one advantage. It slowed Sister Anne down to a jolting twenty miles per hour.

At first, redwood and fir trees formed a dark tunnel. With bracken brushing against the car wheels, they ascended the hill until the ground at their left fell away and they looked down, much as birds might, on a valley of gigantic evergreens. The only signs of human life were a honeycomb of mailboxes set back in a clump of live oak, and a stumpy telephone pole.

Just when Mary Helen feared they were completely lost, another small sign pointed the way up an even narrower road.

"This is just like being way out in the country." Eileen's words bumped up from the backseat.

Mary Helen nodded. Actually, that was exactly why she had chosen to spend a week at this retreat center. Although St. Colette's was only sixty-five miles south of San Francisco, its brochure stressed the remoteness, the quiet, and the access to all the beauties of the redwood forest.

That and the glorious colored pictures convinced her that St. Colette's was the perfect place for her annual retreat. She was so enthusiastic about it that Eileen decided to join her. They both needed it. The two old nuns had spent a particularly difficult academic year at Mount St. Francis College, what with their pilgrimage to Spain having resulted in a murder investigation and its aftermath back home. But better not to think of all that now.

Retreat was the time to "come apart and rest awhile." She had chosen a quiet, beautiful spot in which to greet her God and to realize, once again, His continual, loving presence and the strength of that love.

Mentally, she unpacked her suitcase: her Jerusalem Bible, her book of the Divine Office, a well-worn copy of the Life of Teresa of Avila, hiking shoes, windbreaker, and several cotton skirts and blouses. She'd toyed with the idea of buying a pair of comfortable slacks, the kind that Sister Anne often wore. But a quick comparison of their girths cooled that notion, pronto!

Sister Blanche, the college's science teacher, had insisted that Mary Helen take along a lovely little book full of photographs entitled *Plants of the Coast Redwood Region*. "That way you'll know what you're looking at," Blanche said.

These books, plus the retreat master's conferences, should give her plenty to think about. A Father Percival Dodds was to be the retreat master. She'd never heard of the priest. Lest he turn out to be a bore, just before they left the college she'd tucked *The Chartreuse Clue* into her pocketbook.

"Isn't that a mystery?" Eileen had asked with more innocence than was genuine.

"Isn't religion itself a mystery?" Mary Helen was equal to her old friend. "Aren't we going away on retreat in part to wrestle with life's mysteries? Why, this particular book features a Catholic bishop as a kind of Nero Wolfe. And it was written by a former priest. That qualifies it as a holy book of sorts.

"Furthermore, it fits perfectly into my plastic prayer-book cover. If that isn't providential, I don't know what is."

Eileen simply rolled her large gray eyes.

Although no living soul was behind them, Sister Anne hit the signal lever for a left turn.

Now she gets cautious, Mary Helen thought as the car slowly descended the steep driveway into St. Colette's. Gigantic redwoods surrounded a valley of low wooden buildings with bright orange shingled roofs that she recognized from the brochure. The entrance itself was guarded by a terra-cotta statue of St. Francis holding a rabbit and petting a wolf. Although a few cars were in the parking lot, the center was deserted except for two enormous, noisy German shepherds whose clamor didn't seem to bother the birds swooping down on the brightly blooming flower beds. The dogs, tails wagging, ran up to the car and barked ferociously.

Eileen peered out of the car window. "I never know which end to believe," she said.

"Where is everybody?" Opening the car door, Anne began to rub the huge animals behind their ears. Before long, romping playfully, they followed her toward a half-glass door marked OFFICE. "I'll ring the bell," she said, "to make sure you two get in."

"You go on," Eileen spoke up. "You want to get to your father's house for dinner and you don't have much time to spare. Wish him a happy Father's Day for us."

Anne hesitated, then began to pull the suitcases from the Nova's trunk.

"We'll get in," Mary Helen assured her, raking her fingers through her short gray hair to smooth it. After the ride it must surely be standing on end.

"We are probably just a little early. I didn't expect you to get us here so quickly. Traffic and all," Mary Helen added, hoping she hadn't sounded critical.

After all, Anne had done them a big favor dropping them off. The convent car that Mary Helen signed out for retreat had broken down. Again! Eileen and she would be on the bus, if Anne hadn't offered to drop them. She could just as easily have driven directly to her parents' home in San Mateo to celebrate Father's Day.

"If you're sure." Mary Helen recognized a look of concern in Anne's hazel eyes.

"We will be just fine." Eileen patted her hand.

"What could possibly go wrong in an idyllic setting like this?" Mary Helen asked. She wasn't positive, but she thought Anne did a double take.

"I'll pick you up on Saturday, then. Have fun!" Anne called over the rev of the motor.

"And to think she worries about us," Eileen said, watching the convent Nova exit amid swirling dust and barking dogs.

With Anne on her way, Sister Mary Helen walked to the office door and pressed a small button doorbell. She waited, then pressed it again. No answer.

The top half of the door was made of what looked like wine-bottle bottoms and was impossible to see through.

"Maybe we are expected to walk right in." Eileen glanced warily at the dogs who, tired of chasing Anne's car, were loping down the hill.

"How do?" Mary Helen sang out, pushing back the door. Quickly the two nuns stepped into a lobby of sorts. A sudden draft banged the door shut. The bottle bottoms gave an ominous rattle. That kind of glass, Mary Helen remembered, was all the rage in the sixties. Glancing around, she realized that the entire room had a sixties look: paneled walls, Danish chairs covered in lime-green and orange vinyl, a small swag lamp in the corner.

Beyond was a smaller office with the door ajar.

"How do?" Mary Helen called out again.

An invisible hand pushed the inner door, which closed with a soft click, shutting out all but the low hum of a telephone conversation. Although the words were not clear, the tone certainly was. The speaker was extremely agitated.

"What do you suppose is going on?" Mary Helen whispered.

Eileen set her mouth primly. "Whatever it is, it does not concern us," she said. "Maybe we should step outside."

The heavy bodies of the barking dogs slammed against the front door, rattling the glass again.

"Do you want to?"

"Not on my longest day." Eileen moved closer to Mary Helen.

Without warning the door to the inner office flew open. A short, solid, habited nun with flaming apple cheeks stepped out.

"Sorry to keep you waiting," she said in a high-pitched, distracted voice. "I am Sister Felicita."

At the moment you look anything but blissful, Mary Helen thought, introducing herself and Sister Eileen.

Sister Felicita, smelling faintly of lavender, smiled uncertainly. Her large, pale blue eyes blinked behind rimless glasses. "How can I help you?" she asked, tucking her hands beneath the black scapular hanging loosely from her shoulders and covering her black habit.

Except for a horseshoe-shaped white coif circling a tuft of ash-colored angel hair and a small pointed collar, everything Sister Felicita wore was black: her shoulder-length veil, the nylon stockings filling the gap between her mid-calf skirt and her sturdy black shoes. She's a little "sixties" too, Mary Helen noted wistfully. How easy her packing must be!

Rifling her pocketbook in search of their confirmation letter, Mary Helen tried to determine Felicita's age. The habit, the almost entirely covered hair, and the full face made it hard to pinpoint.

Something about the way gravity was already pulling Felicita into a pear shape made Mary Helen place the nun in her late fifties.

When Felicita's left hand fluttered out from behind her scapular to take the letter, Mary Helen knew she was right. Hands are a dead giveaway.

Just a kid, she thought, congratulating herself. She always considered anyone twenty or more years her junior a "kid." And she fully intended to keep right on doing so, although there were more and more "kids" around these days.

Without warning Felicita's face turned the color of Brie cheese. "You're a week early!" she blurted out.

Mary Helen grabbed back the letter and shoved her bifocals up the bridge of her nose. "It clearly says June twenty-seventh. Isn't today the twenty-seventh?"

"No, old dear," Eileen whispered. "It is the twentieth."

Mary Helen bristled at the "old dear." This was not an age issue. It had nothing whatsoever to do with age. It was a mistake that anyone with a busy schedule could easily make. God knows, her schedule was busy enough to confuse someone half her age.

"Now you tell me!" she snapped at Eileen.

"Now you ask me!" Eileen snapped back. "But, no harm." Always optimistic, Eileen had obviously hit upon a solution. "We can still make whatever retreat we are on now."

"That's impossible." Red splotches returned to Felicita's cheeks.

"Nothing's impossible!" Mary Helen frowned. That was the trouble with "kids"; they couldn't see the options. "What retreat are you having?"

"A diocesan priests' retreat." Sister Felicita said, then giggled. "And frankly, I could use some company!"

+I+   +I+   +I+

Over a cup of coffee in a tiny collation room off the kitchen, Mary Helen explained that Sister Anne had dropped them off, and since they didn't have her parents' phone number and didn't want to disturb her until morning anyway, they were for all practical purposes stranded.

Thoughtfully, Felicita traced small circles on a plastic tablecloth. "Maybe it's providential," she said. "The retreat actually starts tomorrow, but a few of the priests have already arrived. And just as you pulled up I received a phone call from Bakersfield."

"Oh?" Mary Helen perked up. Maybe they'd find out why Felicita was so upset when they arrived.

"The other four nuns . . . There are only five of us here to run this huge place. But that's another story. They went to the funeral of one of our benefactors in Bakersfield. A fine, generous man. . . ."

That's another story, too, Mary Helen thought, hoping she wouldn't get sidetracked.

"Someone had to stay home because of the priests' retreat." Felicita pursed her lips. "They were to be home late tonight. Sister Timothy assured me that the car was in perfect working condition." Red splotches reappeared on her cheeks. "And . . ."

"The blasted thing broke down." Mary Helen finished the sentence. Nuns are the same the world over, she mused. In coifs or out of coifs, Franciscans or Presentations or Mercys, teachers or retreat directors. We all have a Sister Timothy, and at least one sick car.

The loud, persistent clang of what sounded like an enormous gong filled the room and spread down the mountainside.

"That's our bell," Felicita explained unnecessarily. "Do you hear it?"

If I didn't hear that, the next thing I'd hear would be Gabriel's horn, Mary Helen thought, waiting for the noise to die out. It didn't.

"A benefactor gave it to us. It came from the old Berkeley ferry," Felicita shouted above the din. "A little nautical for a mountaintop, but it does the trick. We use it to call our guests to prayer, to the retreat conferences, to meals. Although sometimes Beverly overdoes it."

"Beverly?" In the distance, Mary Helen heard the dogs howling.

"Beverly is our cook. A wonderful chef, really, but a bit on the temperamental side." Felicita's pale blue eyes blinked rapidly. "Something must be wrong in the kitchen. You can always tell by the way she rings."

The clanging stopped as suddenly as it had begun, leaving its echo dying slowly among the trees.

"We had better go before she starts again." Avoiding the kitchen proper, Felicita led Mary Helen and Eileen out a side door and onto a wooden sundeck.

"If Beverly cooks as well as she rings, we are in for a treat," Eileen remarked cheerfully.

If she cooks as well as she rings, Mary Helen thought ruefully, she wouldn't be cooking here!

Although each building was separate, they all seemed to be connected by the sundeck. At least the main ones did. Felicita paused long enough to give them a taste of the panorama.

Drawing in a deep, woodsy breath, Mary Helen gazed out across a valley of redwoods, beyond the gorge to where ridge after ridge of the Coast Range rolled purple in the distance.

A hot sun falling just below the treetops on its slow descent into the Pacific, created a tranquil sky full of lavender and pink. Directly below the sundeck, long blue shadows stretched like fingers over the lawn and drew dark stripes across a sparkling swimming pool. An evening silence covered St. Colette's Retreat House. The heavens were declaring the glory of God. Mary Helen stood rapt in the beauty until the raucous call of a jay perched on the deck rail broke the spell. Apparently he had heard the dinner bell, too.

"Right this way." Felicita, plainly used to being immersed in all this loveliness, seemed anxious to get to the dining room. "We call it St. Jude's," she said, swinging back the heavy door. "He's the patron saint of desperate and impossible cases, as you know."

Eileen shot Mary Helen a warning look. Mary Helen stared back innocently. She had no intention of asking if its name had any connection to the food served, if that was what was worrying Eileen. After all, Mary Helen realized full well that, as hard as Felicita was trying to be hospitable, they were at best uninvited guests.

"When we first began this building, it seemed an impossible feat, so we prayed to St. Jude and—see!"

The two visitors looked around. St. Jude had outdone himself. The dining room was airy and spacious with walls of windows letting in the breathtaking view. Twelve, or maybe fifteen, brown Formica-topped tables were positioned around the room. Each had place settings and orange vinyl chairs for eight. Cylinder-shaped lights hung from the ceiling in groups of three.

"Looks as if a couple of the boys are already here," Felicita whispered.

Sister Mary Helen followed her glance toward the table in the far corner. The "boys," who were seated and sipping what appeared to be red wine, were two grown men in sport shirts and black slacks.

Mary Helen never understood why priests in "civvies"

neglected to change their trousers. Black pants were such a telltale.

"Ah, Sisters, join us." One of the priests, the older of the two, rose and pulled out a chair.

Although Mary Helen did not really know him personally, she recognized him as Monsignor Cornelius McHugh, pastor emeritus of St. Patrick's Church in downtown San Francisco. The monsignor was a senior statesman of sorts, confidant of archbishops past and present. With his regal posture and a full mane of hair the color of winter wheat, his picture at ground-breakings and other official affairs appeared frequently in the *San Francisco Catholic*.

"I'm Father Con McHugh," he said unnecessarily. "And this bright-looking fellow is Father Ed Moreno."

Moreno scrambled up from his chair.

"These two Sisters—" Felicita began the introduction, but Con McHugh interrupted.

"Anyone who reads the *Chronicle* knows who these two are. As a matter of fact, when we saw you come in, Ed said, 'I hope we're going to be safe.' Didn't you, Ed?"

"You're full of it, old man." With a hearty laugh, Ed Moreno shook hands with Eileen, then turned to Mary Helen. She was surprised that the short, wiry fellow had such broad shoulders, big hands, and an almost painfully strong grip. He must lift weights or squeeze clamps or something, she thought.

They had just settled down at the table when the kitchen door was flung open. A large woman in a grease-spattered apron stood there, grim-faced. Her hair, pushed unconvincingly into a net, lay on top of her head like a untidy haystack.

"Are they all here yet?" she asked. Her impatient eyes strafed the room for hidden diners.

"They are on their way, I'm sure." Felicita looked toward the monsignor.

"Just give us five minutes, Beverly," he said with the ease of one used to being in charge. "Then, ready or not, here you come."

Without a word or even a change of expression, the woman disappeared back into the kitchen, leaving the door swinging in her wake.

"I see Heavy Bevy is her usual happy self." Ed Moreno lifted the wine bottle from the floor beside his chair. He filled three more glasses.

"Drink up." Con McHugh pushed a glass toward each of the nuns. "From the looks of things, we might need it."

Mary Helen was not surprised to see Felicita take the first sip. From the tense expression on her face, she needed it. "Salute," Felicita said after the fact.

"Ed, here, works at Juvenile Hall in the city," the monsignor began. Before he went any further, the door to St. Jude's opened and three more men in sport shirts and black slacks sauntered into the large room.

"Get over here, you guys, before Heavy Bevy and her cleaver arrive," Ed called.

Felicita's cheeks blazed. "Shh, Father! What if she hears you?"

"I'll pretend Tom said it." Ed pointed to a tall, curly-haired priest with a crooked grin.

Mary Helen recognized Father Thomas Harrington, the articulate and much televised director of the Archdiocesan Communications Center. "Happy Harrington," he was called because of his easy grin.

"That man could charm honey from the bees," old Sister Donata said whenever she saw him on television.

And how will he fare with Beverly? Mary Helen wondered crazily while the monsignor made the formal introductions.

"This is Father Andrew Carr." He nodded toward a balding priest with a scruffy graying beard.

"We call him 'Handy Andy.'" Apparently Ed Moreno had a nickname for everybody.

"Why is that?" Eileen took the bait.

A flicker of annoyance shadowed the monsignor's face. Obviously he did not like to be interrupted. "Because he's always handy when the archbishop has a chaplaincy to dole out," he said. "Andy is now chaplain to the Police Department, the Fire Department, Alcoholics Anonymous, the Knights of Malta, and the whole Port of San Francisco."

"The guy is so busy he doesn't have time to shave," Ed Moreno quipped.

Ignoring him, Andy smiled at the nuns. "Jealousy is a sad thing, especially in a clergyman," he said.

"Last, and definitely least," the monsignor said, winking, "may I introduce you to Father Michael Denski."

A red flush began at Father Denski's jaw and spread quickly up his cheeks to his too-long sideburns.

"Father Denski is newly ordained. Right, Mike?"

With his smooth, unwrinkled face and wide, almost topaz-blue eyes, he reminded Mary Helen more of an altar boy than of a priest. How new? she wanted to ask. Again, Con McHugh supplied the information.

"It will be two years next week. Right, Mike?"

Father Denski nodded.

"Where are you stationed, Father?" Eileen asked kindly.

"He's got one of those cushy suburban jobs as associate pastor at St. Dunstan's in Millbrae," Moreno answered for him.

"Dunstan's a fine Irish saint." Eileen filled the tense silence that followed. "Nobly born, he became a monk and went on to reestablish monasteries, counsel kings, advise popes, teach at Canterbury. Besides that he was a noted musician and metalworker. And he illustrated manuscripts."

"How long did he live?" Mike Denski asked in amazement. It was the first time he'd spoken.

"If I remember correctly, he died at about seventy-eight," Eileen said, astonishing everyone but Mary Helen with her memory for trivia.

"You better get busy, Con," Ed Moreno teased.

Before anyone else could comment on Eileen's brief hagiography, a stainless-steel serving cart hit open the kitchen door. Beverly, her plain face red and damp with perspiration, launched it toward them like a guided missile.

With an angry thud, she flung down platters of beef stew, plates of steaming corn bread, and a tub of butter.

"If you want dessert, it's here." She pointed to the bottom of the cart, where individual Pyrex dishes full of lemon cup pudding steamed like a row of six-ounce volcanos. "Coffee's in the kitchen. And I'm done for today."

"Thank you, Beverly. This smells and looks delicious," Felicita said politely. "We'll see you then, tomorrow."

"I hope so," Beverly said ominously, leaving Mary Helen wondering if the cook was not coming or if she expected one of them to be missing.

Suddenly the loud, insistent barking of the German shepherds filled the room. "She's gone out to feed Rin and Tin-Tin, the two dogs," Felicita shouted over the din. "The noise won't last long."

As Felicita predicted, the uproar stopped as unexpectedly as it began. "Beverly really loves those dogs," she said apologetically.

In the distance Beverly's car door slammed. Everyone, especially Felicita, visibly relaxed. Like London after the Blitz, Mary Helen thought, watching the plates and platters being passed.

Although the cook's attitude had been unpalatable, her stew and corn bread turned out to be delicious. The priests and Sisters ate leisurely, enjoying good humor and good conversation.

Tom Harrington, quoting Benjamin Franklin, Mary Helen thought, announced a little thickly, "Wine is a constant proof that God loves us and loves to see us happy," and refilled the wineglasses.

While they talked, a slim girl with a nervous face and auburn hair done up in a French braid walked in and out, quickly gathering up the dishes. Felicita introduced her as Laura Purcell.

Long after Laura's last trip, the group continued to talk about their ministries, about the people they knew in common, about new trends in theology, world affairs, and the latest doings of San Francisco's rather autocratic archbishop, Norman Wright, whom Ed Moreno irreverently called "Absolute Norm."

The kitchen was quiet and the sky was filling with stars when Mary Helen, no longer able to stifle it, yawned.

"You're tired," Felicita said—too quickly. Obviously she was waiting for any excuse to call it a night. She looked relieved when Mary Helen admitted that she was.

While the priests talked on, the three nuns excused themselves.

"Sorry you're leaving us," Con McHugh said with a gracious nod. He sounded as if he really meant it.

Outside the sky was navy blue velvet pierced with stars that looked close enough to touch. Gravel crunched beneath their feet as Felicita led them across the deserted parking lot toward the dormitory buildings. "Be careful out here," she cautioned, "it's easy to turn your foot on a fallen acorn or a loose stone."

Slowly the three nuns moved across the dimly lit pavement. The German shepherds, like sentries, flanked them on either side, panting as if they'd just finished a long run.

The stillness surrounding them was so profound that Mary Helen heard a single pinecone fall to the ground. From somewhere a screech owl trilled and, as though on cue, thousands of crickets began wildly rubbing their tiny legs together.

"Is it always this peaceful?" Eileen asked, sucking in the cool night air.

As if in answer, a door slammed and someone ran across the parking lot. The dogs, alert, began to bark.

"Oh, shut up!" an angry voice shouted.

"Laura?" Felicita recognized it. "Is that you, dear?"

"Yes, Sister. It's me." The young woman stopped beneath one of the parking lot lights and waited for the nuns to reach her.

"I was in St. Agnes' Hall using the bathroom," Laura offered, although Felicita hadn't asked. Her thin face was still pink, and soggy. From recent tears, Mary Helen conjectured. A sprinkle of freckles stood out on her red nose. Straggly pieces of auburn hair, escapees from her French braid, hung in her face.

Sister Mary Helen hardly recognized her as the same quiet, intelligent-looking girl who had removed the dinner dishes. Laura looked as if she'd fought a decisive battle.

"What in the world are you doing here so late? I thought surely you'd have gone by now," Felicita said. "You must be exhausted."

Laura gave no indication that she had heard Felicita. "I have something to say to you, Sister."

"Yes, dear?" Sister Felicita blinked nervously. From Laura's tone of voice one knew that what she intended to say was not good.

Instinctively, Mary Helen and Eileen stepped back to give Felicita a little privacy.

Laura's green eyes were as hard as glass. "I quit!" she said, and with a stiff arm, pushed her folded apron into Felicita's unsuspecting hands.

Poor Felicita reeled back as if she'd been struck. "You quit? Oh, no, Laura. Why?"

"Why? I'll tell you why, Sister. I cannot . . . no, I will not, take one more moment of Beverly." Unexpectedly, she exploded like a boiler into furious sobs.

"There, there, dear." Felicita led the girl toward a wooden bench. "What happened?"

"I'm sorry, Sister," Laura hiccuped, "but I am so mad I can't stop crying. She's awful. She's just plain mean. Tonight, she used every pot, pan, and skillet in the whole place on purpose. I've been here, Sister, three months now, and I really need the job. I've tried, but I just can't take her.

"Nothing I do is ever right, no matter how hard I try. When she is nice, it's worse. It scares me, like she wants something from me." Laura shuddered and Felicita put her arm around the thin, rigid shoulders.

"When Greg came to pick me up, she told him to come back in two hours. She knows my car is dead and that he was going to pick me up for the show." Laura's green eyes blazed. "She makes me so mad, I could clobber her with one of her precious pots."

"Who is Greg?" Felicita asked, obviously trying to distract her.

"My boyfriend. Actually, he is—almost—my fiancé."

For the first time, Felicita seemed to remember Mary Helen and Eileen, who were standing a little apart. "Why don't you Sisters wait for me in St. Agnes'?"—she nodded toward the far redwood building with an alpine roof—"until Laura and I get this settled."

"It is settled," Laura said, her lips set in a thin line.

Before Felicita could protest or the other two nuns could

move, tires screeched and a pair of headlights swept across the parking lot.

The dogs pitched forward, barking and nipping at the wheels of a sporty white Camaro. When the driver switched off the motor, they seemed to lose interest and, with a perfunctory bark or two, went chasing after another supposed intruder in the underbrush.

"It's Greg," Laura said, standing up and smoothing her hair from her face. She forced a smile.

The door swung open and a broad-shouldered young man unfolded himself from the driver's seat. Although it was difficult to tell much in the dim light, Mary Helen thought him good-looking in a blond, sun-bleached, surfer sort of way.

"Are you okay, Laura?" he asked.

Quickly, Laura went to him, buried her face in his leather bomber jacket, and began to sob again.

"What's wrong, babe?" he asked. "Are you hurt or something?"

"Hurt?" She pulled herself away. "I am not hurt. I am furious. I am so mad I could scream."

"Sounds like you are," Greg teased.

"This is not funny, Greg," she said, although the anger was already seeping out of her tone.

"Beverly again?" he asked.

"Again! Still! Always! But I'm not taking it anymore, Greg. No matter how much we need the money, I quit!" Laura nuzzled her face back into the front of Greg's leather jacket.

Felicita groaned.

Greg enveloped Laura with his arms, pressed his chin onto the top of her head, and smiled helplessly at Felicita. "She ain't a redhead for nothing, Sister," he said.

The door of St. Jude's opened and a beacon of light spread across the parking lot. "I thought the priests' retreat started tomorrow," Greg said, staring at the laughing clerics framed in the doorway.

"A couple came early," Laura muttered, without ever moving her face from his chest. "That's what started all the trouble, I think."

Ed Moreno raised his hand in a wave and the group strolled across the blacktop.

"Let's go," Greg said quickly, "or we'll miss the last show."

"Maybe tomorrow, when Laura calms down, she and I can talk," Felicita appealed to Greg.

"I'm sorry, Sister." Laura's back stiffened. "I have had it."

With a stiff plastic smile, Felicita watched the car disappear over the hill and the five priests disappear into their building before she sank down on the bench. "She's had it?" Felicita sighed. One tear ran down her soft, round cheek and splashed onto her scapular. "What about me?"

A distinctive buzz reminded Mary Helen that, sitting on the bench, they were nothing more than the entree for the mosquitoes' main meal. "Is there someplace inside we can sit?" she asked.

"There's a small kitchenette in St. Philomena's Hall." Felicita removed her rimless glasses and dabbed her eyes with her snowy white handkerchief. She pointed to the nearest dormitory building.

"St. Philomena? Didn't the Church declare her persona non grata?" Mary Helen asked, more to distract Felicita than anything else.

"Don't tell her." Felicita nodded toward a statue of the saint illumined by one of the overhead lights. Philomena, dressed in her native toga, held a palm frond in her stone hand as a symbol of her martyrdom. "She's the one we prayed to for Beverly."

"Be careful what you pray for." Mary Helen smiled, paraphrasing the old Chinese proverb. "You just may get it!"

Over steaming cups of herbal tea, Felicita spilled out the whole story. "For years we had nothing but trouble finding a decent cook. We were desperate. Then Beverly came along. She had excellent recommendations. And lives not far away, over in the Bonny Doon area." She shrugged. "And so we didn't hesitate when she asked for a two-year signed contract. Actually, we were delighted.

" 'How long can a two-year contract be?' I asked Mother Superior at the time." Felicita scowled at her own foolishness. "Now I know!

"From her first day here, she began to alienate the other members of the staff. First, the women in the kitchen. Then the housekeepers. The ladies in the office. We can't keep a living soul! She even bothers Mr. King, the caretaker." Felicita's eyes blinked in disbelief. "And Mr. King is almost stone-deaf! The only ones who seem to like her are Rin and Tin-Tin. Maybe it's because she feeds them.

"And now, Laura. She's our fourth dishwasher since Beverly came. Do you have any idea how hard it is to find a dishwasher?"

Eileen shook her head.

"Worse than a cook. Next to impossible," Felicita sighed. "I had great hopes for Laura. She's a graduate student in drama here at the university and, as she said, she needs the job. When she didn't quit in the first few weeks, naively I thought she was happy. Actually, I thought Beverly rather liked Laura. She seemed to talk more to her than she talked to any of the others. In a friendly way, I mean."

"Why don't you simply fire the woman?" Eileen's dander was up.

"Our lawyer says she could sue. And Mother Superior fears a suit more than sin itself." Felicita caught herself. "Not that I blame her. We have so little and we've worked so hard for it, it seems silly to risk it all because we can't reason with one woman. That is, unless you've tried yourself."

"I take it you have."

Sister Felicita's pale blue eyes sparked. "Might as well spit in the wind. Pardon the expression. It just comes back at you. She knows she has us over a barrel."

"What exactly does she do?" Mary Helen was curious. The woman sounded like something right out of a gothic novel.

"It's like putting your thumb on mercury. No one who quits ever says exactly why. Most of them try to be kind. Saying such things as 'I need more hours,' or 'the commute is too hard,' or some such thing. And if you ask Beverly what happened, she falls into a rage, slamming pots. You saw her act tonight."

"Calling her on it does no good?" Eileen asked, obviously unable to believe it.

"It only makes matters worse."

"Monsignor McHugh seemed to know her. Maybe he could reason with her."

Felicita sighed. "Many of the priests know her. They come here with their parish groups. Believe it or not, she's worse to priests than to anyone. It is almost as if she hates them."

"How much of the contract is left?" Mary Helen asked, shuffling through her mind for the name of a Mount St. Francis alum who was a sharp contract attorney. She'd call Shirley, her secretary in the Alumnae Office, first thing in the morning.

"A year and two months," Felicita said. She made it sound like a lifetime sentence to Devil's Island.

Wearily, Felicita rose and rinsed out their teacups. "Nothing is up to par," she said, straightening up the counter. "I am continually training new help. No one knows how to make square corners anymore and, I swear, they don't see dirt. Even our staunchest supporters have mentioned it. Nicely, of course. But no one, however staunch, expects to come to retreat and begin by cleaning up the bathroom sink.

"That, plus the priests' being insulted every time they bring parishioners—how long will anyone continue to come?" Felicita suddenly looked very old and very tired. "It's taken us years, decades really, to build up our clientele. And once they are gone . . ."

Silently Mary Helen and Eileen followed Felicita across the deserted grounds. Their hostess insisted on showing them to their rooms in St. Agnes' Hall, although Mary Helen felt reasonably certain that, given the room numbers, they could find their own way.

Suddenly, she felt almost as tired as Felicita looked. Maybe it was the time of night or the herbal tea or just the pressure of preparing for retreat, leaving Mt. St. Francis College, and driving to Santa Cruz. Whichever, she was one guest who did not intend to examine the square corners on the bed, or the bathroom sink, for that matter. She doubted that she'd even get through the first few pages of her new mystery before sleep took over.

The gentle night wind rustled the leathery leaves of the bay trees, almost like wind chimes. The soft hum of the insects rose in the stillness. Ancient redwoods formed a dark, protective rim around St. Colette's, their thick, soft bark producing a profound quiet. Overhead the sky was awash with stars. Mary Helen found the bright North Star and marveled at its nearness.

No one would ever suspect, she thought, yawning as Sister Felicita fumbled with the door keys, that such turmoil could possibly exist in this citadel of peace.

Monday, June 21

Day Two

The mournful and persistent coo, coo, coo of a pair of doves finally woke Sister Mary Helen. Eyes shut, she lay in the comfortable bed wondering how it was possible that someone who slept through foghorns, sirens, garbage trucks, and Muni buses, not to mention the stream of traffic on Turk Street, could possibly be awakened by a mourning dove. Impossible, yet true! Worst of all, she could not fall back to sleep.

The hungry squawk of a blue jay startled her. It sounded so close. Was the bird in the room? Reluctantly Mary Helen opened her eyes. What was it Eileen always said about birds in the house? A sign of death?

She felt a sudden dread, but shrugged it off as nonsense. She had not quite recovered from the shock of discovering a dead body on her trip to Spain last year. That's all it was. If I'm not careful, I'll be expecting dead bodies everywhere.

Furthermore, she thought, searching for her slippers on the cold floor, how would a bird get in?

Shivering in the early morning chill, Mary Helen pulled back the heavy drapes. Below the window, a narrow sitting porch ran alongside the building. A noisy jay with a long, dark crest was perched on the rail. He tilted his head. Bold stump! Mary Helen thought as she and the bird eyed each other.

Beyond the porch lay a pageant of trees—sycamore and redwoods, madrone and spruce—as far as the eye could see. Fog rose from them like incense from some gigantic thurifer hidden on the valley floor. As the mist blended into the overcast sky, Mary Helen felt as if she were about to catch a magical glimpse of Brigadoon. Then with a twinge of regret she remembered that she must wait another whole week to enjoy seven days of all this beauty.

Not that she didn't enjoy her work in the Alumnae Office of Mount St. Francis College. She did. Very much, in fact. But the sudden change of plans—because they really couldn't stay on the priests' retreat—made her realize how much she had been looking forward to this retreat.

Tiptoeing into the bathroom between Eileen's room and her own, she listened for any "awake" sounds. All she heard was a low sough. Eileen was fast asleep.

Sister Mary Helen dressed quickly and warmly, then checked her wristwatch. Six-thirty. She'd have plenty of time for a walk before waking Eileen and calling Sister Anne to pick them up. What a perfect way to make her morning's meditation! Wasn't it William Cullen Bryant or some such poet who wrote, "The groves were God's first temples"?

As an afterthought, Mary Helen grabbed up her book on plants of the region. A guide to the cathedral, she thought whimsically.

Even before she reached the vestibule of St. Agnes' Hall, she smelled the aroma of coffee. Following her nose, she found a small glass electric pot and paper cups.

Felicita must be up, she thought, savoring the hot, rich taste. Most likely, poor Felicita hadn't slept very well. Before they left, Mary Helen must call Shirley about an alum attorney. Her secretary would be in the office by nine. It might make Felicita feel better to know someone else was interested in her problem.

Mary Helen blew on the hot coffee and scanned the notices pinned to the large bulletin board. There was a brief life of the patroness of the retreat center, St. Colette. "The renowned Franciscan mystic," it read, "lived two hundred years after Francis and Clare and reformed the Order of Poor Clares."

She really did a job, Mary Helen thought, sipping her coffee, since the Poor Clares are still one of the most austere Orders in the Church. . . .

There were guidelines on how to make a retreat; a warning about smoking in bed; and a list of the room numbers along with the names of the intended occupants. There was also a rather detailed map of the hillside Way of the Cross. A short blurb explained that the devotion was "a kind of pilgrimage in which one mentally visits the important scenes of Christ's Passion in Jerusalem. The Way of the Cross is made by stopping at fourteen stations indicating the path followed by Christ, bearing His cross from the palace of Pilate to Calvary. Each station is marked by a wooden cross."

Mary Helen studied the map. If it was to be believed, the distance between the crosses was short and the terrain not too hilly.

Zipping up her windbreaker, she left St. Agnes' and headed, literally, for the hills. Ivy partially covered the cliffs and the long shoots of periwinkle ran over onto the path. Sorrel with delicate pink blossoms carpeted the sloping hillside. In the distance she heard a stream gurgling.

Holding tightly to a manzanita branch, Sister Mary Helen straddled a shallow ditch. She began to puff.

A small black and white chickadee balancing on a

quivering tree branch eyed her nervously. "Sick, sick, sick," he drawled.

"You might be right," Mary Helen said aloud, starting to doubt the wisdom of scaling the hillside. At last she reached Station One. The stark wooden cross stretched ten feet into the air.

A sign warning CAUTION: STEEP PATH AHEAD made up her mind. One station was enough for her. The map on the bulletin board obviously had been drawn by an optimist. Or a physical-fitness freak. A sundial marked a fork. Mary Helen chose the flat trail leading to "Madonna Grove."

The grove was a veritable cathedral of gigantic redwoods. Logs created a boundary of sorts and the thick carpet of yellowing pine needles gave it a deep hush. A large terra-cotta Madonna set in a burned-out tree trunk was obviously what gave the clearing its name.

Mary Helen was delighted to spot a handmade wooden bench. Still puffing, she lowered herself onto it. She breathed in the peace. A curious quail appeared from the bracken, gave a sharp whistle, and scurried away. Absently, Mary Helen wondered what had become of the two dogs this morning.

She unzipped her jacket. Already the air was beginning to warm up. Today was going to turn into a hot one. She must remember to pack her bathing suit for next week. Actually, she must remember to buy a bathing suit for next week; then lose twenty pounds so that she'd have the humility to wear it.

In the deep quiet, the buzzing of the insects took on extraordinary volume. They seemed to be swarming just beyond one of the logs. What could it be? A ground nest, perhaps?

Wishing she had brought along a book on bugs as well as one on trees, Mary Helen walked toward the sound. Thousands of insects covered something. But what?

With her finger, she pushed her bifocals up onto the bridge of her nose, and bent forward for a closer look. An angry hornet buzzed dangerously close to her face. An army of bottle flies glinted green in the dawn light. Mary Helen felt a heavy thud in her chest that made her momentarily light-headed. Were those tennis shoes? Were the insects swarming over a pair of tennis shoes and up stiff, unmoving pant legs?

Had someone fallen facedown in the needles? Knocked himself unconscious? That's what happened, she thought. There was an acorn caught in the sole of one shoe. Surely whoever it was had slipped. Last night Felicita warned them that the rocks and cones could be treacherous.

"Shoo! Shoo!" Mary Helen cried, waving her hands. "Get away! Shoo!" she shouted. The insects billowed up like a buzzing cloud, then landed again.

"Shoo! Shoo! Shoo!" Flailing with her plant book, she swatted at the bugs, dislodging some, but it was like trying to shake iron filings from a magnet.

"Be all right. Be all right," she chanted over and over, louder and louder, as if shouting would make it so. Fighting down her repulsion, she grabbed one bug-blackened shoulder. Her hand slipped. She grabbed again. With great difficulty, she rolled the body over.

The mouth hung open. She swatted at the flies crawling along the thin brown scratch of blood that ran from the corner of it down to the chin. Pale blue eyes stared up at her, flat and unseeing. The shirt and leather jacket were blood-soaked.

Where had she seen that face before? It took her a moment to recognize it. Greg! It was Laura's Greg. She didn't even know his last name. "Greg," she pleaded, "please, please be all right." But even as she said it, she knew without question that Laura's Greg was dead.

Recklessly Mary Helen scrambled down the hillside, her legs fighting to stay steady. Low branches yanked at her hair. She slipped on pine needles and felt herself hurled against rough tree bark.

A bevy of frightened quail rose up from the thickets. She covered her face as they flew at her with short, stubby wings.

With trembling hands she clung to a limb, trying to catch her breath. Her temples throbbed. Furtively, she peered around her, waiting for someone to come crashing from the underbrush. But there was only stillness.

She ran forward. A shower of small stones rattled down the path behind her. Sharp twigs scratched at her legs and face. Chest aching, she finally stumbled into the parking lot and the waiting arms of Monsignor McHugh.

"Whoa! What is it, Sister?" He grabbed both her shoulders. "What happened? I heard you screaming." Frowning with concern, he studied her face.

Mary Helen struggled to catch her breath. His eyes were so blue, so keen, so alive, such a contrast to the vacant, unseeing blue eyes staring up from the bug-infested face that she could not bear to look.

"You're trembling." Con McHugh led her to a bench and insisted she sit. Her knees felt too rubbery to resist. "What happened, Sister?" he asked again.

Sister Mary Helen's throat ached. Oddly, she could not manage to get her tongue around the words.

"Calm down." The monsignor smiled kindly. "Are you all right? Are you hurt anywhere?"

First Mary Helen nodded, then shook her head.

Father Ed Moreno, who had come out of his room in St. Philomena's Hall, joined them in the parking lot.

Silently the two priests stood over her, examining her scratched hands and legs. Like a bug under a microscope, she thought wildly, and began to shiver.

"What's all the hollering about?" A sleepy Father Tom, still in his pajamas, appeared on the porch.

"It's Yellin' Helen!" Ed Moreno called over.

He can't help himself, Mary Helen thought, burying her

face in her hands. Without warning, she began to laugh and then to cry.

◆I◆ ◆I◆ ◆I◆

"It simply cannot be true." That was all Sister Felicita said when she finally arrived in the parking lot.

The noise had drawn all the retreatants, one by one, from their bedrooms. They stood around Mary Helen like remnants of a lost tribe, waiting for her to speak. Slowly, painfully, Con McHugh coaxed out the story.

"I'm sure that he just fell," Felicita said. "What is he doing here at this time of the morning anyway?" She sounded annoyed. "It can't be true that he's dead," she repeated nervously.

"Maybe I am imagining things," Mary Helen conceded, wishing that were the case. From the expressions on their faces, she knew that every one of the group shared Felicita's disbelief. This could not be true! Everyone, that is, except Eileen. The color had drained from her face and she stared at Mary Helen in horror.

"If he fell, we'd better get up there." Tom Harrington had slipped on a running suit over his pajamas.

"You're right. Let's have a look." As chaplain of the Police and Fire Departments, Andy Carr seemed the natural leader.

With Felicita close at Andy's heels, the small group wound its way up the hillside trail. Eileen hung back with Mary Helen. Together, they brought up the rear.

"I feel like the kiss of death," Mary Helen said. She did not need a second opinion to know Laura's Greg was dead.

"Don't be silly." Eileen, still pale, patted her hand encouragingly. "Surely you cannot be blamed. We've an old saying back home."

Mary Helen groaned. Eileen could dig up an old saying for every occasion, even, as Mary Helen often suspected, if she had to invent one.

Eileen ignored her. "Nobody knows where his sod of death is."

"Which means?" Mary Helen asked, glad to be distracted, if only for a moment.

Eileen blinked her gray eyes. "That nobody knows where or when he or she will die. That nice young man just fell. So how could you be responsible? Unless, of course, you killed him and we don't even know that the man was killed."

"Is this supposed to make me feel better?" Mary Helen's head was throbbing.

"You can't hang a person for trying." Eileen shrugged, but said no more. Actually, both nuns needed all the breath they had for the trek to Madonna Grove.

The priests and nuns formed a small, stony-faced circle around the body of Laura's Greg. Everyone, that is, except Father Denski. Mary Helen could hear the young priest behind the wide trunk of a hemlock, retching.

"He's dead all right," Andy Carr pronounced with authority.

"I don't even know his last name," Felicita said, as though it was an error in etiquette not to know the surnames of dead bodies found on your property.

"I know it," Mike Denski shouted from behind his tree. "It's Johnson. That is—was—Greg Johnson. He was in the sem—" That was as far as he got.

"Marva Johnson's son." Con McHugh sounded stunned. "She goes to daily Mass at St. Pat's. Poor Marva."

"It's hard to tell who it is with all those . . ." Mercifully, Tom Harrington knew when to stop communicating.

"I thought that was his car here last night," Ed Moreno said, almost to himself.

"How do you suppose he fell?" Felicita scanned the clearing for an errant limb or a recalcitrant rock.

"I don't think he did fall. See those cuts?" Father Moreno pointed to a series of gashes on the dorsal side of the dead man's arm. "It looks to me as if he was defending himself against someone with a sharp weapon. Like a switchblade. Or a long, sharp knife of some sort."

"How do you know that?" Felicita sounded put out. Mary Helen didn't blame her. If Greg Johnson was dead, of course Felicita wanted it to be accidental.

"Ten years in Juvie," Father Moreno said simply.

Any semblance of Tom's usual smile had vanished. "What are you saying, Ed?"

Moreno shook his head. "That it looks to me like—foul play."

Andy Carr's face was grayer than his beard. "Shouldn't we give him the last rites or whatever we're calling it now? Lord, there are four of us priests—well, four and a half, if you count Mike—standing here gawking at the poor devil." Andy looked as if, any minute, he might join Mike Denski. "Shouldn't we give him absolution or something?"

"Ego te absolvo a peccatis tuis in nomine . . ." Monsignor McHugh began the familiar ritual of the Sacrament. No one seemed to notice that he was using Latin. "I absolve you from your sins in the name of the Father and the Son and the Holy Spirit." A resounding "Amen" rose among the redwoods.

The regal old man made the sign of the cross over the body of Greg Johnson. "By His most loving mercy, may the Lord forgive you whatever wrong you have done . . ." The monsignor was mixing and matching his sacraments and his languages. Surely under the circumstances, the Lord did not care. Certainly, the grisly remains of young Greg Johnson did not care either.

+I+   +I+   +I+

At Sister Felicita's suggestion, the group had moved to St. Jude's dining room to await the sheriff.

"It's a very small department and very understaffed." Felicita's voice shook as she poured mugs of hot coffee for everyone. "There are only a half a dozen cars to cover the entire county. I'm not sure how long we'll have to wait."

"It seems to me that a dead body would be a priority." Although he was still deathly pale, Mike Denski was now able to speak. "How many dead bodies are discovered in these mountains?"

"More than you'd expect." Felicita crumpled into a chair. "We've had some awful murders in these hills." She frowned, trying, no doubt, to remember. "What was that one's name? Miller? Muller?"

"Herbie Mullin," Ed Moreno said. "That happened twenty years ago. You're not suggesting it's something like that again?"

"I'm not suggesting anything," Felicita said quickly, as if the mere mention of a psychotic killer might bring one around.

"I haven't thought of Mullin for years." The monsignor stared out the dining room window with glassy eyes. "Poor old Henri. Such a good, gentle man. May he rest in peace."

"Henri?" Mike asked. Obviously he was the only member of the group who did not know that Father Henri Tomic, a priest from Los Gatos, was Herbert Mullin's thirteenth victim.

Ed Moreno filled him in. "A priest-killer would be in hog heaven with this group," he added in an attempt to lighten the mood. No one took up the banter. If anything, his reference to a serial killer darkened the gloom.

Through the large picture windows, Mary Helen watched a hot ball of sun begin to show over the treetops, burning off the morning fog as it rose. She checked her wristwatch. It was just after seven o'clock. Could so much have happened in just one short half hour?

Andy Carr cleared his throat. "That name, Greg Johnson. Something about it rings a bell."

"It should." Mike pulled nervously at his long sideburns.

Andy turned his needle-sharp eyes on the young priest. "Why's that?"

"Because he was one of the seminarians arrested in a Gay Rights demonstration."

"Sure! Now I remember." Andy shifted his large bulk. "The creep got himself arrested and the archbishop was on my tail.

" 'It may create a grave scandal among the faithful, Father, if news that one of our seminarians was arrested were to leak . . .' " Andy did a perfect, if irreverent, imitation of the prelate.

"Is he—was he—gay?" Mary Helen asked. If he was, what on earth was he doing with Laura the evening before?

"Hell, no," Tom Harrington said with a knowing grin. "He's a dyed-in-the-wool troublemaker. That kid is well aware of the Church's official stand on homosexuality and what a difficult position he would put the archbishop in."

He studied the toes of his Gucci loafers. "On the one hand, many of the Church's staunchest supporters—and I could also say wealthiest—oppose anything even touching on the subject. Yet many of the City's gays are Catholic. If the truth were known, the archbishop himself is unsure about his own pastoral position with the gay community.

"If you ask me, the kid got his kicks from watching Absolute Norm squirm. Old Greg was no innocent, idealistic seminarian, you know. He was a real good pot-stirrer. After the incident with the demonstration, the Arch sent him to me for an internship, figuring, I guess, that the kid had a flair for muckraking, so why not use it in the media?"

"Did it work?" Eileen always liked a happy ending.

Tom shook his head. "He was more interested in the office secretaries than he was in the office equipment."

A chuckle went around the room. Once again all the color drained from Mike Denski's face. "Doesn't it strike you as callous . . . no, ghoulish . . . to sit here and laugh when Greg is—"

"Lighten up, Mike," Ed Moreno said, not unkindly. "We're not laughing at Greg's death. If you believe what you preach, Greg is laughing at us. You know that death is what life is all about."

Mary Helen felt a sympathy for the young priest. Accepting death, especially sudden and violent death, takes a great deal of hope and trust in God's promises. Hope, like all other virtues, demands years of practice.

"Then, all of you, that is all except Father Moreno, knew the young man?" Eileen asked in that Irish statement-question way of hers.

"Oh, I knew Greg Johnson, all right." Ed pushed his coffee mug forward for a refill. "When Happy Harrington here couldn't handle him, he came to do some time with me in Juvenile Hall. I'm the one he finally told that he was leaving the seminary. And it was the right decision. The kid did not have a vocation to be a priest."

"More than likely, it was his mother who did," the monsignor said softly. "Poor Marva. Wait until she hears this."

"I think that the archbishop always thought it was my fault," Ed said. "Like I gave Greg a shove or something."

"Did you?" Mike asked the question that was on Mary Helen's mind.

"Actually," Ed Moreno said, sounding a little defensive, "I did the kid a big favor. It just wasn't for him."

"It's really quite a coincidence," Mary Helen said.

"What is, Sister?"

"That all you priests knew the young man. And that we Sisters met him here last night. Then his body appears . . ." She let her words trail off.

Ed Moreno ran his fingers nervously through his thinning hair. "Do you mean it's a coincidence, or do you mean it seems suspicious?"

Sister Mary Helen frowned and cocked her head as if she had not quite heard. That's one of the advantages of growing old, she thought, stalling for time.

His question was a legitimate one. She really should answer it. Yet, for some reason, she did not know how.

In the distance, a car door slammed. Tom Harrington looked relieved.

"Odd the dogs aren't barking." Felicita rose slowly from the table.

And that there are no police car noises, Mary Helen wanted to say, but caught herself. It was too soon after her "slightly hard of hearing" act.

Andy Carr checked his watch. "I guess we were a priority after all, Mike. It only took them a half hour to get here."

"Who's 'them'?" Beverly threw open the kitchen door.

Poor Felicita paled. "Beverly, it's you," she said, trying to recover her poise. "You're early."

"You're the ones who are early," Beverly snapped, her plain, red face screwing up into a scowl. "Besides, who were you expecting, Sister? Chef Boyardee?"

"Good one, Bev." Ed Moreno laughed.

Beverly fixed the group with her small coffee-brown eyes. "I'm here early because I have things to do," she said, her voice suddenly flat and angry, "and I want to do them in peace and quiet. So don't start bugging me to hurry up and fix your breakfast. I'm not in the mood." She pulled the door closed behind her.

"I had better go in and tell her what happened," Felicita muttered.

"I'd leave that to the sheriff." Tom Harrington gave a crooked smile. "After all, he's the one trained for combat duty."

Beverly slammed drawers and cupboards while Felicita absentmindedly refilled the coffee cups until, finally, Eileen put her hand over hers. "I think my back teeth are beginning to float," she said softly.

"Of course. Sorry." Felicita created a mountain of toast using the dining room's toaster. She even managed to slide in and out of the kitchen without incident, for butter and jam.

When the sheriff arrived at last, there was no mistaking it was he. The squeal of tires was followed by the heavy thud of the car door. The high-pitched voice of the police dispatcher squawked out into the morning stillness.

"Sister Felicita?" The man's immense frame filled the doorway of St. Jude's. His tan shirt and forest-green pants gave him a woodsy look. When she didn't answer immediately, he studied his notebook with narrow agate eyes that seemed too small for his head. Almost as if he had been given the wrong pair, Mary Helen thought.

All at once, he was staring at her. Unwittingly, she stared back. She had never in her life seen such a big police officer. He didn't even look "regulation," if there was such a thing.

Not only was he extremely tall, probably about six feet four or five, but he was also broad, with thick hands and feet that seemed even wider than they were because of his highly polished paratrooper boots.

His nose, set a little high on his sunburned face, gave him

a sniffing look. And his light hair was clipped so short that it was difficult to tell its exact color.

He ambled toward the group. With each step his holster rubbing against his basket-weave belt made a creaking sound. "Which one of you ladies is Sister Felicita?" he asked impatiently.

"I am she," Felicita answered, as if she wished she weren't.

"You say you found a body?" He sounded as skeptical as if she'd reported finding a Martian.

"Yes, Sheriff." Felicita seemed to recoil.

"Actually, I found the body." Mary Helen adjusted her bifocals so she could read the name badge pinned to his shirt pocket. He wasn't the sheriff at all. He was a sergeant. Probably one of the few, if Felicita was to be believed. Sergeant Eric Something.

He must have noticed her checking his badge. "I'm Sergeant Eric Loody, ma'am," he said with what struck Mary Helen as a supercilious smile. "Loody rhymes with duty."

A mnemonic device for the old lady, Mary Helen thought, feeling her hackles rise. She took a deep breath. All that coffee must be affecting her nerves. Surely, the deputy meant nothing invidious by it.

"How-do, Sergeant Loody," she said, wondering what Father Ed Moreno would make out of that name.

"And who are you?"

Quickly, she told him, then began to relate the circumstances of her grueling—and gruesome—discovery. "I woke early this morning," she said, "and decided to enjoy the mountains and perhaps to make the stations."

Loody frowned.

"The Way of the Cross?" she offered. When he still looked puzzled, she hurried on. If she took the time to explain every devotion of the Catholic Church, it would be a very long day indeed.

"Anyway, Sergeant, I changed my mind early on. Too steep. And went instead to Madonna Grove, where I found . . ." She stopped. She had to. Her mouth was dry and she felt nauseated.

With a hostile-sounding sniff the officer shifted his gaze toward the priests around the table. "Who are you guys?" he asked.

The monsignor rose, his handsome face almost as white as his hair. "Con McHugh," he said, offering a hand, which Loody failed to take. Apparently sergeants do not shake hands with potential suspects, Mary Helen told herself.

Deftly waving the same hand, McHugh included the other four men. "We are all priests from the Archdiocese of San Francisco," he said, "here at St. Colette's to make the annual priests' retreat."

Loody's eyes swept the group. "Padres, huh?" he said flippantly, then flicked his eyes toward Eileen. "And you're a nun, too, without the penguin suit?"

Eileen's soft wrinkled face colored. From the parentheses forming on either side of her thin, tight lips, Mary Helen knew her friend was hopping mad.

"What's your name, ma'am?" he asked with cold courtesy.

"Sister Eileen," she said in a brogue so thick, one could slice and serve it.

Mary Helen stared at Loody in disbelief. It had been so long since she had run into one that, for a moment, the term escaped her. She had thought that by now the breed was extinct. Could it be that in this day and age, they had stumbled upon an—an—anti-Catholic bigot?

In the distance, a second car screeched to a halt and Mary Helen heard heavy, hurrying footsteps approach the dining

room. The door swung back and a second officer stepped inside.

With a strange sense of relief, Mary Helen shifted her
attention to the new man. Although dwarfed by Loody, he
was tall, young, and clean-shaven with a friendly, open face
and candid blue eyes.

"This is Deputy Foster," Loody mumbled almost grudg-
ingly.

Foster's face colored, as if he were unused to the title. He
touched the brim of his brown Stratton in a stiff cowboy
salute that looked as if he'd copied it from a western sitcom.
In Mary Helen's opinion, however, the hat wasn't a cowboy's
hat at all. If anything, it made Foster look, for all this world,
like a doughboy right out of World War I. Of course, his
fresh-scrubbed face didn't help much either.

"Just picked up the one-four on the radio," he announced
to Loody and everyone else within earshot. "What've we
got?"

Loody sniffed. "Don't know yet, Foster," he said. "I was
just about to find out.

"Anyone else on the grounds except you people?" Loody
asked, making "people" sound as if he had trouble finding a
noun to define their lot adequately. His small eyes jumped
from person to person.

Counting to eight to see how many we are, Mary Helen
thought, uncharitably.

As if on cue, the kitchen door swung open. "I'm Beverly
Benton." Was Beverly eavesdropping?

"Are you a nun too?" Loody asked with a sneer.

Beverly caught him with a glare that could sear metal.
"No," she said, "I am not. I just work here."

Loody gave a noncommittal grunt. "Don't any of you get
any ideas about leaving the place," he said severely.

Then, turning toward a red-faced Foster, he spoke loud

enough for all to hear. "Get down their names and addresses, Deputy. All of them. These guys in their pious getups don't fool me for one minute. I know about their kind. If you ask me, the murderer is right here in this room."

Felicita groaned aloud.

"By the time I'm finished with them," Loody growled, "they'll wish they'd never tangled with the Santa Cruz Sheriff's Department."

If Mary Helen didn't know better, she'd think they were caught in one of those frozen, deep South dramas with the sheriff and Bubba and the Klan.

Before Deputy Foster had quite finished his task, Loody announced in a pugnacious tone that he was cordoning off the retreat house. No one was to leave. No one was to enter until further notice.

"But the other nuns." By now Felicita looked as if she might faint. "They are on their way home from Bakersfield. And priests will be arriving . . ."

"No one is to leave and no one is to enter the premises until I say so." Loody gave a satisfied sniff. His holster and belt creaking, he left the dining room, following a grim-faced Felicita.

Deputy Foster, avoiding direct eye contact with anyone, smiled sheepishly. Then, without a word, he left too. No doubt they were going to view the victim.

"I wonder which one of you did it?" Beverly said, nibbling on a piece of cold toast. Her face was more flushed than usual and wisps of straw-colored hair escaped from her topknot.

"One of us?" Monsignor McHugh sounded genuinely shocked. "Surely, you don't think . . ."

"You were the only ones who were here, weren't you?" Her dark eyes riddled them all. "I wouldn't put it past any one of you." Giving the door a hard jab, she disappeared into the kitchen.

For a long moment the group sat in stunned silence watching the door swing. The monsignor was the first to recover. "How in the world could she think that one of us killed that unfortunate young man?"

"Greg Johnson may turn out to be the lucky one after all," Ed Moreno said.

"Lucky?" Mike looked as if he might lose the little bit he'd eaten. "Why lucky?"

"He is dead, my boy. We are alive and held captive with Heavy Bevy and . . ." It took him a minute, but he came up with a handle. "Eric the Rude."

Even Ed's epithet was unable to lighten the mood. The seven religious sat in what Mary Helen considered an unholy gloom. Still, who could blame them?

Like it or not, they were all suspects. As Beverly had so flat-footedly pointed out, they were the only ones on the premises when Greg Johnson was murdered. Which proved nothing, of course. The hills around the retreat house were open to anyone with the courage to climb them. Or were they? Was the property fenced? Odd that the victim was someone they all knew, however briefly.

"It's a long road that has no turning," Eileen said, breaking into her reverie.

"What does that mean?"

"It means that every cloud has a silver lining." Her brogue was thick enough to let Mary Helen know she was still upset.

"Which is what?"

Despite their attempt to whisper, the priests were listening with interest.

"Sister Cecilia thinks we are safely on retreat. With any luck at all, she may never know this happened."

Cecilia! With all this morning's goings-on Mary Helen hadn't given a single thought to anything else. As president of Mount St. Francis College, Sister Cecilia had weathered the publicity that accompanied Mary Helen's previous brushes with murder and murderers. After the pilgrimage to Spain, Cecilia had mentioned—a bit testily, in Mary Helen's opinion—that her forbearance was wearing thin.

And, although Eileen said it was nonsense, Mary Helen sensed that Sister Therese, who liked her name pronounced "trays," and several of the other nuns were beginning to avoid the two of them as one would a pair of Grim Reapers. Actually, only young Sister Anne found their adventures exciting. Eileen was right. It was best that this whole affair be kept as quiet as possible.

"Surely it's too remote a murder to make the *Chronicle,*" Eileen assured her. Several of the older Sisters at the college read the San Francisco paper with almost religious fervor, missing no item, however insignificant.

Tom Harrington smiled. "They won't need the *Chronicle,*" he said. "The clerical grapevine will have the news up Holy Hill faster than the speed of light."

Mary Helen groaned. Twenty priests were expected at the retreat house. How soon? She had lost all sense of time. Checking her watch, she was surprised to see that it was only a few minutes after eight o'clock in the morning. The significance hadn't dawned on her.

In less than two hours, twenty diocesan priests would be turned away from St. Colette's by the police. Figuring in travel time down the mountain and telephone time, Mount St. Francis would undoubtedly have the news by lunch. Unless, heaven forbid, some priest had a car phone. Then the bad news might arrive as early as the morning coffee break.

From the picture windows of St. Jude's dining room, Mary Helen watched the sun clear the tips of the distant evergreens. Already the room was stuffy and warm. The usually delicious aromas of frying bacon and baking bread coming from the kitchen were cloying.

With an unexpected bang of the kitchen door, Beverly reappeared. Her stainless-steel cart was laden with a platter of bacon and scrambled eggs, fruit juice, and baskets of fresh-baked muffins.

"Your breakfast," she said, as if nothing unusual had happened to disrupt her schedule.

"Won't you join us?" Con McHugh was cordial.

Mary Helen watched Beverly's reaction. Curiously, there wasn't one. As if she hadn't heard, Beverly reopened the door, then paused. "I'd be afraid to," she said, leaving the group in an awkward silence.

With a quick, clumsy sign of the cross, Con McHugh blessed the food and they all sat down to breakfast. No one took very much. Beverly's parting shot had done away with any appetite they might have had.

"What do you think will happen now?" Tom made heavy work of buttering his muffin.

Instinctively all eyes went toward Andy Carr. "Damned if I know," he said. "I'm just the Police Department chaplain. I've never been under suspicion before. What do you think, Ed? You're really more familiar with the system than I am."

Ed Moreno took his time chewing and swallowing. "Beats me," he said finally. "I don't think he can keep us here much longer. With a guy like Loody, however, it's hard to tell. I know what I intend to do."

Every eye was upon him. "What's that, Ed?" Mike Denski played with the end of his long sideburn.

"I'm going to eat up. From the sound of things, Bevy's picked one of us as the murderer. Knowing her, whoever it is is already convicted and condemned. She's just waiting for the execution."

"Which one?" Mike's mouth quivered.

"Who knows?" Smiling, Ed passed the platter. "But if it's me, kid, I intend to have my last meal. Why don't you guys do the same?"

He was just finishing his second helping of breakfast when Beverly reappeared with an empty trolley to clear the table. "I suppose I'll have to do these, too," she said, slamming down a plate. A spoon clattered to the floor.

Eileen bent over to retrieve it and, much to Mary Helen's surprise, did not offer to help with the dishes. Following Beverly into the kitchen was too much like following a lioness into her lair for Mary Helen's taste. Apparently Eileen wasn't that brash either.

Mike Denski's eyes opened wide. For a moment Mary Helen thought he was about to volunteer. The poor guy—Beverly will eat him alive! Instead, he gathered up the remaining cups and saucers, stacked them on the bottom of the cart, and moved them out of the dining room into Beverly's domain in double time.

The rattling and banging of Beverly's dishwashing echoed in the background. "I know she must have some redeeming qualities, but that's the person I would have murdered," Mike said to everyone's surprise.

Mary Helen knew he wasn't the first person to feel that way. Last night an angry Laura Purcell had said the same thing. Laura! She wondered if anyone had told the girl about Greg's death. Surely, Sister Felicita had been too busy. Deputy Loody wouldn't have had the chance yet—if he even knew about Laura.

Poor thing! Last night, her face flushed with rage, she had wept out her anger in Greg's sympathetic embrace, never suspecting what would happen. Mary Helen wondered sadly how they had spent the evening. And if they'd ever made it to the movie Laura wanted to see. What a shock his death would be for her!

"I can't stand that banging much longer." Tom Harrington's handsome face strained into a shallow grin.

"Nothing says that we can't go out on the sundeck to wait for Loody's return." Ed Moreno opened a glass door and stepped out onto the wide wooden deck that ran the length of the building.

Sister Mary Helen followed. Leaning against the wooden rail, she was once again enthralled with the magnificence of the view. Sycamores, redwoods, bays, cypresses, and Ponderosa pines formed a silent sea reaching to the sparkling blue sky.

To her amazement, on the lawn below a brown rock moved. Pushing her glasses up the bridge of her nose, Mary Helen spotted a fluffy white tail and realized that what she thought was a rock was a large brush rabbit pausing to nibble the grass. Many things aren't what they seem, she thought, watching it scurry into the underbrush.

Down the length of the porch were redwood tubs of lacy dianthus, cherry-red patio dahlias, and tufts of Sweet William. Green and white director's chairs, placed at intervals, suggested that the retreatants could enjoy both the view and their solitude.

Father Carr made quick work of pulling several chairs together.

"Like pioneers circling the wagons," the monsignor remarked. "Do you mind?" He pulled out his pipe.

"Circle is now complete with campfire," Ed quipped, but no one seemed to mind.

In fact, Mary Helen rather enjoyed the aroma of his tobacco. There was just a hint of vanilla in it. From somewhere a thrush gave his flute-like call. It seemed impossible that amid so much beauty and tranquillity she had stumbled upon such violent death.

Her stomach roiled. Quickly, before her knees melted, she took the place next to Con McHugh.

The crash of falling dishes reverberated out onto the silent air.

Andy Carr swore under his breath. "You know," he said, "maybe Mike had something."

"Me?" Mike sounded more surprised than anyone. "About what?"

"About someone wanting to kill Beverly." Andy fingered his scruffy beard. "You know, she is tall and blond, not unlike Greg. Maybe from the back in the dark, someone could have mistaken her."

"That's possible." The monsignor pulled on his pipe.

"Come, Rin. Come, Tin-Tin. Come on, boys!" In the distance Beverly could be heard calling the dogs.

"Anything's possible, of course," Mike said, "but people don't just kill somebody because they are rude. What would be the real reason?"

"We all know Beverly," Ed said. "Need you ask for more of a reason?"

A sudden, horrendous thud from the kitchen drove home his point.

◆I◆   ◆I◆   ◆I◆

The familiar sounds of cars, radios, and men's voices announced the arrival of yet more police. Undoubtedly the crime scene unit, the forensic team, and the coroner, Mary Helen speculated from previous experience. Nevertheless, she was surprised when two young men in plainclothes rounded the corner of St. Jude's and introduced themselves as homicide detectives. For some reason she'd never imagined a sheriff's department having its own homicide unit, although it made perfect sense.

"I'm Detective Sergeant Bob Little," one of the men announced.

The first thing Mary Helen noticed about him was that he was not—little. If anything, he was big. Not as big as Loody; although he was almost as tall, his body had the lean, hard look of an athlete's. Big and brown, Mary Helen thought, with brown hair and eyes, a thick brown mustache and a deeply tanned face. Even his slacks and sport coat were shades of brown.

Not that the brown made him dull. On the contrary, it was a warm, amicable brown that showed in his humorous eyes and twitched around his lips.

"This is my partner, Deputy Dave Kemp," he said.

Kemp was Mutt to Little's Jeff. To acknowledge his introduction, the deputy gave a quick nod of his surf-bleached head. His sharp cobalt eyes bounced from one to the other. Nervously he fiddled with the knot in his bow tie. Mary Helen thought it unusual to find such a young man wearing a bow tie and wondered how long before it came off in this heat.

"You're taking over from Sergeant Loody, then?" Father Carr asked, too quickly.

Although his face betrayed nothing, Little's eyes twinkled. "Sergeant Loody will cordon off the areas and post guards, but Deputy Kemp and I will handle the investigation from here on in."

Suddenly the sundeck took on a different air. The green and white chairs were pushed back. The pioneers were rescued. The cavalry had arrived!

Before they began to feel too liberated, Detective Sergeant Little reinforced Loody's directive by asking them to remain at the retreat center. "Just until my partner and I have the opportunity to question each of you," he said, almost apologetically. "I understand you'd be here on a retreat anyway, so no one is expecting you home for a week, right? I'm sure St. Colette's is much more comfortable than being sequestered in a motel."

He gave a wide smile that reached not only his eyes but his entire face. Although the result was exactly the same, being held captive by Sergeant Little was already more bearable.

"You're free to walk around the place," he said. "Just try not to get in the way of the forensic team and, please, don't go back to the crime scene."

Wild horses couldn't drag me, Mary Helen thought. Her stomach lurched at the very idea.

I *I* *I*

Little and Kemp had nearly crossed the parking lot when they saw Sister Felicita descending the hill. "Swear to God, it's Sister Mary Immaculata," Bob Little muttered, watching her.

"Who?" Kemp asked.

Little shrugged. "My high school English teacher. I swear she looked just like that." He studied the approaching figure. It was short with a black veil flowing gracefully over the shoulders and a loose scapular concealing everything but the solidity of the shape beneath.

"From this distance, dressed like that, how can you tell who it looks like?" Kemp asked.

Little nodded toward the nun. "It's those wire-rimmed glasses and those eyes: clear, blue, and—what's the word? Hell, I should remember the word! She was my English teacher. 'Inscrutable,' that's it. Inscrutable eyes."

Kemp shaded his own eyes from the glaring sun. "How can you make out her eyes from here? If you ask me, she's squinting."

"Trust me," Little said with confidence. "I am a man of experience."

"I didn't know you were Catholic."

"I'm not," Little said. "I just went to the Catholic school. I never did convert, although I picked up a big dose of their guilt and the wisdom to realize that Sister knows best."

Actually, Little had been one of the few non-Catholics at Holy Cross High School. In desperation, his frustrated parents sent him there for the discipline. In fact, he suspected his talent for basketball, rather than his adherence to the school's rules, is what saved his hide. That, plus his mother's untiring devotion to the Mothers' Guild, and Sister Mary Immaculata's continued prodding.

Much to his parents' relief and amazement he had graduated from Holy Cross and gone on to the state university. There, again thanks to Sister Mary Immaculata's previous drilling, he was spared from taking "Bonehead English." Actually, he hadn't thought of her much since, only once in a while when the correct word or a line of a poem came back.

When he'd entered the police academy, his mother was finally able to relax.

"She was afraid you'd end up on the other side of the bars," his father had joked. As with all humor, Bob Little recognized the element of truth.

> *"The Brain — is wider than the Sky —*
> *For — put them side by side —*
> *The one the other will contain*
> *With ease — and You — beside."*

Little recited Emily Dickinson aloud. "Sister Mary Immaculata made me memorize that," he said with a grin, "and I've never been able to forget it."

"Whatever the hell it means." Kemp seemed to be tiring of the good nun.

Little shrugged. "I told you she taught English," he said, as if to explain away any aberrations.

Head down, muttering to herself, Sister Felicita almost ran into them. "Excuse me," she stammered, blinking.

Her eyes were clear and blue, Little noted with satisfaction. He wondered if Kemp had caught that.

"I am so distracted, I'm not looking where I'm going. I just can't seem to think of anything but—" Felicita pointed toward the wooded hillside.

Watching the color drain from her face, Little quickly changed the subject. All he needed was to have the little woman faint.

"You must be Sister Felicita." He gave her his friendliest smile. "You're the directress of the retreat center and the one who called in the complaint?"

She nodded, the tears welling up.

"Why don't you go join the others," Little suggested. "We can talk later."

With a nervous bob of her head, Felicita hurried to do just that.

Little and Kemp worked their way up the steep hillside. Loody in his tan and forest-green uniform stood like a giant tree guarding the entrance to Madonna Grove.

Little scanned the clearing. It was small and flat with a carpet of dried pine needles, sheltered from view, and from the rising heat, by tall trees. To one side was a homemade log bench.

Even with all the activity of the crime unit, the place had an uncanny quiet. A peaceful, secluded spot, Little thought, noticing the large Madonna in the burned-out tree stump. A perfect spot for praying. And for murdering.

A camera flashed. "Want to get a look now, Bob?" a man

called. "Or do you want to wait until I'm done? I've only got a couple more."

"Go ahead," Little answered. "I can wait." To tell the truth, he'd prefer to wait forever. The first view of the victim, any victim, was something he dreaded. No matter how often he did it, he never got used to it. The sight, the smell, the fear of death itself—he didn't know what it was. All he knew was that every time, no matter how he tried to prevent it, he had to fight down the sickening sensation of bile rising in his throat and the weak, watery feeling in his knees. This time was no exception.

"Overkill," Kemp pronounced. Little stared down at the victim. Greg Johnson was covered with slashes. His arms where he had held them up to defend himself were criss-crossed with knife strokes. After he had fallen, any one of the multiple gashes and stab wounds on his body could have killed him.

"You got that right," Little tried to keep his voice steady, waiting for the nausea to subside.

"Clearly, a crime of passion. We just need to find out who's passionate about the guy," Kemp said, obviously buoyed up by Little's encouragement.

"In a murder case nothing is nearly as clear as it seems," Little said. In time, Kemp would learn that by himself, but there was no sense letting him turn into an officious know-it-all too. One per department was enough and Loody already was their designated pain in the butt. Judging from the reaction of the dining room, he had just shown his colors to the priests and nuns.

"He was a handsome dude," Kemp said, somewhat subdued. "Has he a significant other?"

Little wondered if that was still the politically correct term.

"I got her name from the nun." Loody, watching from the sidelines, could no longer contain himself.

Little bristled. Although it was hard to put his finger on, there was something about Loody that rubbed him the wrong way. The man was a good officer, exact, hardworking, but he was so self-important, so righteous, so punctilious—now, there was a good Sister Mary Immaculata word—so punctilious. So damn annoying, actually.

Even the way his nose sat on his face, as if he were looking down it at you. That, Little realized almost as he thought it, was hardly fair. No one can be held responsible for the placement of his nose!

"Great!" Little said with as much largesse as he could manage. "Let me write it down." He pulled a small notebook from his jacket pocket.

"The girl's name is Laura Purcell." Loody spelled both names slowly, Little noticed with annoyance. "She goes to the university and worked here at St. Colette's as a dishwasher. Until last night. She and the victim were almost engaged, and according to the nun"—Loody dragged out the word *nun* as if it were a minor offense—"the two went off together last night."

Again, with insulting exactitude, Sergeant Loody read Laura Purcell's address and phone number.

Meanwhile, Kemp, keeping out of the way of the forensic team, was making his own notes. "Looks to me like he was killed right here," he said, his bow tie bouncing on his Adam's apple.

Little, whose stomach was beginning to settle, wondered if Kemp, too, was having trouble keeping his breakfast down. The blood-soaked ground around the body was a mess of smudged footprints. Little knew that if any one of them proved identifiable, it would undoubtedly belong to one of the religious, who in good faith went to see what they could do for Greg Johnson. What they had managed to do, of course, was to ruin most of the physical evidence.

Little pulled on the end of his mustache. What really puzzled him was what Greg Johnson was doing in the grotto in the first place. He was a big fellow. Who or what could have forced him up here without his yelling or running? Or had he been unconscious? If so, how had someone got that much dead weight up the steep hillside? Was he dealing with Godzilla? Two murderers? A murderer with a wheelbarrow? Shaking his head, Little scouted the area for a hint of tire tracks, and silently cursed all do-gooders.

He was glad to see the coroner's men enter the grove with the stretcher and the green body bag. They'd get complete reports from the pathologist and the forensic team. If there was anything else to find, those boys would find it. Right now, he needed to get back to the living. One of them, after all, had the real answers.

+I+ +I+ +I+

A bright yellow ribbon cut St. Colette's off from the rest of the world. The parking lot was overrun with sheriff's cars and men, in and out of uniform, carrying cases and brown bags for gathering evidence. The coroner's gray van stood as a silent reminder of where all this was leading.

The nuns and priests who had wandered over from the sundeck watched, mesmerized by all the activity. Only the hot sun beating down on her head and shoulders reminded Mary Helen of the passing of time.

Finally, Monsignor McHugh broke the silence. "We've none of us said Mass yet this morning." He looked toward Felicita, who had just joined the group. "Do you think that we can concelebrate?" he asked.

Felicita dragged herself back from wherever her mind had

taken her. "Yes, of course." She sounded happy to have something else to worry about. "Just let me get the chapel ready."

"No fuss," the monsignor called to her fleeting back.

But Mary Helen knew he called in vain. As an obvious
expert in the fine art of fussing, Felicita needed some fresh
and new things to gnaw on. And the more the better.

◆I◆ ◆I◆ ◆I◆

The five priests gathered around the stark marble altar in the
Chapel of the Holy Spirit. Behind them a wall of windows let
in all the beauty of the mountainside without any of its heat
or bugs.

Directly above the altar a magnificent stained-glass window depicted the Holy Spirit. Seven cinnabar rays shot down
from an enormous azure dove hovering with widespread wings
over a core of fire that burned and leapt like a torch. The
midday sun caught the colors and sent rainbows skittering
across the marble floor.

"Come up on the altar with us," Con McHugh invited.

And although Sister Felicita and Sister Eileen joined the
men, Mary Helen declined. Not for any theological reason,
but let them guess. Actually, her legs ached. And her hands
and knees still burned from her run down the hill. She preferred to sit in the cool wooden pew and let the words and
ritual refresh her very drooping spirit. With one finger, she
pushed her slipping glasses back onto the bridge of her nose
and waited.

"This Mass is offered for the repose of the soul of Greg
Johnson," the monsignor began. He made a few loosely connected remarks about Greg and St. Aloysius Gonzaga, the
Jesuit whose feast the Church celebrated on this day and who
was the protector of students.

"Not that he did a very good job with this kid," Ed

Moreno quipped irreverently. He'd snatched the thought right out of Mary Helen's mind.

Appropriately, the monsignor chose the first reading from the Book of Wisdom. "The just man, though he dies early, shall be at rest. For the age that is honorable comes not with the passage of time, nor can it be measured in terms of years. . . ."

Poor boy surely did die early, Mary Helen thought sadly. He couldn't have been more than twenty-eight or twenty-nine. She prayed for his family and for Laura.

The monsignor's deep voice resounded in the still chapel. "Having become perfect in a short while," he read, "he reached the fullness of a long career; for his soul was pleasing to the Lord, therefore He sped him out of the midst of wickedness."

Wickedness itself, not God, is what had sped Greg out of his young life, Mary Helen reflected with annoyance. Why blame God when it is human wickedness all along? But whose? She wondered, suddenly. Whose wickedness had destroyed Greg Johnson's life?

✦I✦   ✦I✦   ✦I✦

"Eternal rest grant unto him, O Lord." The final blessing was shattered by the ringing of the Berkeley ferry bell. Apparently for Beverly, tragedy or no, it was business as usual.

Like automatons, the group filed into St. Jude's dining room and stood amid the tables in a tense tableau waiting for Beverly to appear.

Much to their obvious relief, it was Detective Sergeant Little who pushed open the swinging door. "I thought my ringing that bell would get you," he began. His friendly voice bounced off the silent walls.

A thin chuckle ran through the group.

"There's no law that I know of against eating during a murder investigation."

Again, they all laughed appreciatively.

"Actually, we might all think better if we're not hungry. And since Ms. Benton prepared a hot lunch, I suggest we eat it."

Before Little had finished speaking, Beverly wheeled in a cart laden with platters of steaming spaghetti oozing with meat sauce, baskets of French bread, and bowls of crisp green salad.

The condemned ate a hearty meal, Mary Helen thought, spotting the lemon cups left over from last night's supper. Now cold, they were arranged on a heavy silver tray.

With no more finesse than she had displayed on the previous evening, Beverly flung things down on the Formica tabletop.

Although Deputy Kemp jumped at one thud, Little continued to smile pleasantly. Nerves of steel, Mary Helen thought, watching him choose a place next to the monsignor.

With the cart unloaded, Beverly frowned at them, then started for the kitchen.

"Ms. Benton," Little's voice stopped her. "Please join us. There's plenty of room. There," he pointed, "next to Sister Felicita."

Both women looked as if they'd just been given a death sentence. Felicita was the first to recover her composure. "Surely," she said, moving over to make additional room.

To Mary Helen's surprise, Beverly's face flushed as she lowered herself into the plastic chair. Do I detect shyness? Mary Helen wondered.

The table, clearly designed to seat eight adults comfortably, was quite a squeeze for eleven. Somehow, by pulling chairs up to the corners and straddling the table legs, they managed.

Oddly, no one suggested moving to an adjoining table. Mary Helen wasn't really sure why. Perhaps it was Little's unspoken expectation that they all sit together. Or perhaps, like her, no one wanted to miss a moment of the interplay between Little and the group. Not that she'd admit it.

Fascinating chap, that Little! Good night nurse! She was beginning to sound like one of the English thrillers she'd been reading recently.

Regardless, he was a personable young man, yet very commanding. What was the old saying? "An iron hand in a velvet glove"? Or was he more of an "iron fist"? Time would tell.

By way of blessing, the monsignor made a wide, airy sign of the cross over the food, which looked to the untrained eye as if he were shooing flies. "Benedic nos, domine . . ." Apparently distraught, he reverted to Latin.

After a ragged "Amen," they began to pass plates in almost retreat silence. Lack of elbow room didn't seem a problem since no one was doing much eating. More food was being shoved around the plates than was being shoved into mouths. Only Little seemed to have an appetite.

He broke his French bread. "Where are you folks from?" he began, as if they were all participants at a convention, meeting casually at the luncheon table.

One by one, he drew the priests into conversation. Soon they were all so relaxed that the monsignor—ostensibly a suspect—not the detective, brought up the subject of murder.

"You know, Bob," he began. (To Mary Helen's amazement, they were now all calling him "Bob.") The monsignor's handsome face was stony and he played with his unused spoon. "I was wondering about the boy's mother."

"Do you know his mother?" Little seemed surprised.

"Yes, indeed. Marva Johnson. She's one of my parishioners, so to speak. Actually, she lives way out on Geary, not far from the beach. St. Thomas's parish. I was there, years ago, as an assistant pastor. When I was moved downtown to St. Patrick's, she switched to that parish."

"A groupie," Ed Moreno quipped.

The monsignor's blue eyes sparked and his cheeks flamed in an unexpected show of temper. Unexpected, that is, by Mary Helen.

"Sorry, Con," Ed said quickly, "lousy timing." Obviously, this side of the regal monsignor was well known to Father Moreno.

Clearing his throat, Monsignor McHugh continued. "Marva's been a widow for years. She lives alone and her only other child, a daughter, moved with her family to Wenatchee."

Little frowned.

"Washington," the monsignor added, "where those red Delicious apples grow. The point I am making"—his sonorous voice rose—"is that in my opinion Marva should not receive this news over the phone. If someone could go personally to the house . . ."

Little looked sympathetic. "Gee, I don't know, Monsignor," he said in a deceptively bungling way. "I was going to notify the next of kin right after we'd finished here."

"You haven't called his mother yet?" Young Mike Denski looked stricken. Obviously, if he were dead, he'd want his mother to be the first to know.

"I didn't even know he had a mother yet. A living mother, that is," Little answered patiently.

"Where on Geary does she live?" Eileen, who was being uncustomarily quiet during the meal, perked up. No doubt she had a plan.

As soon as the monsignor gave the address, Mary Helen knew what it was. Marva Johnson lived very close to Kate Murphy. Kate, a San Francisco homicide inspector, was an alumna of Mount St. Francis College and a close friend of the two nuns. Over the years, Mary Helen's unfortunate stumbles into murder had really cemented that friendship.

Eileen was right. Kate was a good one to break the news to the poor woman, if there was such a thing as a good one to deliver bad news.

"We have a friend in homicide with the San Francisco Police Department," Eileen began. Mary Helen wondered what the detective's reaction would be. Little listened with interest. If he was surprised, it didn't show.

"She lives on Geary too," Eileen continued. "Quite close to Mrs. Johnson, actually. Maybe if you called Kate Murphy, Detective Sergeant, she could go to the woman's home. They may even know one another."

"If you ask me, that's the perfect solution." Andy Carr spoke up. Of course, no one had asked him, but as chaplain to the Police Department, he must have felt that the decision was his business.

Little seemed to be considering Eileen's suggestion. "Let me think about it," he said, and everyone, including the monsignor, seemed satisfied to wait.

The food was passed around the table a second time and appetites and conversation both began to pick up. Even Beverly let down some of her guard. One of Eileen's "old sayings from back home" came to Mary Helen. "Men are like bagpipes. No sound comes from them till they're full." At this table it was certainly proving true.

Helping himself to more spaghetti, although Mary Helen wondered how he could eat another bite, Ed Moreno told his latest Hillary Rodham Clinton joke. The men laughed uproariously and Mary Helen managed an indulgent smile. If the truth were known, she thought that Hillary jokes were wearing very thin.

Adroitly, Little won their confidence, put them at ease, and knocked down any barriers they might have to being interviewed. Mary Helen would lay odds that this detective with his deceivingly boyish grin was one of the Sheriff's Department's leading homicide investigators. He wore the air of a natural confidant, a talent that defied logical explanation, even hers.

On the other hand, his partner, Kemp, did not have such luck. He sat stiffly. Mary Helen watched his cobalt eyes sweep over the priests like searchlights. It was absurd, almost blasphemous, to think that he suspected one of these men. They were upright men, dedicated men, good and holy men.

The monsignor had spent a lifetime of service in the Church. Ed Moreno, quick-witted and always ready for a joke, used his humor to brighten the lives of those of God's children who had ended up in jail. Tom Harrington, with his trademark crooked smile and that soothing voice, adroitly spread the Gospel message of love and forgiveness. His radio and television shows went out to literally thousands of listeners and viewers all over the country. Most of them received peace and consolation from his words.

Then there was Andy Carr, whose zeal impelled him always to be available for a chaplaincy. Mary Helen wondered if sometimes, late at night, he lay awake, fed up with the entire bunch of organizations he served, and imagined himself free of them all. Mike Denski, with his whole life before him, had solemnly and generously offered it to God's service.

It was outrageous to imagine one of them as a murderer, yet she was unable to shake Beverly's earlier taunt. "I wonder which one of you did it? You were the only ones here."

After all, they were all human. Under pressure, the monsignor had shown his hair-trigger temper. Tom was a bit too showy and glib to be completely genuine; Andy, too eager to please. Mike had all the earmarks of a mama's boy, and funnyman Ed would be a psychologist's delight. Did he use humor to cover his real emotions?

None of them was perfect by any stretch of the imagination, but—murderers? "Corruptio optima pessima," St. Thomas Aquinas had declared centuries ago. "The best things corrupted become the worst." And no one had yet proved him wrong, Mary Helen thought gloomily.

Looking toward Eileen, she wondered what her friend was thinking. At the moment, Eileen was preoccupied with wiping spaghetti sauce off her chin.

Without warning, the door to St. Jude's banged as if pulled by a fierce wind. All heads turned toward the entrance where Laura Purcell stood frozen.

Her auburn hair billowed wildly around her face, which was as white as the shorts and halter top she was wearing. Her eyes were wide.

"Sorry, Sergeant." A red-faced Deputy Foster appeared behind her. "I told her no one was allowed in the crime scene, but while I was explaining that to the occupants of the next vehicle, she jumped out of her car and ran by me."

Little raised one large hand to the deputy, dismissing the slip up as unavoidable. Foster relaxed. "This is one popular place," the deputy said, truly amazed. "I had to turn back at least twenty cars already this morning. Seems they came for a retreat, whatever the heck that is."

Before Detective Sergeant Little could comment, Laura was across the room.

"What happened?" she asked with a breathlessness that sounded as if, indeed, she had been running.

"First, ma'am, may I ask your name?"

Laura told him. "I used to be the dishwasher here," she said, and threw her arms around the unsuspecting Felicita. "Sister"—her voice was almost a sob—"I was so afraid something had happened to you."

Felicita, cheeks flaming, straightened her rimless glasses.

"Thank you, dear." She patted the young woman's hand. "I am just fine."

"Who is it, then?" Laura's glance shot around the table. Although it didn't seem possible, her face lost more of its color. "Is it one of the retreatants?" she asked.

In the empty silence that followed, Mary Helen wondered who should, who would, answer her question.

Beverly narrowed her eyes and Mary Helen could almost hear the wheels of cruelty turning behind her stare. Detective Sergeant Little must have recognized it too.

Unfolding himself from his chair, he took a deep breath and put his arm around the girl's shoulder. Reassuringly, he walked her out of St. Jude's.

Laura's screams reverberated down the mountainside. Mary Helen shivered. Like the keening of a banshee outside the door, she thought, letting us know that death has visited the house and that Detective Sergeant Little has just broken the news.

◆I◆   ◆I◆   ◆I◆

Inspector Kate Murphy slammed the car door, covered her ears with her coat collar, and waited for her partner, Dennis Gallagher, to come around from the driver's side. She was freezing. A thick, drizzly fog covered Geary Boulevard all the way from 25th Avenue to the beach. Everything was wet and dark.

It was only two-thirty in the afternoon and already lights shone in windows on both sides of the wide street. The houses with no lights probably had nobody home. A perfect giveaway for after-school burglars, Kate thought, stamping her feet to keep warm.

The two homicide inspectors had left the Hall of Justice in downtown San Francisco, where a weak summer sun had managed finally to burn off the fog. They had driven out into this pea soup and on the way Kate had tried to explain their mission to her partner.

"Detective Sergeant Bob Little from the Santa Cruz Sheriff's Department called," she said.

"Called you? Why would he call you?"

"That's what I'm trying to explain," Kate snapped. This task was going to be difficult enough without getting the needle from Denny.

"Just asking, Katie-girl. No need to bite my head off."

"Sorry," she said, and she was. It was not his fault that she found herself in this predicament. "A young man by the name of Gregory Johnson was found murdered in Little's jurisdiction. It so happens that his mother lives on Geary, very near my house. Little asked if I'd do him a favor and go over and break the news to her in person. It's not the sort of thing a mother wants to hear over the phone."

Or at all, Kate thought, wondering just how she could bear it if someone came to tell her that her son, John, was dead. The very idea catapulted her stomach into a spasm.

She had been teary for three full days after she took him to the baby-sitter for the first time. Her decision to go back to work was an agonizing one, but one she felt was right for all of them. Once it was made, she wrestled for weeks with child care. Her mother-in-law was still a little cool about her choice of Sheila Atkinson. But Kate felt that Sheila was best for John. She was an old friend. John liked her and enjoyed playing with her children. Plus, they lived only a few blocks away. Kate knew that her tears were ridiculous, but she had shed them nonetheless.

Even now, eight months later, she still felt a pang when she dropped him off. Perhaps the cruelest blow of all was that John enjoyed being there. Each morning, he threw her the briefest bye-bye kiss and ran cheerfully down the front walk to Sheila's without ever looking back.

"Do you know the Johnson woman?" Gallagher interrupted her woolgathering.

"I don't really know her," Kate admitted. "I know who she is and when we meet in the Safeway or at the cleaner's, we say 'Hello' and 'How are you?' She's lived in that pink house up the block forever. In fact, my father used to call it the 'pink palace.' Maybe because it's two stories high and painted what he considered an odd color for a house.

"Anyway, I've seen Marva Johnson around the neighborhood since I was a kid. As far as I can remember, there never was a mister. Only the two kids, Janice and Greg. Both went to St. Thomas grade school, although neither one was in my class. Both are younger than I am."

Kate was going to say "much younger," but maybe that wasn't true. When you are in elementary school, the age difference between first-graders and eighth-graders is light-years. Somehow, when you're twenty-nine and thirty-six, the difference doesn't loom as large.

Gallagher turned his head to peer at her over his horn-rimmed glasses.

"What is it?" Kate wished he'd keep his eyes on the traffic.

"Do you know this Little?" he asked, running the light on yellow.

Kate shook her head.

"Then, this guy has got to be the luckiest damn cop in Santa Cruz—no—in the whole state of California. Or maybe he's one of them psychics. Don't they have a lot of psychic types over there in Santa Cruz? I mean, Kate, if you don't know each other, how in the hell did he manage to pick you out of all the cops in San Francisco to call? How did he manage to hit on a neighbor of the victim's mother to ask to do this particular favor?"

This was the part of the explanation Kate dreaded. She knew well Gallagher's opinion of Sister Mary Helen and Sister Eileen's becoming involved in crime, any crime, least of all homicide.

"Well," Kate stalled, "it was a coincidence, of sorts. You see, Greg Johnson's body was found on the grounds of St. Colette's Retreat House and it so happens that . . ."

Gallagher's whole body stiffened. Even the tips of his ears turned red. Whether or not it was her imagination, Kate felt his heat warming her entire left side.

"I hope. No! I hope to hell that this is not leading where I think it is." Gallagher's voice was dangerously calm.

"It is." Kate waited and felt a sudden perverse pleasure—like sticking a pin into a balloon and waiting for the bang.

Gallagher ranted and sputtered for several blocks, lamenting the state of the Catholic Church, liturgical change, women's ordination, the pope's wanderings, modern convents in general, and these two nuns in particular.

"You sound like a regular old tight-ass," Kate said, tuning out the familiar tirade. Was Denny worse, or was it that while she was on maternity leave she had forgotten how irascible he could be? One thing was for sure, neither her absence nor her presence improved his disposition. She was glad when he finally petered out and they drove the last few blocks to the pink palace in silence.

"Lead the way." Denny came around behind her.

A faded brown Mercury, shaped somewhat like a landing barge with pontoons, was parked in the driveway. Apparently Mrs. Johnson was home.

Gripping the banister, Kate mounted the slippery terrazzo steps leading to the front door. This was a part of her job that she truly hated. Her words, no matter how gently put, would shatter a life. Thank God there were a dozen steps. She needed time to summon up the courage to say them.

She pushed the doorbell. Marimba notes echoed through the silence. They were followed by a series of quick, nervous footsteps.

"You're doing the talking. Right?" Gallagher looked unusually pale. He was no good at breaking bad news either.

Kate nodded. The front door opened a crack. A wary brown eye peered at them over the night chain. "Yes?" The voice was low and gravelly like the voice of an aging smoker.

"Mrs. Johnson? It's me, Kate Murphy from down the block."

Recognizing her, Mrs. Johnson closed the door enough to slide off the chain. When it reopened, the muscles in her face were tense. Her lips stretched over her teeth in a forced smile.

"What is it? What's wrong?" Mrs. Johnson tugged at the front of her blue woolen cardigan, then folded her arms around her in a protective bear hug.

Before Kate could answer, the woman pulled the door wide. "Come in," she said, with a sudden need to defer the news. "It's freezing out there."

The inside of the pink palace was anything but palatial. The decor was eclectic, although Kate guessed it had been designed more by circumstances than by choice. Much of the furniture had a "late fifties" look mixed with several pieces not quite old enough or expensive enough to be called heirlooms.

The living room had a rich, loamy smell, since what Mrs. Johnson lacked in interior decoration, she made up for in houseplants. On every table, shelf, and nearly every ledge water stains showed beneath pots of violets. There were pink, pale blue, purple, and white violets; sprawling African violets;

lavender Persian violets; miniature violets like tiny jewels in clear, square Lucite containers.

The room itself was a veritable hothouse. The furnace thudded, reminding the unaware that it was creating most of the effect.

"Sit down, please." Mrs. Johnson ushered them to a slip-covered sofa that shared a wall with a large television set. She faced them from a padded rocker, presumably "her chair."

Kate shed her coat and introduced her partner. "Mrs. Johnson," she began, wishing she didn't see the panic in those flat brown eyes or the thick, knuckled hands twisting and untwisting the edge of the sweater. "I'm afraid I have come with some very bad news for you—"

"Greg." Mrs. Johnson's hoarse voice cut her off. "It's Greg, isn't it?" Her eyes narrowed into a hard stare. "My boy is dead, isn't he?"

Kate nodded.

The woman bolted up from her chair, leaving it rocking violently. Then, as if she didn't know where to go, she sat down again. "How did it happen?" she asked.

"He was . . . murdered. Stabbed," Kate said as gently as she could. "I'm so sorry."

A tear ran down Mrs. Johnson's stony face. Kate tried to put her arm around the woman, but the narrow shoulders were rigid. "Let me get you some tea, Mrs. Johnson," Kate said. "Or perhaps some brandy. You've had an awful shock."

Mrs. Johnson shook her head. "I'm fine," she said, then added, "There's bourbon under the sink."

Kate returned from the kitchen with a hefty shot of liquor in a jelly glass. "Is there anyone who can stay with you?" she asked. "Janice, maybe?"

The woman snapped in indignation, "Janice moved away and doesn't come around any more than she needs to since she married that good-for-nothing husband of hers."

"Good-for-nothing?" The last time Kate saw Janice John-son passing her front window, she had been stylishly dressed and elegantly coiffured. If anything, Janice Johnson appeared to be very well heeled.

Mrs. Johnson took a small sip of her drink. "I simply asked her about having children, is all. I could tell she was mad. Feeling guilty, I wouldn't doubt, but instead of admit-ting it, she told me it was none of my business. I told her that as a good, God-fearing mother, it was my business." Mrs. Johnson shook her head sadly.

"And I am ashamed to tell you the kind of language she used to her own mother. I never allowed either of my chil-dren to use God's name in vain, you know. I had my strap for that kind of talk. So, I know she didn't pick it up in this house. It must have been from him. And no wonder. Do you know what he does for a living?" The woman didn't wait for an answer. "He sells drugs."

"He's a drug dealer, ma'am?" Gallagher asked.

"Not the kind you mean, Officer. Although he's just as bad. Worse, if you ask me. He sells drugs to pharmacies and doctors and he doesn't care a fig what kind they are. He sells birth control pills, those condoms, or whatever you call them."

Kate knew exactly what she meant, and from the sound of Gallagher's muffled cough, so did he.

"I told Janice that husband of hers was doing the Devil's work for him." She began to rock. "And now Greg's gone, too. I knew it. I knew something awful was going to happen." Her hands were shaking. "I warned him about it."

"About what?" Kate asked, realizing that Mrs. Johnson was in shock. But maybe they would uncover some small truth that she could pass on to Detective Sergeant Little.

"I warned him," she repeated, almost to herself. "I told him about that girl. 'You cannot tempt the Lord, thy God,' I said."

"What do you mean?" Kate prodded gently.

"Exactly what I said. With those immodest, low-cut blouses and her tight jeans and that wild hair. Looking like a streetwalker." She fiddled with the top button of her cardigan. "That girl was nothing more than an occasion of sin for my boy, and I told him so, too," she said with a triumphant gleam in her eye.

"And what did your son say to that?" Gallagher spoke at last. As the blustering father of five grown children, he had plunged head-on into hair length, curfew, dropping out of school, premarital sex, and drugs. But Kate was sure that even he knew better than to insult his sons' girlfriends, let alone meddle in his daughters' marital intimacies.

Mrs. Johnson's face tightened. "I would be ashamed to tell you the filth that came out of my son's mouth, Inspector." She was crying now. "But I knew it was the Devil talking and I told him so. 'Fornicators, idolaters and all liars, their lot shall be in the lake that burns with fire and brimstone,' I said."

The furnace thudded again and Kate bloused out her sweat-soaked shirt.

"And he left here saying that he was over twenty-one and that he'd do as he pleased, even if it was to marry that girl!"

"What is her name?" Kate asked, feeling a certain sympathy for "that girl."

"Laura Purcell." Mrs. Johnson spat it out as if it were a curse.

"What was it you warned Greg about, Mrs. Johnson?" Kate tried to steer her back to her original statement.

The woman snapped, "Sin, Kate, temptation, damnation. I just told you."

"Yes, but prior to that, you said, 'I knew it was going to happen. I warned him.' What did you mean?"

"That he would end up dead, of course."

"And why is that?"

The narrow face twisted into an acid grin. Her eyes shone. "Because the wages of sin is death, dearie. Because the Lord God said in his wrath, they will be tormented day and night, forever and ever." She shook her head sadly.

"But she wouldn't let him go, even if he came back to his senses. No, they were too steeped in their sin. And with him in the seminary once . . ."

Kate hadn't realized that Greg had studied to be a priest.

"I begged him to come back to God; to come back to the Church. But, no. He was running around at all hours, sleeping anywhere. My Greg would have been a good priest and he would have made it, too, if it hadn't been for that Father Harrington."

"Father Tom Harrington?" Kate recognized the name of the archdiocese's official spokesman. She often saw him on television and his picture was frequently in the *San Francisco Catholic*.

"They call him 'Happy Harrington,' you know." Mrs. Johnson's voice held a twist of bitterness. "But I have other names for him."

"Why is that?" Kate asked.

Mrs. Johnson took another sip of bourbon and went on as if she hadn't heard Kate's question. "I wouldn't be a bit surprised that if it isn't that girl, he's the one responsible for my Greg's death. In fact, I wouldn't put it past him and that girl to be in it together. My Greg was fine, just fine, until they assigned him to work with that one."

Her head jerked up and she stared at the blank television screen. "It was afterwards that my son started having trouble with his vocation. They sent him to work in Juvenile Hall. Greg never would tell me, his own mother, what happened.

He lied to me. He said nothing happened." Her voice dropped. "He didn't learn to lie in this house. I took care of liars. Something awful did happen, I know it. I hold that one responsible."

"You hold Father Harrington responsible for what, Mrs. Johnson?"

"For Greg's fall from grace." Her words came out in a sort of hiss. "For his turning to sin, for his leaving the seminary."

From somewhere a grandfather clock struck the hour. Its low, vibrating bong filled the room like a death knell.

"The Devil is all around me." Marva Johnson shivered in the stifling room. "But God is my shield, my protector. He took my son and I am glad. 'The Lord giveth and the Lord taketh away.' I would rather see my Greg dead than living in sin. I would sooner kill him myself than let him continue on the path to perdition."

She stood up abruptly, moved toward a window ledge, and plucked a wilted leaf from the base of a furry African violet plant. "The Lord said, 'If your hand or your foot causes you to sin, cut it off and throw it from you; it is better for you to enter life maimed than with two hands or two feet to be thrown into the eternal fires. And if your eye causes you to sin, pluck it out and throw it from you . . .' "

The woman turned and fastened her gaze on Kate. It was then Kate knew that what she suspected was true. In that moment, she caught the unmistakable laser glint of a fanatic burning in Marva Johnson's flat brown eyes.

+I+ +I+ +I+

"The mother from hell," Gallagher said as soon as they were back on the freezing sidewalk. "The next time one of my kids gets the gall to complain, have I got a comeback." He unlocked the door. "That old lady gives me the creeps," he said. "How about you?"

Kate nodded. "You really never know what's going on in somebody's head, do you?"

Billows of fog rolled up the boulevard and Gallagher switched on the headlights. "You're right. To look at her, you'd think she was Whistler's mother. Then she opens her yap, and she's a bucket of nuts with those Bible quotes bouncing around like popcorn. If you ask me, she'd be the perfect candidate for that bunch that was going to stone the gal taken in adultery." Gallagher ran his hand over his balding pate. "What are you going to tell Little?"

"I don't know." Kate watched the car lights make small tunnels in the drizzle. "That the victim's mother accused his girlfriend, one Laura Purcell, of murder? That she accused a leading priest in the archdiocese? That she said with quite a bit of conviction that she'd gladly have done it herself? That she's unbalanced? I don't know. What should I tell him?"

"All of the above, Katie-girl." Gallagher let out an exaggerated sigh. "Jeez, I'm glad the whole damn mess is on his plate and not on ours."

They drove a few blocks in silence, listening to the tires swish against the wet streets. "Be sure you tell him—hear me good, Kate—be damn sure you tell him, that no matter what he thinks to the contrary—not to let those two nuns get involved. They look pious and helpless, like two old sweethearts, but we know better. They are nothing but a pair of colossal pains in the you-know-where. Are you listening to me, Kate?"

Kate nodded, but said nothing. She had the feeling that despite Gallagher's warning, Sisters Mary Helen and Eileen were already in this, knee-deep.

✦I✦ ✦I✦ ✦I✦

Directly after lunch, Detective Sergeant Bob Little set up his command post in the small gift shop off St. Colette's main lounge. It struck Mary Helen as a strange place, but she supposed the detective had his reasons. Maybe he figured it would be harder to lie in a room filled with religious pictures and statues. To her way of thinking, if you murdered someone, lying about it, even with a saint staring at you, was small potatoes.

"Be around somewhere so we can find you" was all that Little said to the group. Yet, one by one, they inexplicably wandered into St. Colette's lounge and huddled together in a remote corner of the room as far away from the gift shop door as possible.

Someone had tried to make the enormous room cozier by grouping goldenrod and Chinese-red couches in small conversational squares around coffee tables. Here and there, a teakwood table, a silk scatter pillow, or a porcelain figurine of a geisha girl in a kimono reinforced the Oriental color scheme.

"There's strength in numbers," Eileen said, climbing over Con McHugh's long legs. She perched on the end of a hard vinyl couch.

Mary Helen followed her, taking care not to step on Tom Harrington's highly polished Gucci loafers. She settled down on the other end.

"We've got to stop meeting like this." Ed Moreno edged his wiry body between Mike Denski and Andy Carr. "See no evil, speak no evil, hear no evil," he said, referring, of course, to the three of them squeezed together on the couch.

"Who's which?" Mike asked, his eyes darting from Andy to Mary Helen.

"Who cares?" Andy said rather savagely.

"Well, we know you're not 'speak no evil,' " Ed quipped. Even Andy smiled.

They sat there, knee to toe. Like survivors on a raft, Mary Helen thought. Clinging to one another for dear life. There was no denying someone had brutally stabbed Greg Johnson. They had all been here and they were all here now. Except Felicita.

She had gone with Laura. The poor girl was so overwrought that Little suggested Felicita give her a hot toddy and put her to bed.

Even from the dining room they had heard Laura's protests; then a sudden silence. Undoubtedly she had agreed, although Mary Helen doubted if she would sleep. She had probably realized a bed was the one private place where she could lie down and cry her heart out.

"Where do you suppose Beverly is?" Eileen asked.

Mary Helen had forgotten about Beverly.

"Maybe she's in the kitchen." Andy Carr toyed with his beard. "Or maybe she's the one in with Little," he suggested unconvincingly, staring at the floor.

Monsignor McHugh groaned. "Anyplace but making another meal," he said. Apparently, the last two he'd consumed were still fighting it out.

With an unexpected bang, a side door slammed, letting in a burst of warm air and Sister Felicita.

"If I had a heart, I'd be dead," Eileen whispered.

"Sorry!" Felicita's black veil was askew atop her tousled angel hair. Her face was as flushed as if she'd wrestled with demons and barely won. "I feel about twenty years older than Methuselah," she said.

Sister Mary Helen squeezed over to make room.

"Is it still Monday?" Felicita plopped down beside her.

"As far as we know." Ed Moreno was trying his best to lift the mood.

Felicita's eyes flicked around the square. "Has Detective Sergeant Little called anyone yet?"

Con McHugh shook his head. "No one, unless it's Beverly, since the rest of us are all here."

"Did you get Laura calmed?" Mary Helen asked, trying to make conversation.

"That poor girl." Felicita's pale blue eyes flooded. "I only wish there were something I could do to make this all go away."

Her wish fell like a pall on the assembled religious. No sound was audible from the gift shop. Every attempt at conversation fell like a kamikaze pilot on a mission. Tom Harrington toyed with the obi of the geisha's kimono.

"This is slower than your confession line, Con," Ed Moreno tried again. When Con McHugh didn't rise to the bait, even Ed fell silent.

The relentless summer sun thudded against the plate-glass windows. With each passing minute the temperature in the lounge rose and the morale of those sitting in it plummeted.

Finally, the gift shop door opened and a florid-faced Beverly emerged. Without a word, she hurried from the room.

Deputy Kemp, minus his bow tie, stood by the open door. That gift shop must feel like ladies' night in the Turkish bath, Mary Helen thought, watching the deputy focus on her.

"Sister." He nodded pleasantly. "Can we see you now?"

"May we," she heard Little's voice correct. Congratulations to your English teacher, Mary Helen thought, following Kemp's lead.

The small room was windowless and stifling. Mary Helen took the chair, still warm and moist from Beverly, across from Bob Little. She scanned the walls and shelves and almost gasped aloud when she read the saying on the poster behind Little's head.

"Truth will rise above falsehood," it read, "as oil above

water." She wondered if it was a coincidence or if Little had tacked it there intentionally.

Bob Little's tall good looks seemed unwilted by the heat. He studied her with friendly brown eyes—eyes that must drive the young girls gaga, Mary Helen thought.

He asked her to retell the events of the morning, which she did in detail. Deputy Kemp scratched away in his notebook as Little gently eased her through her grisly discovery.

"Did you see anyone on your way down the hill?" he asked when she'd finished.

"No. No one."

"Whom did you run into first?"

"Monsignor McHugh."

"Then?"

"Father Moreno came out of his room, and shortly after that Father Tom Harrington came out of his in his pajamas. But you can't suppose . . ."

"Don't worry." Little's face broke into a smile. "We don't suppose anything yet. We're just trying to get the facts straight, Sister. Can you remember hearing anything out of the ordinary during the night?" he asked. "Or in the early hours of the morning?"

Mary Helen thought. Actually, she had heard nothing at all until the cooing of the mourning dove awakened her. "I slept the sleep of the dead," she blurted out, instantly wishing she could reswallow her words. Little didn't seem to notice.

When Mary Helen left the room, she was feeling restless. The very thought of sitting in that hot, sticky lounge was too much. She needed some exercise. A walk around the grounds might clear her head. It might clear up something else that was bothering her as well. Where had those big dogs gone? The last time she saw them, they had loped off to chase something in the underbrush.

"Sister Eileen," she heard Deputy Kemp say, "may we see you next, please?"

+I+   +I+   +I+

Choosing a shady footpath, Sister Mary Helen approached a screen door leading to the kitchen. She was surprised to hear voices coming from inside. Beverly and a man were talking. His voice sounded vaguely familiar, but she couldn't put her finger on exactly whose it was. They were talking softly, but from the tone the conversation was heating up.

Mary Helen eased toward the door. Both backs were toward her. Beverly fanned herself and ran her free hand up the untidy haystack of hair piled on her head. Beside her was a broad, thick tan-shirted back belonging to a man with short reddish hair. Sergeant Loody! Of course!

What kind of business could he have with Beverly? And why wasn't he guarding the murder scene?

Even policemen need a coffee break, Mary Helen thought, hurrying past the door before they spotted her. She was in no mood for a confrontation or even a conversation with either of them.

She followed a secluded wooded trail up the hillside. Thankfully, it was far away from Madonna Grove, yet had the same wilderness beauty.

Live oak, white-barked sycamore, and waxy madrone shaded the path. Fragrant yellow broom and sword fern grew along its sides. Mary Helen walked a wide berth around the bright red poison oak leaves and stooped to examine the ballerina-shaped fuchsia blossoms.

Amid all this peace and beauty, how could she have discovered something so heinous? She breathed in the fragrant air.

The angry buzz of swarming insects snagged her attention.

Her stomach jumped and her hands felt cold and shaky. Was this going to happen every time she heard bugs buzzing? Was her mind going to conjure up imaginary evils even in this idyllic setting?

She moved toward the noise. They were after something. Bravely she stole a glance and her stomach pitched forward in a sickening lurch at what she saw. Her question was answered. There, lying rigid and stiff, in a field of miner's lettuce and buttercups, were the two German shepherds. Except for their arched necks and their open, bulging eyes, they might have been asleep. The sound of her screams filled the silent woods.

"It was louder than the Berkeley ferry bell," Eileen said later, but Mary Helen never did believe that.

◆I◆   ◆I◆   ◆I◆

Deputy David Kemp was the first to hear the scream. Eileen was the first to recognize it.

"It's Sister Mary Helen," she said, her brogue thick.

Detective Little threw back his chair. He heard it bang against the gift shop wall as he followed Kemp out the door.

The two men ran toward the noise. Surprisingly, the little old nun, Eileen, was not too far behind, puffing but keeping up.

"Atta girl!" he wanted to call over his shoulder, but he needed all his breath to keep going himself. Too much time with Terry and not enough working out, he thought ruefully.

"What the hell's Loody doing here?" Kemp pointed to the enormous figure bursting through the screen door by the kitchen. "Isn't he supposed to be guarding the scene?"

"Maybe he needed to take a leak," Little said, then hoped that Sister Eileen hadn't heard him.

"Aren't there enough trees in the woods?" Kemp called.

Before Little could answer, Mary Helen stumbled into the clearing, her face the color of pabulum. She swayed. He grabbed her. Her whole body was trembling.

"What is it, Sister? What happened?"

With great effort, Mary Helen sobbed out her grim discovery.

"Get somebody up there," Little shouted, keeping his arm firmly around her.

Eileen caught up. Slowly, the two of them half walked, half carried Mary Helen toward the kitchen. Beverly filled the doorway.

"What you need is a good strong cup of coffee." Little nodded toward Beverly, knowing she heard him. Without any change of expression, she went inside.

Where had he seen her before? He knew he recognized her from somewhere, yet he could not put his finger on where. A woman of her stature was hard to forget. This was his first visit to St. Colette's, so it hadn't been here. It had bothered him all during lunch. If he thought about it long enough, he knew he'd remember.

That was why he had called for her first, although his interrogation had shed no real light. Beverly Benton, forty-one years old, had lived in the Bonny Doon area of Santa Cruz for about two years. Alone. Before that she had lived in San Francisco, working as a chef at an upscale restaurant on Kearny Street.

She said that the job was "too pressured" and so she had moved from the city and found work at the retreat house as their cook.

She had never been married, had no immediate family, and didn't know the victim, other than that he was Laura Purcell's boyfriend.

Last night, she had stayed home alone watching reruns on

television and had gone to sleep early because today the priests' retreat started and she knew it would be a busy week.

She added, with the first bit of emotion Little had seen her show, that she had no good reason to kill Greg Johnson.

When he asked, "What about a not so good reason?" she had actually smiled. Maybe she even had a sense of humor.

Bob Little felt Mary Helen sag in his arms. "We're almost there, Sister," he said.

"If you ask me, she needs something stronger than coffee." Beverly reappeared with a full snifter. Little caught the distinctive smell of brandy. With surprising gentleness, she held it up to the old nun's lips. Eileen hovered nearby.

"Sister looks like she's in good hands," Little said. He was anxious to get up the hill to check out this latest development. Who the hell kills dogs? "If you think she needs a doctor, just let one of the deputies know."

Mary Helen's back stiffened. "A doctor is totally unnecessary." She sniffed. "There's plenty of life left in the old girl yet." The flint in her eyes left no doubt in his mind that what she said was true.

By the time Little arrived at the new crime scene, Kemp had summoned the forensic team. Carefully they studied the ground around the two animals, searching for anything that might be useful. Deputy Foster, looking as if he had been hit with the flu, stood to one side. "Looks like poison," he managed.

Loody's face twisted with disgust. He stared at the two German shepherds. "What kind of a son of a bitch poisons a dog?" he asked, kicking viciously at a rock. It ricocheted off a tree trunk with a *ping*, narrowly missing one of the forensic team.

The man stared up angrily. "Take a hike, will ya?"

Before Loody could answer, Little grabbed his arm. "I need you back at the parking lot," he said with all the good humor he could dredge up. "With everyone else up in the hills, you never know what kind of nut will wander in."

Loody hesitated, then, much to Little's relief, he followed him down the hillside. Little felt he didn't need any insurrection among the troops.

"What was going on in the kitchen?" Little made sure they were out of earshot before speaking.

Loody's small eyes became even smaller. "What do you mean?" he asked.

Little shrugged. "When I was running toward the screaming, I saw you barrel out the kitchen door. I was just curious what you were doing there. Maybe you happen to know the cook from somewhere?"

"It was as hot as hell in that grove and I was sweating like a pig. I needed a glass of water, that's all," Loody said, too quickly.

"Just wondering." Obviously this was not the time or place to get the truth out of Eric Loody. He'd wait. "Make sure no one crosses the line, will you, Sergeant?" he said, pointing to the bright yellow cordon.

Loody scoffed. "Just let 'em try!"

◆I◆ ◆I◆ ◆I◆

Bob Little paused by the kitchen door. Sister Eileen gave him an "okay" signal. Confident that Mary Helen was in good care, he continued to the gift shop.

Back in the small, airless room, Little closed his eyes, deep-breathing as Terry had taught him, purposely trying to relax. I still have "miles to go before I sleep," he thought, remembering Sister Immaculata's penchant for making her students memorize poetry. He usually chose Frost. At least he understood the stuff.

After a few minutes, he ran his finger slowly down the list

of names. Monsignor McHugh, Cornelius J. Might as well start with the top banana. Besides, he was the one who knew the victim's mother. Marva. Little remembered the name because it was so odd. Like naming a baby "Wonder Woman." If Terry and he ever had a child, he wondered what they'd name it. Something a lot more ordinary than Marva or Cornelius.

Thinking about a child was really far-fetched. Terry and he hadn't even decided on a permanent commitment. They had their careers. Terry was on the way to becoming a highly paid architect and he considered himself a successful cop.

True, they had lived together for a little over two years in a small gem of a Victorian built on a short street off East Cliff that dead-ended at the beach. The cottage belonged in Terry's family and was once undoubtedly the only dwelling on the cliff.

The place reminded him of a gingerbread house, but Terry loved it. Probably had something to do with being an architect. When pushed he had to admit that its location was ideal. The soothing rhythm of the waves, the ever-changing sky, and the long stretch of beach provided a perfect place to forget crime. But—back to work . . .

"Monsignor Cornelius McHugh," Little called from the doorway. "May I see you next, please?" He wondered absently if the other kids had called him "Corny."

The monsignor, sitting stiffly in St. Colette's lounge, rose from a Chinese-red couch. Slowly, almost painfully, he walked the length of the room and crossed the threshold into the stifling gift shop.

"It's a sorry way to begin a retreat," he said.

It's a sorry way to begin anything, Little thought. A trickle of sweat slid down his back. Where the hell was Kemp? Somebody needed to take notes.

He didn't have to wait long. Kemp, his face red from coming down the hill, threw open the door and pulled the notebook from his breast pocket. "Ready," he said, clicking his ballpoint pen and waiting for Little to begin.

✦I✦ ✦I✦ ✦I✦

Two hours and four priests later, Detective Sergeant Little was happy to hear a knock on the door. The room felt like a sauna and his rear end ached from sitting on the small, hard chair. Kemp's face had an unhealthy glow and not only was his bow tie off, but the first three buttons of his shirt were open. Before long he'd be stripped down to his T-shirt.

"Sorry to disturb you, Sergeant." Sister Felicita peered at him through her rimless glasses. "There is a lady—Inspector Kate Murphy—on the telephone."

Little had almost forgotten about Murphy. He checked his watch. Nearly quitting time for her. Maybe she'd gleaned something from the victim's mother. He sure hoped so. He was getting no place fast with these clerics.

"Take a break, Dave," Little said, and followed Felicita outside. A breeze was picking up. Thank God. Maybe the night would cool off so he could get some shut-eye. Things always seemed clearer after a good night's sleep.

Sister Felicita ushered him into a small office, carefully shutting the door as she left.

"Sergeant Little," he said, picking up the receiver.

"Inspector Murphy here." Her voice was energetic, especially for the end of the day, Little thought, but then she hasn't been cooped up for hours in a sweatbox.

Kate Murphy got right down to business. "My partner and I dropped by Marva Johnson's home and notified her of her son's death."

"How did she take it?" Little asked, realizing what a dumb question that was.

"She was shocked, of course, but somehow not surprised."

"How's that?"

"She strongly disapproved of his lifestyle."

"Which was?"

"Promiscuous, from her point of view. She thought his girlfriend Laura Purcell was 'a tramp.' Her words."

Little was surprised. If anything, Laura had seemed to him like the all-American coed type. Somebody that anyone's mother would approve of. His sure would. "So?"

"So, if Laura didn't lead him into trouble someone else would."

"Other women?"

"Not only women, anyone, even priests. He was in the seminary, you know."

Little did know. He had learned that much, anyway, from his interviews with the clergymen.

"She implied that if he hadn't met Father Tom Harrington—he's a prominent priest here in San Francisco—" Kate explained.

"I know who he is. I just spent a half hour talking to him," Little said.

"He's there too?" Kate sounded surprised.

"Why do you ask?" Little's heart sank. Don't tell me he's a pedophile or some damn thing, he thought. So much had been in the media lately about the sexual abuse and indiscretions by priests, and even bishops, that the impact was gone. It just left him with a sad, sick feeling.

"I had the impression that it was a nuns' retreat," Kate said.

With a sense of relief, Little cleared his throat. "No. There was just a little mix-up with your two nun friends. Actually, it is, or was supposed to be, a priests' retreat. It could happen to anybody."

Kate chuckled. "Things happen to those two that don't happen to just anybody," she said.

Oddly annoyed that Murphy seemed to be making fun of the two old ladies, Little shifted gears. "Let me get this straight, Inspector. The mother suspects the girlfriend because she's a tramp. And/or Father Harrington? Why?"

"Apparently her son worked with him at the Archdiocesan Communications Center. Not too long after, he left the seminary 'to do the Devil's work for him,' direct quote."

"His mother said that?"

"That isn't all. She implied that maybe the girl and the priest were in it together. She finished off our conversation by saying that she'd sooner have killed him herself than to let him continue living in sin."

Little's mouth went dry. "Is she a nut or what?" he asked bluntly.

"A nut of the worst kind. A religious one!"

"Do you think there's any truth in what she says?"

"That's up to you to find out, Sergeant," Kate said cheerfully, "and good luck!"

◆I◆   ◆I◆   ◆I◆

"Jeez, Kate, I thought you were going to warn the poor devil about the nuns," Gallagher said the moment she replaced the receiver.

"I intended to," Kate said, feeling along her desktop for her earring. She found it under a pile of reports and clipped it back on her earlobe. "But I got the impression that he didn't want to hear it."

Gallagher's eyebrows shot up. "Why the hell not?"

"I don't know why. Just something in his tone told me to let it be."

Gallagher checked the electric clock on the detail wall. "He's only been with those two, what? Nine, ten hours now? You're probably right. He still thinks they're a couple of harmless old sweethearts and you're a jaded, cynical lady cop."

Quickly Kate cleared off her desk, pouring the remains of her cold coffee into the plant on its edge. She balanced the paper cup on the mountain of trash in the can. It was Monday, her day to pick up the baby at Sheila's and her husband's turn to fix dinner.

She wondered if tonight Jack would actually cook something or would he get takeout? Not that it mattered much, as long as he didn't bring up moving to Marin County again. She was as set against going as he was set on it. Lately, their discussions were beginning to shed more heat than light on the subject. What she wanted tonight was a peaceful dinner.

Gallagher snatched up his jacket from the back of his chair. "You're right," he said, "better to let that guy Little learn about those nuns the hard way."

"Better for whom?"

"Who cares?" he said, following Kate out of the homicide detail. "As long as it's no business of ours."

◆I◆　　◆I◆　　◆I◆

"About ready to call it a day?" Dave Kemp was waiting for Little when he got off the phone.

The two men walked together into the parking lot. The sun, moving below the redwoods, sent long, cooling shadows across the shimmering blacktop. The forensic team was packing up. A van from the animal shelter had arrived to pick up the two dogs. Only one green-and-white sheriff's car remained in the lot, Loody's.

Eric Loody loomed like a lone sentinel beside the bright yellow police barrier, a second deterrent to anyone tempted to enter.

"Anything happening?" Little asked him.

"It's been pretty quiet for the last couple of hours." The top of Loody's large nearly hairless head was a strawberry red. "I convinced all those padres that came here to go home." His small eyes narrowed even farther. "There must be some souls to save or whatever it is they do, somewhere else. A carload of nuns tried to get in. One little mouthy one told me it was their right."

He sniffled. "I told her she had the right to remain silent, the right—"

"So all went peacefully?" Little interrupted. It was all he could do not to shout his disgust at Loody's bullying. A carload of nuns, for chrissake!

Beside him, Kemp shifted. His partner must be reacting the same way.

"Everything was peaceful," Loody said, unaware of the effect he was having on them.

"What time is your replacement coming?" Little asked.

"Should be any minute."

"See you tomorrow then." Waving to the forensic team, Little and Kemp crossed to their unmarked champagne Ford. At least, the owner's manual in the glove compartment said the color was champagne. Little thought of it more as "tugboat gray."

"How about a cold one before we go home?" Kemp turned the key and flipped on the air conditioner. Little loosened his tie, waiting for the hot blast of air to cool.

The two detectives found a quiet booth at 99 Bottles of Beer on the Wall, a trendy place on a side street in downtown Santa Cruz. True to its name, it did have ninety-nine different kinds of beer, all on display along the wall.

When they arrived, it was nearly empty. Too early, really, for the serious happy hour crowd; too late for even the most leisurely businessmen's lunch.

A couple of women laden with Gottschalk's department

store bags were sitting at the bar sipping something foamy and red. The younger of the two glanced over her shoulder appraising Kemp and himself, Little thought, almost as if they were designer dresses on a sale rack.

Her eyes flicked for a moment on Little, then honed in on Kemp. It's almost as if Terry shows, he thought, searching the vacant room for a waitress. In the end, Kemp, obviously unaware of anything but his thirst, went to the bar. He carried back two cold Elephant malts, the beer of the day.

Both men took long swallows, then stopped to savor the taste in silence. "Milk of the gods," Little said at last.

Kemp nodded and licked his upper lip. "Okay," he said. "Where are we?"

Little's eyes burned. He closed them for a minute. "So far, what we know for sure is that all the priests were acquainted with the victim. The nuns had met him. We know that everyone we talked to had the opportunity to kill him because they were all there last night.

"That is, if Greg Johnson was killed at St. Colette's. And from the looks of the scene, he was. The question is—how did the killer get Johnson back to St. Colette's and up that hill without him making a racket? And apparently he didn't because someone would have heard him holler. The place is so quiet and sound carries." His brown eyes riveted on Kemp.

Obviously unable to shed any light on the question, Kemp took another swallow of his malt. "We don't have a motive either," he said, finally. "Although from the looks of the body, I'd guess it was what the media call a crime of passion."

Little nodded. "Inspector Murphy, the call I got from San Francisco, says the victim's mother thinks that it could be the girlfriend. I suppose she could get him to follow her up the hill."

"Laura Purcell." Kemp supplied the name.

"Right, or maybe the priest, Tom Harrington."

"The smiley guy with the Gucci loafers?"

"The same. Murphy said something about the mother saying she'd do it herself."

"The mother?" Kemp's eyes opened wide in disbelief. "Why?"

"For religious reasons."

Kemp finished the rest of his drink in one gulp and called over for another. "So, what's your gut feeling?" he asked, wiping the foam from his mustache.

"Too soon," Little said honestly. "We need to hear from the forensic boys tomorrow. And we need to know where Greg Johnson was last night after he left Laura."

"If he left her," Kemp added.

Little waited until the waitress set down Kemp's drink. "I know I've seen that Beverly somewhere, but I can't place her. Check on her first thing in the morning, will you, Dave? Tomorrow, I'll talk to Laura. See if this case becomes clearer."

"What about your gut feeling?" Little asked out of courtesy. Kemp shrugged as Little knew he would. Gut feelings take time to acquire.

"Another beer?" Kemp asked.

"No." Little patted his stomach. He wanted to get going. Terry should be home from work by now. Maybe they could get in a game of beach volleyball before dinner. Better get some exercise unless he wanted little old nuns beating him up hills.

✠ ✠ ✠

"Her color is coming back," Felicita whispered.

Mary Helen bristled. If there was anything she detested, it was being talked about as if she weren't there. But she held her tongue. No doubt Felicita was concerned and trying to be kind.

"Do you think we should help her back to her room? Lying down for a while might help," Felicita said.

Eileen did not answer. She knew better.

When Beverly asked, "Should I get her some more brandy?" Mary Helen knew it was time to speak up. More brandy and they'd be carrying her to bed.

"I wonder what she'd say if she could speak?" she said ironically. Then added, "I'm really just fine." She didn't want to sound too unappreciative. "It was just such a shock finding those animals." She stopped. The color in Beverly's face drained and unexpected tears brimmed in her coffee-brown eyes.

"They were good dogs," she whispered. Mary Helen reached out to squeeze her hand and, to her surprise, Beverly let it be squeezed.

"Why don't you get some fresh air?" Felicita suggested, and Mary Helen didn't argue. Reluctant to trust her legs too far, Mary Helen eased into one of the canvas director's chairs on the deck outside St. Jude's. Taking a long, relaxing breath, she gazed out at the vista. The sun, inching toward the mountain of evergreens, sent wide shadows from the wooden railing down the length of the porch. A breeze rustled the fern ever so slightly. Although the sun was several hours from setting, the night cool was already in the air.

Thank God, Mary Helen thought. Despite the fact that she herself was not a native San Franciscan, she had lived there long enough to have a native's abhorrence of heat. As far as she was concerned, seventy-two degrees Fahrenheit was God's temperature and as warm as any place or any person needed to be.

Satisfied that Mary Helen was comfortable, Felicita bustled away on some errand or other. Beverly, apparently embarrassed by her own lapse into gentleness, recovered enough to make several pointed remarks about "people who had nothing else to do." Mary Helen did not doubt that they'd soon hear her saucepans banging, even from this distance.

Eileen pulled up a deck chair close to hers. "Where are the priests?" Mary Helen whispered. They seemed to be alone, but one never knew.

"I imagine they've all taken to their rooms for a siesta. Heaven knows after the day we've had, we can all use a snooze. I thought I'd swallowed my heart when I heard your scream."

Mary Helen hesitated. Wasn't your heart already swallowed? she wanted to ask, but thought better of it. Eileen was obviously upset. Her brogue gave it away, that and the way she was pressing her stubby fingers together.

"By the way, what were you doing up there? Alone," she added, as if it were an accusation.

"I was simply taking a walk." Mary Helen hoped she sounded offended. "What else would I be doing?"

"Don't give me that malarkey. What were you looking for?"

Mary Helen wanted to defend her innocence for a few more volleys, but she really felt much too weary. "If you must know, I was looking for the dogs."

"Why ever?"

"Because they were so noisy when we first arrived. Then this morning not a sound from them. It just didn't make sense. Either someone had coaxed them away or . . ." Suddenly Mary Helen felt light-headed.

"Do you suppose someone silenced those poor creatures so that he could get onto the property undetected?" Eileen asked hopefully.

Mary Helen knew where her friend was heading.

"A perfect stranger." Eileen shivered. "Perhaps one of those serial killers that Father Moreno mentioned?"

"That doesn't explain what Greg Johnson himself was doing here." Mary Helen hated to splash cold water on Eileen's theory. Frankly, it was the explanation she was hoping for herself: Somehow, a crazed killer slipping onto the property, silencing the dogs, then attacking the first victim he stumbled across seemed more palatable than the murderer being someone you knew. It did not, however, explain Greg Johnson's presence at St. Colette's.

"We'll have to ask Laura what happened after they left here," Mary Helen said.

"You can't suspect Laura, can you?" Eileen's gray eyes welled up with sympathy. "She was so upset when she found out that Greg was dead. No one could have put on that haunted look or those agonizing screams. Not even a drama student," she added quickly.

The Berkeley ferry bell gonged out the advent of the day's final meal. The two old nuns slowly rose to join the rest of the group in St. Jude's.

The dining room and the kitchen area were oddly silent. "Beverly's gone home early," Felicita announced when they all assembled. You could hear her relief. "She set out a cold buffet and we can pick up."

The nuns, pros at pick-up suppers, led the way. The line moved quickly, since, as both nuns knew, the speed of the line is always in direct proportion to the amount of food being taken.

With little enthusiasm and half-filled plates, the group settled once again at the Formica-topped table. The long, hot day had taken its toll on them all.

Mike Denski, staring straight ahead, seemed to have aged ten years since last night. A tight-lipped line replaced Tom Harrington's usual crooked grin, while across from him, Andy

Carr looked as if someone had let out all his air. Even Ed Moreno was silent and morose. Perhaps the worst of all was Monsignor McHugh. Tonight the venerable old man looked every bit his age.

"Would anyone care for a glass of wine?" Felicita offered cautiously, as though the idea might be offensive in the light of the day's events.

"A meal without wine is like a day without sunshine." Tom Harrington pushed his wineglass toward her.

"Who said that?" Ed asked. "Gallo Brothers?"

"I could skip any more sun," Mike Denski said softly.

"Use a little wine for thy stomach's sake." Loosely quoting St. Paul, the monsignor put a pious spin on the question and settled the matter once and for all.

Although the wine didn't raise anyone's spirits appreciably, or, Mary Helen suspected, improve anyone's digestion either, it did bring on a mellow mood. She watched as, one by one, they relaxed.

"I guess this has been about the longest day of my life," Andy Carr said finally.

No one spoke, but there were nods of agreement.

"What I can't understand is why the police are questioning us." Denski's face was flushed. Nervously, he curled the piece of hair at the end of a long sideburn.

"Why wouldn't they? We were here, after all," Ed Moreno began logically. "Each one of us, priests, I mean, knew him. That's quite a coincidence, don't you think?"

"Not really." Andy Carr's voice was flat. "This is a small archdiocese and we have very few vocations. The chances are pretty good that we'd all know any young guy who was in the seminary."

"True enough." Tom Harrington twirled the stem of his wineglass. Felicita leaned forward and they all watched as she refilled it.

"What kind of a fellow was Greg Johnson?" Mary Helen wondered aloud. "Why would anyone want to murder him?"

Her question hung frozen on the air. What a moment before had been a pleasant enough conversation became dead silence.

"What do you mean?" Con McHugh asked icily.

"I'm just curious," Mary Helen said. "I only saw the boy once. At first meeting, despite his rather dubious seminary career, he seemed like a very nice young man; not the kind of person someone would kill."

"I see." McHugh sounded relieved. "I've known Greg almost all his life. And he was a nice boy, actually a good boy, always thoughtful and considerate of his mother. He grew up to be a fine, upstanding young man."

"No wonder he had to sow a few wild oats after he entered the seminary," Tom interjected, almost as if he were talking to himself.

"What does that mean?" The monsignor stiffened.

"His continual flirting with my secretaries is what it means." Tom's eyes flashed.

"Nobody'd kill a young guy for that," Ed Moreno quipped, a cautious eye on the monsignor's flushed face.

Andy Carr grinned. "Except maybe his mother." He cleared his throat as if for a pronouncement. "I think, if anything, his death may have had something to do with his Gay Rights connection."

"Get serious," Ed said. "You'd hardly kill a guy for one protest march, Andy. Not even Absolute Norm was that mad."

"So, what you're saying," Mary Helen broke in, "is that there was really no reason, that you know of, anyway, why someone would want Greg Johnson dead?"

"My point exactly," Mike Denski burst out. "It could

have been a mistake. Whoever killed Greg might have meant to kill someone else."

Mary Helen studied the young priest. His altar boy face blazed with emotion, his eyes, two points of light. Obviously, he wanted to believe that Greg Johnson's death was a mistake. Did he think the intended victim was Beverly? He'd mentioned her earlier in the day. Why? Mary Helen wondered. And most important of all, why did he want it to be true?

"Don't you think it's odd that the police haven't talked to Laura?" Tom Harrington interrupted. His glass was empty again.

Laura! That was where she and Eileen had left off. As difficult as it was to imagine her stabbing Greg so viciously, Mary Helen had the gnawing feeling that Laura was somehow involved.

"Didn't you see her?" The monsignor answered Tom's question with one of his own. "She's nothing but a young girl. She'd not have the strength." His keen blue eyes swept over the group and his nostrils flared. "And, if you ask me, she was too broken up to have committed the crime—or any crime at all."

Ed Moreno shifted in his chair. "Look, Con, somebody did it. I know it's hard to imagine that it was an innocent-looking coed, but killers come in all sizes and shapes and they can be very persuasive."

"Yet, I simply cannot believe . . ."

"Do you know her, Con?" Andy asked softly.

The monsignor's cheeks flamed. "Not really. Greg introduced me to her last night."

"Last night?" Tom blurted out. "Where the hell did you meet Greg last night?"

For a moment the old man looked stung; then, with a

regal toss of his winter-white head, his gaze met Tom's. "I was taking my usual walk before retiring, and Greg and Laura passed me in Greg's car. Since I know both him and his mother, common courtesy prompted him to stop and say hello."

"What time was that?" Andy asked.

The monsignor stiffened.

"Whoa, fellas." Ed Moreno raised one hand. "We are beginning to sound like something right out of *Top Cops*."

Andy Carr looked offended. "Hell, Ed, we're only trying to get a handle on what happened."

Unexpectedly, Ed Moreno turned his attention to Mary Helen. "If anyone has a handle on anything," he said, "I'm putting my money on this woman."

"Me?" Mary Helen was genuinely startled.

"You!" he said with a knowing grin. "You've had quite a bit of experience."

One by one, Mary Helen saw signs of recognition in the other priests' eyes. Only Felicita was in the dark.

"Sister here has collaborated with the San Francisco Police Department on several occasions," Ed explained.

Felicita looked as if she might faint.

"So, Sister," Ed taunted, "what are your thoughts? Who do you think our murderer is? One of us? Laura?"

"I do not have the slightest idea," Mary Helen said curtly. And she didn't.

Not for the first time, she wished she had the enviable powers of some of the detectives who peopled her murder mysteries. She wished that in the presence of the guilty, the hairs on the back of her neck would stand up, or that her mustache, if she had one, would twitch. It would make life so much simpler.

Unfortunately, at the moment she had no sensation

whatsoever, except that of being totally and absolutely exhausted.

I   *I*   *I*

With a minimum of urging from Sister Felicita, the group piled their dishes in the sink. The leftover ones spilled onto the serving cart.

"Beverly's not going to be very happy in the morning," Ed Moreno remarked, balancing his plate on the stack.

"At least she'll have something concrete to complain about," Felicita answered with a toughness that hadn't been there yesterday.

The group dispersed quickly, leaving the three nuns alone in the large, empty kitchen. "Has anyone looked in on Laura?" Mary Helen asked without thinking.

The expression on Felicita's round apple face more than answered her question. "Besides you, I mean," she added quickly.

"Not that I know of. That nice Sergeant Little said that he'd wait until morning to ask her any questions."

Nice, yes, but wise? Mary Helen wondered. Questioning her today, hysterical though she was, might be a waste of time. On the other hand, he could receive the real answers to his questions. Regardless, it was too late now.

"I think I'll bring her over another hot toddy to make sure she sleeps." Felicita was thinking aloud.

"By now, the poor thing might welcome visitors," Eileen offered hopefully.

Mary Helen could tell that Eileen was dead to chat with the girl. She herself was, too. Felicita peered at them through her rimless glasses. "If she's awake, maybe you can talk to her and discover what really happened."

Mary Helen was startled, although she knew she shouldn't be. After Ed Moreno's remark about her involvement with the police, Felicita expected a miracle. The way those priests gab, it's a marvel any of them can keep the seal of confession, she fumed.

"I have no way of discovering what really happened," she said.

But Felicita refused to be dissuaded. She placed the steaming cup on a tiny plastic tray and led the small procession across the parking lot to St. Philomena's Hall and Laura's bedroom.

Under a thin sheet, the girl was curled into a fetal position with her auburn hair fanned out across the pillow like a halo of flame. Crumpled tissues had rolled out of her partially clenched hand. Her halter and shorts formed a small white pile on the rug where she had dropped them. The room was dim and the soft, low rustle of her breathing was the only sound.

"She's asleep," Felicita whispered, unnecessarily.

Since none of them had the heart to wake her, Felicita cautiously closed the door and left Laura in peace, at least until morning. In the hallway, she stared down at the tray in her hand. "Would either of you be interested?" she asked.

"You take it and go off to bed." Eileen's face crinkled into a sympathetic smile.

"After I call St. Anthony's I'll probably need it," Felicita said.

"St. Anthony's?"

"That's the convent where the nuns are staying until this mess is settled. Mother Superior is beside herself with all the negative publicity, and Sister Timothy is acting as if I should do something about it!"

Without another word, Felicita turned on her heel, and

with her black scapular flapping behind her, disappeared down the long, silent corridor.

Outside, the setting sun had changed the distant wooded hills into gray silhouettes, stark against a peach backdrop. "What about you, old dear?" Eileen asked. "You must be dragging. Do you want to head for bed too?"

Mary Helen was tired, yet she doubted that she'd sleep right away. It was still too warm and her mind was too full.

"How about a short walk?" she suggested, and Eileen silently fell into step. A soft breeze sent a shower of golden oak leaves across the acorn-strewn path.

After several minutes, they settled on a wooden bench overlooking an oval pond. Someone had hollowed the space out of the hillside, filled it with water, then added large orange-gold and black carp. Fragrant white water lilies floated beside flat pads. Cleverly, the pond's creator had topped it with chicken wire to keep out swooping birds and scooping beasts.

Probably that same someone had hammered into the ground a small iron sign that declared BE STILL AND KNOW THAT I AM GOD.

Mary Helen stared vacantly at it, her thoughts anything but still. Instead they swam and splashed through her mind like the fish in the pond.

Who killed Greg Johnson and why? Was it Laura Purcell? Although they knew little about her, she seemed like a hardworking, wholesome girl. Besides, the two of them had acted as if they were very much in love. What motive could Laura have to kill him?

The tail of a carp broke the surface of the dark water. . . . Was it one of the priests? Did one of them share a secret with Greg, one so deep and so savage that it made murder a necessity?

Of course not! There was no reason to believe that either Laura or one of the clergy stabbed that young man to death.

"A penny for your thoughts." Eileen's voice was soft. "Or are they the fifty-cent variety?"

"We don't even know how Greg Johnson came to be at the retreat center this morning," Mary Helen stated.

"It's a sure bet it wasn't voluntary," Eileen said.

"No, I mean he must have come in a car, but whose? What time was he killed?"

"Won't the forensic team know?"

"They will," Mary Helen said. "But how will we?"

"Sergeant Little may tell us?"

"Why would he?" Mary Helen asked, and for once, Eileen was stumped.

"What about Beverly?" Eileen was off on a new tack. "How does she fit in, or does she?"

"It was the oddest thing. Before I found the dogs . . ." Mary Helen stopped. She felt her stomach roil.

Eileen looked as if she might say something sympathetic, but Mary Helen glared. Even a hint of sympathy and she knew she'd go to pieces. Another hysterical female was the last thing this investigation needed.

"Before I went up the mountain trail," Mary Helen said, rephrasing her sentence, "I noticed Beverly and Sergeant Loody together in the kitchen. They were talking, and the conversation was heated."

Eileen's gray eyes lit up. "He burst out of that door when you started screaming. Almost as if he were guilty for being there and wanted to look as if he were on the job."

"Are you making that up?"

Eileen looked offended. "As they say back home, 'Two thirds the work is the semblance.' "

"No, not that part. The 'looking guilty' part."

"Well, he did burst out of that kitchen. And Beverly is

such an angry woman." Eileen brightened. "Maybe they are in cahoots!"

"Wishful thinking," Mary Helen said. "Only in mystery stories are the two least likable characters the murderers. And not always then."

A persistent mosquito buzzed near her ear. She swatted at it. "It's either move or become a late dinner," she said, slapping again at her neck.

A fearless blue jay eyed the pair and hopped closer to the bench. Cocking his head, the bird gave a raucous caw.

"Maybe they're all trying to tell us to go to bed." Eileen pushed up from the bench. "Things are always clearer after a good night's sleep."

Deep shadows covered the pathway. The sky, or what little of it showed between the tall evergreens, had turned a graphite gray. Something rustled in the underbrush. Probably a squirrel or a chipmunk settling in for the night, Mary Helen thought. She wished she'd remembered to bring a flashlight.

"Too, too, too," a low call echoed above them. The gigantic black pupils in a pair of glossy yellow eyes stared down from a branch. Eileen grabbed Mary Helen's arm. "An owl."

From somewhere below came the sound of slow, deliberate footsteps. Pine needles crunched. Twigs cracked. The two nuns froze.

"Maybe a deer?" Eileen whispered.

Mary Helen listened. "Too heavy."

"A big deer?"

"Not enough feet."

The steps passed close below them. Mary Helen felt Eileen stiffen. She braced herself. It was too dim to make out anything but a large hunched form. The murderer perhaps, stalking another victim?

The vanilla smell of pipe tobacco wafted up on the night air.

"It's the monsignor!" Eileen let out her breath. "Didn't he say he usually walks before bed?"

"Let's wait," Mary Helen suggested. "If we call out, we'll probably scare the poor man to death. We don't need another dead body."

When they were sure that the monsignor was safely out of earshot, the two quickly made their way toward the parking lot. Fortunately, Felicita had remembered to turn on the night lights.

"I wonder if the monsignor telephoned Greg's mother?" Eileen nodded toward the pay phone just inside St. Agnes' Hall. "And I wonder how Kate made out with her today. I am feeling a little guilty for putting Kate in that position. Why don't you call her?" Eileen suggested, digging in her coin purse for change.

"Why me?" Mary Helen protested, but they both knew it was more for form than for anything else. Mary Helen was dying to call Kate Murphy.

✦I✦ ✦I✦ ✦I✦

"Dammit! What now?" Jack Bassetti said when the phone rang. He stared across the table at Kate as if it were her fault; as if she had somehow willed it to ring right in the middle of their discussion. Their argument, really.

If I could have, I would have, Kate thought, staring right back.

"Hold that thought," Jack said gruffly, and went into the front hall. He picked it up on the fourth ring. Kate heard him attempt to sound polite. Thank goodness the baby was asleep. Little John was so sensitive to everything around him. Their angry voices would surely have upset him.

"It's for you," Jack growled.

Kate recognized Mary Helen's voice immediately and knew exactly what she wanted. She cut short the old nun's apologies for calling so late and for getting her involved again and plunged right into her interview with Marva Johnson.

"What was it she accused Laura of, exactly?" Mary Helen asked.

"Of leading her son astray. Of generally being his downfall. Nothing specific. 'An occasion of sin' is the way she put it, I think."

"What do you suppose she meant by that?"

"That they were living together, I assumed." Kate flushed, remembering a time when, before they were married, Jack and she had lived together. Mary Helen was not judgmental then, nor was she now.

She did seem genuinely shocked when Kate told her Mrs. Johnson insinuated that Father Tom Harrington might have had something to do with the murder.

"What possible reason?" she asked. "Did she explain?"

Kate didn't have the answer. "Something that happened when Greg was assigned with Father Harrington?" she guessed.

"Do you think there is any truth in that?"

"I wouldn't discount it completely, but I wouldn't put too much stock in it either. Remember Marva Johnson actually said that she'd sooner have done it herself than let Greg continue on the road to perdition."

Kate heard Mary Helen groan. "What do you make of it?" she asked.

"I'd say that the woman is a bit of a religious fanatic," Kate said. "You know, very sure, very righteous."

And we all know there is absolutely no cure for self-righteousness, Mary Helen thought. Thanking Kate for her time, she hung up.

+I+   +I+   +I+

"Another murder, right?" Jack said, the moment she reentered the kitchen. "I rest my case, Kate. Where does the
victim's mother live? Right on our own block. And you want
to raise a kid in this city?"

Kate wanted to kick herself for telling him about Greg
Johnson. It gave him more ammunition for the battle they
had been waging for months. Like most battles, it had started
with a small scrimmage. Jack was assigned a child rape case.
Actually, the little girl was about the same age as their John.
Jack was deeply moved, as well he might be. The case was
appalling. Kate admitted that much.

The fight escalated. Jack watched her bundling up John
for the baby-sitter, and threw in the weather. "We both grew
up here," Kate countered, "and neither of us has terminal
frostbite, do we?"

"Hon," he had said one night, "several of the guys in my
detail are buying in Cordero. I think that's where the
O'Connors live, too, isn't it?" he asked, tossing in a detective
from homicide. He proceeded to make the small Marin
County suburb sound as if it were the safest city in America.

"Whitebread!" Kate announced, unmoved.

"Where is this kid going to play?" he asked one Saturday.
"On Geary Boulevard? Talk about telling a kid to go play in
the traffic."

"Where the hell do you think I played," Kate shouted.
"And all the other kids that grew to old age in this neighborhood?"

"That was then. This is now," Jack said in that annoyingly patient tone of his.

Over the last few weeks the subject had become open

warfare. Undoubtedly, tonight they were having the most decisive battle of their marriage. Kate did not want to move. She loved San Francisco. She loved this old house that had been her parents'. She wanted to live right here. She wanted to raise her family here with streetcars and fog and ethnic diversity and all the charm and beauty and culture that San Francisco offered.

"I'm not suggesting New Zealand, for chrissake, Kate. It's only twenty minutes away."

Kate would have hollered about traffic on the Golden Gate Bridge if their front doorbell hadn't rung. "Who the hell is that?" Jack shouted, stomping out of the kitchen.

"Ma!" Kate heard him say. "What are you doing out this late at night? What's wrong?"

"What am I? Some sort of Cinderella. I turn into a pumpkin at midnight, Jackie? Besides, it's only a little after nine o'clock." Loretta Bassetti pushed her way past her son and headed for the lighted kitchen. "It's my bridge night. I was at Mrs. Molinari's around the corner. It was her turn. When I went into her kitchen for a glass of water, I could see your kitchen light still on."

And you were trying to find out why, Kate thought.

"Since I was so close, I decided to pick up my good Dutch oven. God knows when you'd return it, and I need it for your sister Angie's birthday dinner on Friday night. You haven't forgotten your sister's—" She stopped midsentence. Her glance jumped from the table, cluttered with dinner dishes, to the stove, where her pot sat, still unemptied and unwashed.

"What's wrong?" She crinkled her short nose, as if to sniff out the tension.

"Wrong? What do you mean?" Jack smiled stiffly.

"What do you mean, what do I mean? This is your mother you're talking to, Jackie. It's nine-thirty at night. You two are still sitting at the table, the dishes not done. The faces on you look like you have just received a death sentence." She caught her breath. "Something is wrong with the baby?"

"No, Ma. The baby's fine."

"You wouldn't lie to me, would you, Kate?" Her bright brown eyes grew large, panicky.

"Loretta, the baby is absolutely perfect. In fact, he's upstairs sound asleep." Kate flushed. For a minute, she thought her mother-in-law might climb the stairs to make sure. That's all she needed tonight, Mrs. B. in full bustle.

"Sit down, Ma," Jack said, trying hard to sound hospitable. "Let me fix you a cup of coffee."

"Not on your life." His mother clutched her handbag in front of her bosom like a shield. "If the baby's okay, then I've walked in on the middle of a fight. So, I'll go."

But not before you've put in your two bits' worth, Kate thought.

Predictably, Mrs. Bassetti dived right in. "Every young couple has fights. It wouldn't be normal not to. Best for the in-laws to stay out of fights. Only muddies the water. But remember"—she shook a pudgy finger in warning—"it is not good to go to bed angry. So, I'll let you settle this before you're up all night."

"Ma, sit down. Really, we are not angry. We are not even fighting. We were discussing." Kate knew from his expression that he wasn't even fooling himself.

"What kind of a discussion makes two faces look like yours?"

Innocently, Jack stepped into his fatal error. "I was just talking to Kate about the possibility of our moving to Marin County."

Mrs. Bassetti flopped into a chair as if she'd been punched. "Move?" she said, hardly audible.

"Yes, Ma, move. To a better climate, a safer community. A place where a kid can play outside on flat, traffic-free streets."

His mother raised her chubby hand as if to ward off his attack. "You, Jackie, my own son, want to move my only grandchild away from me? Across a bridge?"

"Twenty minutes away, Ma, forty at the most. To sunshine."

"You want to take my little family across a bridge?" Even Kate thought she made it sound like across the Sahara Desert.

"For chrissake, Ma. You're willing to drive alone through Golden Gate Park at ten o'clock at night. Why couldn't you drive across the Golden Gate Bridge?"

"Bridges scare me," she said. Her eyes filled with unexpected tears.

"Nothing living or dead scares you!"

"Don't you dare raise your voice to your mother! And you, Kate?" Before Kate could reply, she answered her own question. "There would be no fight if you wanted to go, too."

Mrs. B.'s backbone stiffened. She reached over and patted Kate's hand. Any coldness between them disappeared in that instant. Kate had an invincible ally. She almost felt sorry for Jack.

With blazing eyes, Mrs. B. turned on her son. "What kind of a man did I raise? What kind of a man wants to take his wife away from her family home? The place where she has lived all her life—a nice place—and transport her to Marin? Bad enough you let her work and strangers take care of your child."

Oh, oh, thought Kate, here it comes. But she was wrong. Child care was small potatoes compared to a move.

"Now you want to move away from your family. Why? What is wrong with us?"

"Ma, you're getting crazy. It's just that I think it might be a better place to raise a kid." Jack ran his fingers through his dark curly hair.

"What do I hear? You call your own mother crazy? Then you say I didn't raise you in a good place? What was wrong with your home? It wasn't good enough for you? Your father, God rest him, would turn over in his grave if he knew that the house he worked his fingers to the bone for wasn't good enough for his big-shot son."

"Nothing was wrong with my home."

"What then? You turned out to be a criminal or you have TB from the fog? No. You turned out to be a cop and you are never sick." She considered that for a moment. "What you are getting is a little thick in the middle, Jackie. Even Mrs. Molinari thinks so, and she has bad eyes. Maybe you need more exercise. You get that thickness from your father's side. None of the Bassettis exercised enough."

Foolishly, Jack took the diversion as a concession. "So, Ma. It's getting late. Maybe you should get through the park."

Acting as if she didn't hear or see him, Mrs. B. turned her full attention on Kate. "Some of his friends have moved over to Marin. That's what it is. Jackie was always like that, even when he was little. No mind of his own. He had to have what his friends had, even if it wasn't good for him. I remember, one time, BoBo Spencer down the block got a BB gun. Nothing would do but Jackie wanted one too. His father said no, it was too dangerous. Jackie threw a fit. Acted like we had deprived him of his heritage. When BoBo shot out Mrs. Brady's windows and she called the police, it wasn't such a good thing." She stopped and gave a satisfied smile.

"If she brings up the motor scooter, I swear I'll strangle her," Jack mouthed to Kate.

"Then there was the time with the motor scooter . . ."

"I am a grown man, Ma!" Jack shouted. Even Kate jumped.

A piercing wail drifted down the stairs. Mrs. B. turned on her son. "See what you have done, grown man? Shame on you! Your yelling frightened that sweet baby." Before either Jack or Kate could react, she ran up the steps.

"God, she can get to me," Jack said by way of apology.

"You walked right into that one," Kate couldn't resist remarking.

"Why did I think she'd be on my side?"

Kate kissed him gently on the cheek. It was warm and moist. "If she has to choose between you and that baby, pal, you're history."

"See, John, sweet baby, Mommy and Daddy are not mad." Mrs. B. stood in the kitchen door bouncing her grandson.

John's round, downy face was pink with sleep. His tiny lips turned down threateningly. He looked from his mother to his father to his grandmother. His brown eyes were wary. Where the pajama top stretched to reach the bottom, small patches of tummy showed through the gap, reminding Kate of how fast he was growing. He'd need a new pair soon.

"See Daddy kiss Mommy," Mrs. B. cooed.

Jack kissed Kate on cue. Kate kissed him back and Little John did look happier. Maybe her mother-in-law had a point.

"Everyone kiss Nonie." Mrs. B. extended her face.

John giggled when his father bussed Nonie's cheek, and stuck out his arms to be taken.

"What kind of a grown man wakes up his own child by yelling?" Mrs. B.'s pleasant tone did not betray the sting of her words. She put the child into her son's arms. "By the way, Jackie," she called, heading for the front door, "he has a full diaper. Not even moving to Cordero can change that."

•I•   •I•   •I•

The nuns sat on two hard plastic chairs in the dimly lit vestibule of St. Agnes' Hall. In a low voice, Mary Helen filled Eileen in on the details—which were amazingly few—that she'd missed listening to only one side of the phone conversation with Kate Murphy.

"Father Tom, Laura, his mother, are suspects," Eileen shook her head in disbelief. "That's what Kate said?"

"Not exactly 'said,' but that's my impression."

The two old friends sat in perplexed silence, each chewing on her own thoughts. The throb of insects filled the air as the redwood forest settled down for the night. A moth blundered into the vestibule. Drawn to the light, it hit again and again against the heavy glass fixture, unaware that the glass was the only thing saving it from cremation.

All the poor creature is doing is knocking himself senseless, Mary Helen thought. Watching the fluttering moth, she felt much the same. "Why don't we call it a night?" she suggested.

"I can't stop thinking about Laura." Eileen set her chin. "I know she didn't have anything to do with his death. Nothing whatsoever!" she said in a "that settles that" tone of voice.

"Then, you think it was one of the priests? Father Harrington, perhaps?"

Eileen narrowed her eyes until they were almost slits. "Certainly not!" There was a reproach in her voice. "Just look at those men."

"I have looked at them," Mary Helen said, more for the sake of argument than for anything else. "They all appear to be good, dedicated priests."

"Appear to be?" Eileen was aghast. "You make them

sound like 'whited sepulchers . . . full of dead men's bones.' "

"I never said a thing about sepulchers and bones. You know as well as I do." She closed her eyes and dug to remember that complicated discourse. " 'Things either are what they appear to be; or they are, and do not appear to be; or they are not, and yet appear to be.' " She opened her eyes and smiled, satisfied. "Epictetus," she said.

Eileen stared at her. "So you are saying that one of the priests is guilty?"

"Of course not! I'm just saying things aren't necessarily what they appear and that these priests are, after all, only human."

"Then you should say what you mean," Eileen snapped. "The March Hare."

A wild howl from a coyote pierced the still night air. The plaintive wail made Mary Helen shudder. Suddenly she felt an overpowering weariness. Her legs, even her arms, were leaden. It had been a very long day.

"If not Laura or the priests, who then?" Eileen was on a roll. "The mother? That seems too unnatural. Sister Felicita? Of course not. She can't even fire a cook. How could she possibly kill someone? And Beverly? What reason would she have?"

At this point Mary Helen saw no reason to comment since Eileen was answering her own questions.

"Then, who? Nobody—that's who."

"Somebody did," Mary Helen said with her last bit of energy. "That's the only thing we are sure of."

Eileen glanced over and stopped. "You look like death warmed over, excuse the expression, old dear, and here I am babbling on and on."

She took Mary Helen's arm and helped her up. "Will you be able to sleep? Or will you be awake all night stewing?"

"Right now, I feel as if I could sleep for days," Mary Helen whispered as she followed Eileen.

The narrow hallway was dark and still. Each step creaked on the waxed linoleum as they moved toward their rooms. The single sharp squawk of a quail carried up from the woods. The silence was so profound that even the jiggle of their doorknobs sounded loud.

How could someone have committed murder and not one of us hear anything? Mary Helen slipped into her cotton nightgown. Voices, sounds, magnify at night. She punched up the pillow under her head. It was very odd that nobody heard anything, she thought, stirring to find a cool spot on the sheets. It was the last thing she remembered thinking clearly all night long.

Tuesday, June 22

St. John Fisher,
Bishop and Martyr

St. Thomas More, Martyr

Day Three

The moment Sister Mary Helen awoke, her mind switched on. That phenomenon was happening less frequently these days, she reflected, her eyes still closed. Most mornings she needed a few seconds to remember what day it was and at least one cup of strong coffee to start her juices flowing.

But not this morning. Laura was on her mind immediately. She needed to talk to the girl before Sergeant Little did.

Opening her eyes, she was amazed to find that the sun, filtering through the evergreens, sent long, bright slashes across the bedclothes. The air, scented with pine, was alive with the chirps and peeps and whistles of birds, all foraging for breakfast.

I must have overslept, she thought, and tried to focus on her watch. Without her glasses, the face was nothing but a blur. Hoping it wasn't as late as it felt, Mary Helen groped on the nightstand for her bifocals and was relieved to discover it wasn't even eight o'clock. Surely the sergeant wouldn't be here yet!

A small spider in the corner above the closet bounced down the wall on a single thread like a miniature mountain climber. "Get up . . . get up," a woodpecker called sharply. At least, that's what it sounded like just before he began his steady tapping on a tree trunk. Despite his injunction, Mary Helen still lay thinking.

Last night her mind was muddled with possible murder suspects: Laura, the monsignor, Greg's own mother, Father Tom, Beverly, and Sergeant Loody; and yes, even poor flustered Felicita. Yet, no one had a reason.

But this morning it seemed quite clear. At the end of my mind, "beyond the last thought rises . . . a gold-feathered bird" of an idea, she thought crazily, as insistent as those blasted birds making all that racket outside her window.

Her idea was quite simple. If I can't figure out "who dun it," I'll figure out who didn't. If I can't find out who had a reason, I'll find out who didn't have one. It amounts to exactly the same thing, she thought, swinging her feet out from under the covers. Laura seemed the logical place to begin.

From a police point of view, Mary Helen knew that the girl bore all the earmarks of a chief suspect. She had had opportunity. Undoubtedly, she had been the last person— save one—to see Greg Johnson alive. Means: the weapon, a heavy sharp knife, was not hard to come by. As the dishwasher in a well-equipped institutional kitchen, Laura had easy access to one. And finally, motive. As his fiancée, she was surely more emotionally involved with him than anyone, except, perhaps, his own mother. Maybe they'd had a bitter lovers' quarrel. Laura did have a redhead's temper. Or Greg had found another girlfriend. Father Tom mentioned the young man's penchant for the ladies and Laura crazed with jealousy . . .

Even as she thought it, Mary Helen did not believe it. She was as convinced as Eileen that Laura Purcell was innocent of murder. Call it intuition or a hunch, but in her bones, Mary Helen knew that Laura genuinely loved Greg and was shocked by his death. No one, not even Sarah Bernhardt, let alone an undergraduate drama major, could have put on such a convincing performance.

Still, there was no denying that Laura was the most likely suspect. If the real murderer was to be found quickly, Laura was the first one who should be eliminated.

After she'd firmly crossed off Laura, Mary Helen would vindicate Greg's mother. Marva Johnson was also an unlikely suspect. She would hardly have been in the area. Furthermore, if every mother who said she'd like to "kill" her child was up on charges, there'd be increasingly fewer mothers left in circulation.

And after Mrs. Johnson? Well, she'd have to see where the Spirit led.

Sister Mary Helen was nearly dressed when she heard a cautious tapping on the bathroom door. Sister Eileen peeked around its edge. "Up and at 'em, are you?" she said. "And let me guess. It's off you are to visit Laura?"

Mary Helen could tell by the touch of the brogue that Eileen was upset. "I wasn't going without you, if that's what's bothering you." She sat on the edge of the bed and put on her sturdy walking shoes. "I was going to ask you—actually beg you, if necessary—to come along."

"And what if I wasn't dressed?"

"I'd wait, of course," Mary Helen said, wondering why she hadn't thought to wake Eileen. She really did want her friend along. Unreasonable as it seemed, Felicita was counting on her to clear up this mess. Mary Helen needed all the help she could get.

Without another word, Eileen disappeared and returned,

obviously mollified, with two cups of steaming black coffee. "What's our plan?" she asked. And Mary Helen told her.

✦✦✦

The two nuns stopped outside Laura Purcell's bedroom and listened. Nothing! Mary Helen opened the door a crack. If Laura was still asleep, she wouldn't waken her. Poor girl was going to need all the rest she could get to face the day.

"Who's there?" a flat voice asked.

Without any further invitation, they entered. Laura, propped up in bed by two large pillows, stared glassy-eyed. A white sheet pulled tight across her breast and tucked under her armpits left her thin tan shoulders bare. Waves of tousled auburn hair spread across the pillowcases. Her face, wrinkled from sleep, was puffy and pink from weeping.

The moment she saw them, Laura's eyes filled with fresh tears. "Why did they kill my Greg?" Her soggy face pleaded with them to give her a reason, and her voice teetered before she broke into wild, uncontrollable sobs.

Good night nurse! Mary Helen sighed. This is no time for hysterics. What we need is answers. The girl must "tough up."

Mary Helen was relieved when Eileen stepped into the bathroom and returned with a damp washcloth. She vaguely remembered reading that a cold, wet washcloth across the face shocks a person out of hysteria. Or was it out of a temper tantrum?

Whichever, Eileen applied the cloth across Laura's swollen eyes more like a compress than a shock treatment.

"Quite frankly, I am afraid you make the best suspect," Mary Helen said, hoping her remark would have the effect of a cold cloth.

Laura gasped.

Direct hit! "But I don't think you did it," Mary Helen added quickly.

Once bitten, twice shy, Laura peeked out from the end of the compress. "Why don't you?"

"Because I believe that you were genuinely shocked and disconsolate when you heard the news."

Slowly, Laura removed the cloth. Tears ran unheeded down her face. "I am so scared." She sounded like a bewildered child. "And my heart hurts. I love Greg. We love one another."

With as much compassion as possible, Mary Helen began the questions she knew Sergeant Little would ask. "When you left St. Colette's Sunday night, Laura, where did you and Greg go?"

"To the late show. Actually, the last show." Dully, Laura gave the names of the theater and the movie, as well as the time it showed.

All easily checked, Mary Helen thought, and easily fabricated. "Did anyone you know, actually either of you knew, see you there?"

Laura was silent for what seemed much too long. "The kid at the candy counter might remember us. Greg argued with him about getting more butter on his popcorn."

"He might," Mary Helen said, although she doubted it. Half the people who buy popcorn at a show must complain about the little squirt of melted margarine that sits right on the top of the box.

"What did you do after the show?" she asked.

"We went home to our apartment." Realizing what she had said, Laura's lips began to quiver.

Mary Helen pretended not to notice. "Did anyone see you going in?"

"On the way we picked up a bottle of champagne at the 7-Eleven. Maybe the guy there would remember." Laura brightened. "Not too many people buy champagne in the middle of the night."

Mary Helen nodded. Not at the 7-Eleven, she thought, but didn't say so. This was not the time to turn into a wine snob. "And?" she urged.

"When we got home, we drank some to celebrate my quitting St. Colette's and then we made love. Greg was feeling 'bubbly' and he wanted to try some of the stuff we saw in the movie, but I just got sleepy."

"About what time do you figure you fell asleep?" Mary Helen asked, before Laura felt obliged to supply any further details.

"I don't know. I was asleep when the phone rang."

Ah! Now they were getting somewhere. "The phone rang? What time was that?"

"I never opened my eyes," Laura said. "Greg answered it. It's on his side of the bed." She placed the washcloth across her face and lay back on the pillow. "He said it was about three-thirty."

"Did he say who was calling?" Whoever called was undoubtedly Greg's killer. Mary Helen tried not to get her hopes up.

"All he said was that it was a nurse from the hospital."

Mary Helen waited.

"I only heard one side of the conversation." Laura sounded defensive. "I could tell it was serious, so I didn't want to ask too many questions."

"Do you know what hospital?"

"Like I said, I didn't ask. I just assumed it was St. Mary's in San Francisco."

"Why did you assume that?" This conversation is like cleaning spinach, Mary Helen thought testily. You have to turn over every leaf looking for dirt. None of it just floats out.

"Because the emergency was his mother and she lives in

the city," Laura said in a tone she'd use on a slow learner. "Besides, he didn't write down anything, so I figured it was someplace he was familiar with. I wanted to go with him. When I asked him if he wanted me to go, he said no." She smiled and the ends of her mouth nearly disappeared under the compress. "He said his mother would have another coronary if she saw me. So I just assumed it was a heart attack. Except, I do remember thinking it was funny she had our number. Greg doesn't give out our number to anybody. But I was a little fuzzy from the champagne. He told me he'd call.

"When I woke up in the morning, I had an aching head and when I felt his side of the bed, it was empty and he hadn't called. I tried St. Mary's, but no Marva Johnson was registered. Around noon, when I still hadn't heard from him I was beginning to get panicky." She swallowed, then cleared her throat.

"He's not like that, you know. He's super-responsible. He told me his mother was real strict when he was a kid and he had to be on time and polite and everything. Anyway, I tried a couple of hospitals in San Francisco, but she wasn't there either. I even tried her house in case they released her. I was going to pretend I was selling something if she answered. But she didn't.

"So, I picked up my own car at the gas station and came straight to St. Colette's to talk to Sister Felicita. Mrs. Johnson was real religious. At least, that's what Greg said. So I figured if she had to go to the hospital, she might insist on a Catholic one. I know Sister Felicita has a thick book in her office with the names of all the Catholic stuff."

Kenedy's *Official Catholic Directory*, Mary Helen thought.

"Maybe she'd help me look up some Catholic hospitals around San Francisco. And when I got here, the police . . ." Laura bent her head and began to weep quietly into the already soaked washcloth.

"Let me get us some coffee," Eileen said, tiptoeing out of the bedroom in search of some.

Gently, Mary Helen put her hand on Laura's shoulder. Words are meaningless in such a tragedy, but sometimes the touch of another human being brings comfort. She waited, absorbed in her own tangled thoughts, while Laura sobbed out her grief.

Was the caller a woman? Mary Helen wondered. Laura had said "a nurse." Mary Helen dismissed that. Gender was no longer a factor. Today male nurses were common.

Where could the killer safely meet Greg? The emergency room in a hospital was a good place. People are preoccupied and tend not to notice others coming in or out. From what Laura said, it was obviously a place he knew. Could it have been near Laura's apartment? Whatever the details, if Laura Purcell was telling the truth, she could be removed from Mary Helen's "who dun it" list. She wondered apprehensively if Sergeant Bob Little would feel the same way.

And Marva Johnson? Had Mary Helen dismissed her too readily? Was she really in the area? If so, why? This new development necessitated another quick call to Kate Murphy.

+I+   +I+   +I+

Inspector Kate Murphy's head felt as foggy as the real stuff billowing past the fourth-floor windows of the Hall of Justice.

"What is it, Katie-girl?" Dennis Gallagher handed her a cup of coffee. "You look like you've been up all night."

Kate sniffed the steaming liquid. "Axle grease," she said, and set down the cup on the corner of her desk. Actually the corner was the last place remaining to set anything. Untouched folders and forms covered the surface, silent reminders of how distracted she'd been for the last few weeks. "Is this left over from yesterday's shift?" she asked, pointing to her cup.

"Careful," Gallagher whispered, intending to be overheard. "O'Connor made that pot himself. If you don't find the aroma irresistible, he's liable to get his feelings hurt."

The detectives scattered around the homicide detail guffawed and some added their own comments about O'Connor's coffee as well as about his feelings.

At the moment, Kate wished that O'Connor's feelings weren't the only thing she could hurt. Face burning, she glared in his direction, but his back was to her. She fought down the urge to cross the room and throttle him. He and his damn propaganda about Cordero were responsible for her restless nights. Even her dreams were being invaded by cozy Hansel and Gretel cottages on sunny, tree-lined, traffic-free streets where clean, happy children played while supermommies with saccharine voices served healthy treats. Yuk!

"What's wrong?" Gallagher asked. His question startled her. "Are you sick or something?"

Kate shook her head and rummaged through her desk drawers, hoping to find an abandoned tea bag.

"You're not pregnant again, are you?" She noticed the alarm in her partner's voice.

"Of course not!" Kate growled. How could she be pregnant? Jack and she had barely touched each other for weeks. Unexpected tears filled her eyes and she turned her head quickly, hoping that Gallagher hadn't noticed.

"What is it, Kate?" he asked with genuine concern.

Kate was afraid to tell him. She felt sure that Gallagher would back up Jack. He always did. "A man is the head of the house. A wife's place is at her husband's side. Blah, blah blah!" She could just hear it. What she didn't need this morning was another irritant!

"What is eating you, Katie-girl?" Obviously Gallagher was not giving up easily.

The sharp ring of her phone cut through the awkward silence. Relieved, Kate picked up the receiver. To her surprise, it was Sister Mary Helen.

"How are things going?" Kate asked warily.

"Nothing more has happened, if that's what you mean." Sister Mary Helen was all business. "I was wondering if you'd have time this morning to do me a favor?"

Kate surveyed the stacks of papers covering her desk. She couldn't be much farther behind if she tried. "Sure," she said without much enthusiasm.

"Is something wrong?" Mary Helen asked.

Even her phone voice was giving her away. "No, Sister," Kate said quickly, then wished she hadn't.

Gallagher glared over his horn-rimmed glasses. "Sister?" he hissed. His eyes burned like two small blue flames on the end of matchsticks. "If that's the Sister I think it is, tell her to stay the hell out of police business."

"You tell her yourself." Kate held out the receiver.

For a split second, it seemed as if he might. Then, cursing under his breath, Gallagher loosened his tie and stomped to the coffeepot for a refill.

"Kate? Are you still there? Kate?" Mary Helen's voice crackled over the long-distance wires.

"Yes, Sister. I thought Denny wanted to talk to you, but apparently he doesn't."

"Inspector Gallagher?" Mary Helen sounded delighted. "I'm so glad he's interested in this case. Two of you on it will make it easier, I'm sure."

Interested is hardly the word, Kate thought, putting her hand over her other ear to block out the returning Gallagher's snorts and muttered invectives. "What is it you wanted, exactly, Sister?" she asked.

Mary Helen told Kate about her plan to eliminate the least likely suspects first, about her talk with Laura, and about Greg's late-night phone call. "Laura Purcell," she concluded with a finality that amazed even Kate, "is innocent."

Without so much as a breather, the old nun went on. "Marva Johnson seems the second least likely suspect," she said, "and since we are unable to leave St. Colette's yet, perhaps you can check up on Marva. Was she in the hospital the night Greg was killed?"

"She didn't mention it when we went to see her," Kate said. "And it seems to me she would have, unless, of course, she deliberately lured him out and killed him herself."

Mary Helen acted as if she had not heard. "I'm convinced Marva had nothing to do with her son's death." Mary Helen paused. "Although stranger things have happened," she conceded.

Promising that she would talk to Marva Johnson, Kate hung up. Stranger things have happened, she thought, surveying the stack of folders on her desk: a child "accidentally" drowned in the bathtub while her mother supposedly went to answer the phone; a Japanese tourist shot in broad daylight in Golden Gate Park; a fatal stabbing at a prestigious Pacific Heights address, possible suspect the victim's lawyer husband; an elderly lady in the Richmond bludgeoned to death in her own home by an intruder for ten dollars and some change.

A foghorn bleated and O'Connor, who had come to work in a short-sleeved shirt, complained loudly about the weather. Probably making another convert to sunny, crime-free Cordero, Kate thought morosely.

"Let's get out of here, Denny," she said, afraid that in her present frame of mind, even she might begin to see his point.

"Where to?" Gallagher asked, watching Kate dig through the piles on her desk. He rubbed his hand across his bald pate and unnecessarily smoothed down the few gray hairs that crowned it.

Finally Kate resurrected a folder. "Mrs. Gertrude Rosen, widow," she said. The file contained all the information on the elderly woman murdered in her home. The interviews of her neighbors were incomplete. Today might be a good day to go door-to-door. Furthermore, the crime took place only a few blocks away from Marva Johnson's home. Only a few blocks away from where I live, too. The thought jerked her to her feet.

"Another murder, right in our own neighborhood," she imagined Jack saying. Maybe he was right. Maybe the city was no longer a safe place to bring up kids.

"What's the address?" Gallagher asked, sliding automatically into the driver's seat.

Kate read it to him. "We've had precious little luck getting her neighbors to answer their doors," she said.

"Maybe they're afraid." Gallagher swung into traffic. "Can't blame them. Jeez, killed for ten lousy bucks."

"And Sister Mary Helen wanted us to stop by Marva Johnson's again . . ."

Gallagher turned his head. "Watch out," Kate shouted, grateful that a messenger on a bike nearly collided with them. All Gallagher's anger poured out on the boy, who was too far away to hear or care.

The ride out to the Richmond district did nothing to raise Kate's spirits. This morning she was more than usually aware of the graffiti scrawled across the Muni buses and along walls and sides of houses. Much of it was gang-related.

She noticed more homeless people asleep in doorways or panhandling on corners with homemade signs. Even their dogs looked more scabietic. Drivers seemed more aggressive, honking horns and flipping fingers at little old ladies doing their best to keep up with the flow.

Twin Peaks appeared like shadows in the fog, and she wondered if the sun would ever break through. The moist sea smell that always invigorated her felt damp and cold. The Victorians with their towers and turrets and Turkish cupolas looked drab. Even the fellow emptying the parking meters in his fishing hat failed to make her laugh. Was Jack right? Was it time to go?

They were nearly at Marva Johnson's home before Gallagher broke into her spell. "You haven't said a word for miles. Either you are sick or something is very wrong."

"I told you, it's nothing." Kate tried to sound cheerful.

"I ran into your old man at the Hall this morning, on the elevator." They had stopped for a traffic light and Gallagher tapped his thick fingers on the steering wheel. "He looks as bad as you do."

Kate felt her face burning. "What do you mean?"

"Don't get your dander up now, Kate, but I've known you since you were a kid. You wouldn't have to be a detective to know that something's upsetting you. And from the looks of Jack, it involves him, too. Now, it's none of my business," Gallagher said.

When did that ever stop you? Kate wondered.

"But I think you may be having some sort of a row."

"What makes you think that?"

"More than forty years of marriage."

Despite herself, Kate laughed. "We never fight." Her voice trembled and she tried in vain to steady it. "At least, we never used to, but for the last few months, we have been arguing about a move. It started out as a civilized discussion, but it is moving into downright war."

"What kind of a move?" Gallagher sounded apprehensive.

"Jack thinks it would be better for the baby if we moved to Cordero."

To her amazement, Gallagher said nothing except "And you?"

"Me? I love the city. I always have. As far as I know so has Jack. It has an energy, a verve that makes me feel alive. I want little John to grow up here. Experience the same feelings I did. I always thought Jack wanted that, too. After all, we both grew up here. We have a perfectly nice house, paid for, in a perfectly good neighborhood. But I don't know if it's worth hanging on to my opinion. Our fighting is affecting everything, Denny, and I do mean everything!" Kate fumbled in her purse for a tissue and noisily blew her nose.

"That reminds me of the old Irish couple?" Gallagher said. "On their wedding night, they vowed never to go to sleep angry with one another. And they never did, although one time, they were awake for three months."

Kate chuckled and waited for her partner to comment. Gallagher always had some free advice, solicited or not, and nine times out of ten he agreed with Jack. His silence was so out of character. He simply cleared his throat. What was it? Could it be that this time he agreed with her? That was it! And the words simply stuck in his throat.

Kate began furiously to twist a lock of her hair. With both her partner and her mother-in-law on her side, was she so right after all? She almost never agreed with either of them on anything. Now to agree with both of them at once? It gave her pause.

＊I＊ ＊I＊ ＊I＊

A few minutes before nine, Detective Sergeant Bob Little turned into the driveway of St. Colette's Retreat House. He was surprised to see Beverly's old brown Chevy just ahead of him. He hadn't expected to see her.

He was even more surprised to see Sergeant Loody wave

her right through. If he wasn't mistaken, there was a grin on Eric's sunburned face. The sly old devil! "Morning, Sergeant," Little said.

With a perfunctory nod, Loody touched the rim of his doughboy hat. His large face, Little noticed, was once again frozen into his sniffing look.

Little parked his car up next to St. Philomena's Hall and waved across the lot to Beverly. In all the confusion, he supposed no one had told her not to come today, so she had. At least the food would be good. The very thought of food made his stomach growl. He could hardly wait until Beverly rustled up some breakfast. He'd had nothing but a cup of coffee. Lately Terry had been too busy with work to grocery-shop, and for some reason it never occurred to him to do it, so their cupboard had hit an all-time record for bare. This morning he'd been unable even to rout out a piece of dried bread or a hunk of mildewed cheese.

When Little arrived at Madonna Grotto, Deputy David Kemp was already there. "Going to be another hot one, huh?" Kemp pulled on his bow tie.

Although the giant redwoods were doing their best to block out the heat, the temperature was rising quickly.

"What's the forensic report?" Kemp asked, knowing that was what Little had waited for.

"Just like you thought, Dave, Greg Johnson was killed here. They found traces of ordinary white cotton in his mouth and on his wrists and ankles. Apparently, he was gagged and tied before he was brought here. Some rock and soil samples stuck in his tennis shoes. They're checking to see if they can make a match. Threads from a car were on his clothes. Those too need to be checked. It's only a matter of time, even though most everything around the scene itself had been thoroughly trampled by the time we were called. Looks like the victim was stabbed around four on Monday morning.

Give or take an hour or so. The old nun stumbled on the body around seven."

"So that's why nobody heard him holler." Kemp swatted at the gnats that swarmed up from the floor of pine needles. "You gag and tie the guy, drive him here at, say, four or four-thirty in the morning, and get away before anyone's up or it's light enough for anyone to see you." His eager cobalt-blue eyes fastened on Little for approval.

"Unless the murderer never left," Little said, not because he believed it. He just wanted to keep Kemp honest.

Kemp gave a good-natured shrug. "So, what else did you get from forensics?" he asked.

"That the cuts on the dorsal side of his arms indicate that the kid tried to defend himself against his attacker, who was shorter than he was. There was a recent bruise on his temple, which looks like he hit his head against something sharp. The edge of a car door or something. There are seven separate stab marks scattered across his chest, two on the nape of his neck, and one on the left occipital bone. The stroke that finally killed him was the one that pierced his heart."

Kemp's face paled. Little didn't blame him. The thought of the anger that must have provoked such a savage attack could make anyone lose color.

Kemp cleared his throat. "Anything special about the knife?" he asked. "Anything that could give us a lead?"

Little shook his head. "Just your common ordinary fillet knife. Your wife probably has one just like it in her kitchen."

Kemp winced.

"An overdose of tranquilizers is what killed the dogs, if that's of any interest."

"Why not use the knife again?" Kemp asked.

"Maybe the death of the dogs was accidental."

Kemp looked surprised. "How do you figure?"

"There was really no need to kill them, only to quiet

them. . . . Who knows how many grams of Valium a German shepherd can safely handle?"

"A vet," Kemp said.

"Well, then, we know that our killer is probably not a vet, don't we?" Little asked facetiously.

Above them a red-headed woodpecker bored into the bark of a tree. A brown squirrel sat on his haunches, nervously nibbling an acorn while a swarm of gray-and-white pygmy nuthatches pecked among the fallen pine needles. Actually, the yellow ribbon cordoning off the area was the only sign that a murder had been committed in this peaceful grotto.

"Nothing more here." Little took a final look around. The large blank eyes of the Madonna reminded him of Laura Purcell's eyes. "Maybe we should talk to the girlfriend," he said, although he wasn't looking forward to it. Too much like torturing a wounded animal. The two officers descended the steep path toward the main building.

"Did you find anything on Beverly Benton?" Little still could not place her, although he'd known from the moment he laid eyes on her that he'd seen her somewhere before.

"Nothing much more than we already knew, except that she has no outstanding warrants for her arrest."

"Too bad." Little ducked his head to avoid a tree branch. "At least we'd have accomplished something."

"Maybe when we're finished here, I can run over and talk to some of Benton's neighbors, if you think it's necessary."

Little grunted. He wouldn't know that until after he'd questioned Laura Purcell.

Kemp pointed to the massive shape of Eric Loody guarding the entrance to the parking lot. "At least we're safe from intruders and the press," he quipped.

"Maybe it's the people already in here that we should be afraid of," Little said. "Which reminds me, see if you can find

Sister Felicita and ask her to gather up all the retreatants' car keys. I'll call the boys at Crime Scene."

Watching Kemp disappear into St. Agnes' Hall, Little placed his call. "I want all the cars on the property checked for hair, fiber, dirt, leaves, bloodstains, anything that could be used as evidence on how the victim was transported," he said.

He was relieved when the deputy answered. "Yeah, yeah, yeah! You don't have to tell us how to do our job. And, by the way, we found the victim's car." Little listened eagerly while the officer filled him in on all the details.

When Kemp returned, his coat pocket jingling with car keys, Little pulled back the door to St. Philomena's Hall and gave him the news about Johnson's Camaro.

"Where'd they find it?" Kemp asked.

"In the emergency parking lot of Dominican Hospital, right here in Santa Cruz."

"Find anything?" Kemp stamped dust from his polished shoes.

Little shook his head. "Nothing much. The keys were still in it. The complete door, including the handle on the driver's side—all wiped clean." A trickle of sweat ran down his back and he wondered how long before he could shed his sport jacket.

"He must have met his murderer there," Kemp muttered. "Did anyone remember seeing anything unusual?"

"Nothing. A deputy asked around, but no one remembers seeing him either. Emergency was exceptionally busy on Sunday night, what with it being Father's Day. It was pretty much what you'd expect. Broken bones from hikes and picnics, burns and cuts from kitchen accidents, traffic accidents, domestic violence. One dear old drunken dad even got himself shot by his son-in-law. I imagine by three in the morning, the emergency staff was too tired to notice if Jack the Ripper was in the parking lot."

Kemp smiled. "Not your typical Hallmark holiday, right?"

"Not at the emergency room anyway," Little said.

"Any signs of Johnson's blood in the area?"

"None, so far."

"Then Johnson must have gone in another car with someone he knew. Someone who could make his getting in seem plausible. Or maybe that's when he got the bump on the head." Kemp unhooked his bow tie and the top two buttons of his shirt. "God, it's hot!" he said.

"The autopsy report shows our boy consumed quite a bit of alcohol. There is the possibility that he was a bit sloshy when he met his murderer."

"I wonder where they went."

"No one knows," Little said. "Not yet, anyway."

Softly, Little knocked on Laura Purcell's bedroom door. The nervous knot in his stomach reminded him of how much he was dreading this interview. He wondered what her reaction to him would be this morning.

During his years with the Sheriff's Department, he had been the bearer of bad news to dozens of next of kin and it never got any easier. It was impossible to predict reactions. Shock made some stoic. It made others babble, while still others refused to believe the news, as if denying it made it disappear. Some cried. A few, like Laura, became hysterical. One thing he had learned was that the initial reaction was no indication of whether or not the person had committed the crime. One case in particular he remembered. A distraught husband, hell-bent on avenging his wife's violent death, turned out to be her murderer.

Little knocked again.

"Just a minute," a hoarse voice called out.

When Laura Purcell finally answered the door, she was wrapped in a pink chenille bedspread with clearly nothing underneath it. Embarrassed for her, Little watched her pad barefoot across the room, then settle herself, cross-legged, in the middle of the rumpled bed.

All the color drained from her face, she clutched the spread under her chin and stared at him. Long strands of auburn hair pulled by static electricity took on a life of their own. Her whole pose took on a Medusa-ish appearance.

Little tried his friendliest smile. Eyes glassy-green, Laura continued to stare. Obviously she was waiting for him to speak first. "Were you able to get any sleep last night?" Little asked. One look at her and you wouldn't have to be a detective to know the answer.

"Some." She sounded as if someone had opened a spigot and drained out all her energy.

"Do you feel up to telling me what happened Sunday night?" Little asked gently.

"I guess," Laura said.

Kemp took out his notepad. Fear skittered across Laura's face. It was the first bit of emotion she'd shown since the two detectives entered her bedroom.

"Do you mind if Dave takes a few notes?" Little asked.

Laura shook her head, although everything about her shouted *Yes, I mind very much.*

"Sunday night? After you left here?" Little coached. "Can you remember what happened, Laura? Try not to leave out anything. Even if it doesn't seem important to you, you never know what bearing it might have on the case."

In a flat, detached voice, Laura recited the events of Sunday night as if she'd done it all before: the movies, stopping for champagne; the details of their lovemaking.

Kemp coughed nervously. My fault, Little thought, avoiding his partner's glance. I asked her to be specific. Laura continued, zombielike. A single tear ran down her cheek when she told him about the early morning phone call, waking and finding both Greg and the car gone. She didn't make a move to wipe it away.

"You know the rest," she said, and fell into a brooding silence.

◆I◆   ◆I◆   ◆I◆

"What do you think, Dave?" Bob Little asked, once the two men were outside the building.

"You got what you asked for, all right. And then some!"

Even through his tan, Little felt his face burn red. Terry thought that this blushing business was sweet. He thought it was a damn pain in the butt and he had no desire to find out what Kemp thought.

"Well, she pinned down the time. Right on the mark with the coroner," he said, pretending that was what Kemp meant. "And the phone call. What do you think about that?"

"It sounds to me like a ploy to get him away from Laura's house." Kemp wiped his forehead with a clean handkerchief. "Let's get the hell out of this heat."

"Unless his mother really was in some kind of an accident." Little thought he smelled the aroma of sizzling bacon coming from St. Jude's.

"Which can be easily proven with a couple of phone calls."

Little nodded. "I'm starving," he said, hoping Kemp hadn't heard his stomach growling again.

In silent agreement, the two men started toward the air-conditioned dining room. "One thing for sure," Kemp said, "whoever placed that call is our killer."

"Unless, of course . . ." Little paused and pulled back the heavy dining room door. "Our Miss Laura made up the whole damn thing."

✦I✦ ✦I✦ ✦I✦

When the nuns stepped out of St. Agnes' Hall, Sister Mary Helen spotted Sergeant Little as he and Deputy Kemp strode across the parking lot. She froze. They were headed for the dining room; exactly where she intended to go. She could not investigate with them hanging about, listening. How could she ask her next "unsuspect" questions in front of two detectives? They'd surely never stand for that.

"What's the matter, old dear?" Eileen asked.

"Our plan has been foiled."

"Which plan?"

"To go through the list of the least likely suspects."

"Whom were we considering next, Felicita or the monsignor?"

"Exactly," Mary Helen said.

Eileen's bushy gray eyebrows shot up. "Are you listening to me?"

"Of course I am listening." Mary Helen hoped she looked offended. "It's just that to my mind those two are neck and neck. I'm not sure which I'd consider first. I was going to let the Spirit lead where She will. But if they're both in the dining room . . ."

Eileen sniffed. "Do you smell it?"

"Of course!" Mary Helen said with a sudden surge of high, if not holy, spirit. "It's Yardley's Lavender."

Just then, an unsuspecting Sister Felicita rounded the corner.

✦I✦ ✦I✦ ✦I✦

Even in the dim hall light, Felicita's face shone red. From her glare, which easily could have singed them, Mary Helen guessed that the high color was a mixture of anger and frustration.

"What is it you want?" she snapped, proving Mary Helen's theory.

"Nothing, really." Mary Helen tried not to sound too calm. She knew from experience that when you are in a dither, there is nothing like saintly serenity to send you right over the top.

"How are you doing, Sister?" Eileen asked gently.

"Terribly, if you want to know." Felicita, eyes blinking furiously behind her rimless glasses, dared either of them to say something pious.

Both nuns knew better.

"My phone has not stopped ringing since it woke me up at six," she said. "I'm lucky I even had a chance to get dressed."

Wisps of ash-blond angel hair sprang over the rim of her coif as if the whole headpiece had been hurriedly set in place. Even her scapular hung a little crookedly, bearing out the truth of her statement.

"Sister Timothy is calling every few minutes, acting as if it's my fault that they're all stranded. From what she says, Mother Superior is about ready for apoplexy over the scandal this incident will cause. She can't even bring herself to say the word *murder*."

Mary Helen doubted that any mother superior worth her salt was that delicate and was about to say so, but she wasn't given the chance.

"According to Timothy, I am to avoid all contact with the press. Do you know how difficult that is to do?" Felicita's eyes leveled on Mary Helen.

Mary Helen nodded. If anyone does, I do, she thought, remembering her own uncomfortable notoriety.

"Have you any idea how many reporters have called?"

The question was obviously rhetorical. "If that big Sergeant Loody wasn't at the entrance, the place would be swarming with them. Every time I hear an airplane, I'm afraid they're taking aerial photos."

"No one could blame you for that," Eileen said reasonably.

Felicita gave her a decided "it shows what you know" look.

Eileen refused to be put off that easily. "The best thing to do is forget about Sister Timothy and Mother Superior, in fact all the nuns at St. Anthony's." She waved her chubby hand as if to encompass all the nuns in the entire world. "Forget about the press. There is nothing you can do about any of them. Deal with what's going on here and now."

"Here and now?" Felicita winced as if Eileen had hit an exposed nerve. "Here and now?" She pointed to the parking lot, where an official-looking car and three equally official-looking men stood with satchels and brown bags. Sergeant Little must have ordered some further investigation, Mary Helen thought, momentarily distracted from Felicita's ravings.

"Those men are going to search the priests' cars," Felicita said in the same tone she might use to denounce a sacrilege. "And the young officer, that Kemp with the bow tie, came to my room. I didn't even have my coif on yet."

Deputy Kemp has seen much worse sights, Mary Helen thought but knew better than to say.

"He asked me to get their keys! As if I don't have enough to do, I have to do his job, too!"

That was puzzling! What was he looking for? "Did you?" Mary Helen asked.

"Did I what?"

"Get the keys?"

"Indeed I did. Although I must admit Father Tom was a little short when I asked him for his."

Mary Helen perked up. Could his reluctance to part with the keys to his new Mazda be significant?

Felicita let out a noisy breath. "From the looks of him, I woke him up. Although I don't know how anyone could sleep with the phone ringing and the doors slamming.

"And on top all this, as if I need another thing, the man from D-Pest Control called." Felicita's apple face blazed. "It's time for our monthly spray. If Detective Sergeant Little allows it, we are scheduled for tomorrow morning." She stared, waiting for the two nuns to get the full impact.

Whatever it was, it completely skimmed past Mary Helen. This morning she'd noticed one tiny spider in the corner of her bedroom, which seemed pretty normal for a mountain retreat.

"Have you a serious bug problem?" Obviously Eileen drew a blank too.

"Actually, it may be fairer to say that the bugs are having a human problem, since they were here first." Felicita's blue eyes sparked.

A novel approach, Mary Helen thought, waiting for Felicita to continue. It didn't take long. The bug man really stuck in her craw.

"Do you have any idea how much time it takes to go with the bug man from building to building showing him every new problem area?"

Both Mary Helen and Eileen readily admitted that they didn't. If Mary Helen remembered correctly, the pest control company at Mount St. Francis College simply sent out a fellow holding a cylinder with a long, thin pipelike squirter attached to it. He walked around the buildings' foundations and did just that, squirted. Next time she saw him, she'd have to look more carefully. Obviously, she was missing something.

"It's an all-morning job!" Felicita's lips stretched in a thin, angry line. "Sister Timothy's all-morning job! That was her last message. She had a list of trouble spots on her desk." She pulled one hand from beneath her black scapular and waved the offending paper at them.

"And as if I didn't have enough to worry about!" By now Felicita had a full head of steam and apparently no complaint whatsoever was to be left unstated. "Beverly just phoned!"

Beverly! Mary Helen had completely forgotten about Beverly.

"Do you know where she is?" Felicita's voice was trembling. "Here! She is here in our very own kitchen demanding that I get over there. She shouted something about needing more supplies if she's expected to feed the Sheriff's Department as well as the priests and nuns.

"That woman!" Felicita strained the words through her teeth.

"Calm down, Felicita," Eileen said. "You're wearing yourself to a frazzle!"

Mary Helen held her breath. If anything could really agitate her, it was being told to calm down. Much to her surprise, Felicita did.

Deliberately she let her stiff shoulders sag, and glanced down at her wristwatch. "You're right. It's not even ten o'clock in the morning and I'm ready to go back to bed and stay there."

"How about a cup of coffee?" Eileen's gray eyebrows shot up. "I bet you haven't eaten a bite yet. We've an old saying back home," she began with a bit of a brogue. "There's no tragedy that doesn't seem worse on an empty stomach."

Mary Helen was almost certain that Eileen had made that up to fit the moment, but her point was well taken. Furthermore, Mary Helen herself was hungry.

Whatever its origin, Eileen's "old saying" seemed to be

working. Together the nuns crossed the parking lot. The whole place was so idyllic, so tranquil. The sword fern and bracken cast lacy shadows along the edges of the blacktop. Mary Helen stopped and took a deep breath. Fragrant yellow scotch broom gave the air a sweetness. Violets grew in wild clumps and bright blue periwinkle spread up the hillside where chattering birds swooped between the tall trees and bounced on the branches of the oleander. The statue of St. Philomena with her anchor and her martyr's palm watched over it all with blank plaster eyes.

The crime team, absorbed in picking, dusting, measuring, and bagging things, was the only reminder that a grisly murder had taken place.

The sudden slam of a car trunk sent Felicita's rollercoaster emotions soaring again. "What will Mother Superior say when she finds out they went through trunks?" she wailed. "We'll lose all of our clients!" Frustration was driving her close to tears.

"If Mother Superior has any sense at all," Eileen said gently, "she'll know you are doing the very best that you can. Even angels can't do better than their very best!"

That quick dip into seraphic theology mollified Felicita for the moment. Mary Helen was grateful. They were nearing the dining room door. If she wanted a chance to proceed with her "unsuspect" plan, she'd have to ask Felicita a few questions, cross her off the list. Considering the state of Felicita's nerves, this was probably the best chance she'd have.

"Sister, I was wondering," Mary Helen began, hoping she sounded as if the idea had just occurred to her. "Early Monday morning, did you hear anything or see anyone?"

Felicita looked piqued. "You mean the morning that you found the body?"

Was she just sensitive or did that sound like an accusation? Whichever, Mary Helen chose to ignore it. "Yes," she said a little crisply, "that morning."

"I was asleep. Sound asleep. I heard nothing. I told Sergeant Little that." Felicita hesitated. The color drained from her face, leaving two round red circles high on her cheekbones. "You don't think for one minute that I had anything to do with . . ."

Raggedy Ann in a coif, Mary Helen thought crazily, surer than ever that it was Felicita and not Mother Superior who could not bring herself to say the word *murder*.

Before Felicita uttered another sound, Beverly slammed out of the kitchen door. She held a pancake turner like a scepter in her right hand. "Get that man out of my kitchen," she shrieked at the three of them.

Felicita gulped.

"What man?" Mary Helen asked.

"That priest! That Father Ed!" The rage emanating from her coffee-brown eyes made them look as if they were "perking."

Felicita caught her breath. "What in the world did he do?"

"I know what he calls me," Beverly hissed. The yellow haystack of hair wobbled uncertainly under her hairnet.

Prudently, Felicita did not ask for specifics. "I'm sure he's just joking."

"Well, he can keep his jokes to himself." Beverly's blazing eyes narrowed. "A little of that bastard goes a long way." She faced Felicita with a fury turning cold and dangerous. "Are you going to tell him or am I?"

Turning on her heel, Beverly banged the kitchen door hard enough for the glass to rattle.

"All I need now is a broken window," Felicita said dully.

"That would be the least of your worries," Eileen observed cheerfully. Obviously she was trying to buoy up the mood!

Felicita stiffened. Her pale blue eyes had the vacant look of one whose thoughts are somewhere else. "You know, Sisters"—each word fell with a thud—"I can really understand how a perfectly good person can be driven to murder!" Nervously she twisted the end of her long black scapular. Her face was stony. "Before this thing is over," she said in a perilous whisper, "I just may kill someone myself."

✦I✦ ✦I✦ ✦I✦

When Mary Helen pulled back the door, she immediately felt the tension in St. Jude's dining room. The breakfast was set out buffet-style, and men moved down both sides of the long table with a forced air of concentration. They stopped at chafing dishes full of fluffy yellow scrambled eggs and bacon and at baskets overflowing with muffins.

Here and there, an elastic smile snapped and a too hearty laugh echoed in the quiet. Sister Felicita, who had burst into the dining room ahead of them, disappeared through the swinging door into the kitchen. Mary Helen heard the rumble of angry voices coming from behind it.

Several wary sets of eyes shifted toward them. "With those same expressions and striped suits, we could all be in an old Cagney movie," Mary Helen whispered.

Eileen "humphed" in agreement.

Despite the strain in the room, Mary Helen found the aroma of coffee and freshly fried bacon irresistible. "Doesn't everything smell delicious!" she exclaimed aloud.

Con McHugh, regal in any circumstance, straightened up in front of the scrambled eggs. "Please join us," he said, offering Mary Helen his plate, "ladies first."

Without a second thought, she took it and stepped in line

ahead of the monsignor. This presented the perfect opportunity to talk to him, if the room hadn't been so unnaturally quiet. Once they sat down, maybe things would be more relaxed.

Sister Eileen slipped in line behind Andy Carr and was giving a conversation her best try. Poor Father Carr, blinking bloodshot eyes, attempted to act alert. "Did you sleep well?" Mary Helen heard her ask pleasantly.

"Take a look at his face, Sister," Ed Moreno called from the end of the line. "He looks as if Amtrak ran through his room last night and he was directly in its path."

Carr frowned and fingered his beard, which looked grayer and scruffier than it had yesterday. "What's the matter with my face?" he asked good-naturedly.

This brought groans and guffaws from the other priests. "Do you want me to tell you?" Tom offered.

Mary Helen took advantage of the horseplay to wait for the monsignor. If her plan was going to go according to schedule, he was next on her list of "unsuspects."

"Sister, here's a seat."

She felt her heart drop when Sergeant Little offered her the empty chair beside him. But her luck was holding.

"After you," Monsignor McHugh said, and they crossed the room together to join the police officer.

Maybe this was going to be better than she expected. The sergeant might ask questions of his own. She would simply piggyback on them.

Scarcely had Sister Mary Helen been seated when, as if by some silent agreement, the table filled up. Crowded as it was, no one chose another spot in the large dining room. It was as if no one wanted to miss anything that was said.

An unnatural silence descended on the group. Sergeant Little ate hungrily, glancing up every few bites to smile or to pass the salt and pepper. Forks scraped on plates. Ice clinked in water glasses. A butter knife clattered to the floor.

Finally, Tom Harrington could stand it no longer. Mary Helen watched him muster all the poise and polish of a television host. "Bob," he addressed Sergeant Little in a deep, commanding voice. "Can you tell us why you asked for our car keys?"

Little finished jockeying the last bite of egg from his fork, wiped his mouth, and set down his crumpled napkin. Slowly, his brown eyes as sharp as any red-tailed hawk's, he studied each one in turn.

Mary Helen followed his gaze. Did he see what she saw? Eminent, regal Monsignor McHugh, whose square shoulders sloped a little this morning under the burden of her grim discovery. Capable, generous "Handy Andy" Carr, a man's man, confidant of policemen, firemen, alcoholics, and you-name-its. Young, idealistic Mike Denski with the too-long sideburns and the guileless blue eyes. Tough, wiry, witty Ed Moreno, whose chestnut hair was just beginning to thin. Handsome Tom Harrington with the crooked grin, who, as the saying goes, never met a stranger. Or was he seeing only the cold, calculating face of a killer? She waited for him to speak.

"Your car keys?" Little's smile was friendly. "Thanks so much, by the way, for cooperating with the Sister. I wanted the keys to your cars"—he paused dramatically. Mary Helen felt that he had played this scene innumerable times before.

"—because Greg Johnson was driven here to be killed. I am checking to see if it was in one of your vehicles." He gave another friendly smile.

An electric silence stunned the room. The monsignor's distinguished profile turned the winter-wheat color of his hair. For a moment, Mary Helen feared he'd go into shock.

"One of us?" Unexpectedly, it was young Mike Denski

who recovered his voice first. His tone was high, squeaky, and definitely enraged. "Are you telling me, Detective Sergeant, that you suspect one of us is a murderer?" He didn't risk the answer.

"Why, why—we're—we're—" he stammered, as though trying to remember exactly what they were. "We're priests, for God's sake!" he said finally. "Priests help people. They encourage people to live. They don't kill them."

"Bob knows that." The police chaplain in Andy Carr spoke up. "He's just doing his job."

"But to even suspect that one of us . . ." Denski was breathless with rage.

The lad "doth protest too much, methinks," skittered through Mary Helen's mind.

"We do have original sin, you know," Tom said. Then added with a touch of sarcasm, "I'm sure they told you that in the seminary."

Denski's eyes searched his fellow priests in disbelief. "None of you is saying anything. Does that mean that you agree with him? That the killer could be one of us?"

When no one answered, Denski jumped up. His chair clattered to the floor. Tom, who was beside him, righted it.

Mike Denski's young face burned. His eyes darkened. He turned them on Little. "I can't swallow that you really believe . . ." Suddenly he was speechless.

Ed Moreno shrugged. "Every barrel has a few bad apples, kid. Remember Rasputin? And wasn't Richelieu a cardinal?"

"Now is hardly the appropriate time for a Church history lesson," the monsignor said, each word dropping like a cube from an ice maker.

"I didn't say I believed or disbelieve it, Mike." Little's voice was still calm and friendly. "I'm just checking it out. Like Andy says, it's my job."

Somewhat appeased and, Mary Helen suspected, a little

embarrassed, Denski sank back into his chair. She cleared her throat. "What I can't believe," she said, remembering her own trek up the pathway, "is, regardless of how Greg Johnson came here, that someone got him to the grotto."

Pushing her bifocals up the bridge of her nose, Mary Helen studied Little, waiting for his explanation.

The sergeant touched the edge of his mustache. "You hit it right on the head, Sister," he said with a wide smile. "That's the real puzzler. I'm working on the easy stuff first. After we figure out who brought Johnson here, the perp himself can tell us how he persuaded the victim to walk up there."

His glib answer did not satisfy Mary Helen nor, she suspected, him either. "Did the murderer have the knife to his throat?" she wondered aloud. "Or were two people involved? One would need to be very intimidating. Or was Greg unconscious? Then, the murderer needed something to transport him. A place like this must have a wheelbarrow. Most likely he was motivated—or persuaded—to climb that hill for a reason we are unaware of." She looked at Sergeant Little.

"I told you this lady was great," Ed Moreno burst out.

Mary Helen's face flushed. Sergeant Little looked puzzled. Mary Helen sighed; not that Holy Hill murder business again! She'd prefer that the sergeant—in fact the entire Sheriff's Department—stayed in the dark about that. It made her digging so much easier. In her experience, as soon as a police department, any police department, knew that she was looking into things, they became excessively touchy, which, of course, made everyone's life more difficult.

She pursed her lips and gave Father Moreno her best schoolmarm face, willing him to be still. He didn't seem to notice. Grinning around at the others, Ed was about to spill the beans when Sister Felicita exploded like a sonic boom from the kitchen door. Her face was mottled and her pale eyes blazed.

"And you!" she shrilled, startling everybody. One short finger pointed directly at Father Moreno. "You stop it! Do you hear me? You stop calling Beverly names! In fact, you stop talking to Beverly altogether. I'm having enough trouble around here without you getting her all upset. Do you understand?"

With searchlight eyes, she swept the group. "Do you all understand?"

A charged silence followed the question. Felicita herself stood clenching her fists. Her bottom lip quivered.

A meek "Yes, Sister" rose from somewhere followed by a self-conscious hush. Mary Helen wondered who would break it. If she were betting money, she'd put it on Eileen. Something inherent made her old friend want to set things right. She hoped Ed Moreno wouldn't try a joke. Anything close to humor would surely send Felicita into tears.

The situation was saved by the unexpected appearance of Laura Purcell. The oblique rays of sun coming through the plate-glass windows showed off every wrinkle and pucker on Laura's white shorts and halter. Strands of auburn hair, still unsmoothed, waved like an aura about her head. The unhealthy gray of her face made her green eyes darker, more haunted.

"You must be hungry, dear," Felicita said, apparently glad of the distraction. She scurried away.

Shivering despite the mounting heat, Laura made her way to the table. Mike and Tom shifted to make room for her and Andy drew up an extra chair.

"How are you feeling this morning, Laura?" the monsignor asked kindly.

Laura was about to say something when Felicita reappeared with orange juice. "Start with this," she said, "and then tell me what you feel like eating."

Woodenly, Laura did as she was told. The others watched in silence while she sipped the juice.

"Is there anything I can get you?" Eileen had been quiet for longer than Mary Helen expected.

Tears hung in the corners of Laura's eyes. "Just get me Greg's killer," she said in a tone of cold fury. "Tell me who he is and . . ." She closed her eyes and drew in a deep breath. "I will do such things—what they are yet I know not—but they shall be the terrors of the earth."

Sister Mary Helen was startled. Not so much by the young woman's ferocity as by her ready and apt command of Shakespeare. *Othello*, wasn't it? But then, why not? After all, Laura Purcell was a drama major.

+I+   +I+   +I+

Kate Murphy slammed the car door. Stamping her feet against the cement sidewalk to keep warm, she waited for her partner to lock up. It wasn't even safe to leave a police car unlocked anymore, she thought, disheartened. Above her the bruised June sky shifted, and in the distance a foghorn roared a single baritone blast.

"I guess the old lady's home." Gallagher pointed to Marva Johnson's faded brown landing barge of a Mercury in front of the pink palace. Both looked cheerless. Only the terrazzo steps glistened in the dripping fog.

The marimba sound of the doorbell echoed in the silent house. Cautiously, the front door cracked open. A wary brown eye took them in.

"Oh, it's you two again." Mrs. Johnson's voice was low and gravelly. She pulled open the door just wide enough for the two detectives to slip inside, then slammed it shut and leaned against it.

She shivered. "That cold would go right through you, if you aren't careful." She pulled her blue wool cardigan closer around her.

Kate was startled at the woman's appearance. Overnight her face had turned a ghostly white, and deep, tired lines seemed spread over it. Patches almost the color of her sweater brooded under her eyes. Her gray bubble of hair was stiff and flat where she had slept on it.

Looking at her now, Kate thought she might very well have just been released from a hospital. She followed Mrs. Johnson into the living room. By contrast with the chill outside, the heat of the house was stifling. The pungent soil-smell of the potted plants choked Kate, and perspiration trickled down from her underarms.

She glanced toward Gallagher, who already was running his finger around his shirt collar. She'd better make this quick!

Oblivious of the temperature, Mrs. Johnson sat in her padded rocker. On the end table beside it, a cigarette burned in an ashtray, unnoticed. Methodically she pushed back and forth, back and forth. A soft squeak timed each rock. At her insistence, Kate and Gallagher perched on the edge of the slip-covered sofa.

Marva Johnson's face tightened. "Have you found my son's killer yet?" Her glinting eyes turned on Gallagher. "Is that what you've come to tell me?" The thin lips stretched into a tight smile. "That you've discovered what I've known all along? That it was that girl, that Laura, who led my boy to his death?"

Gallagher cleared his throat. "No, ma'am," he said. "My partner's come upon some new information and she'd like to ask you a few more questions."

How smoothly Gallagher made that handoff, Kate thought, watching Marva Johnson's eyes shift toward her. Everything about him said that he didn't want to touch this lady with a ten-foot pole, to use one of his own favorite clichés.

"Mrs. Johnson." Kate's voice was soft. "Laura Purcell informed us that your son received a phone call at about three-thirty on the morning that he was killed."

The woman's lips curled into a sardonic grin. "And what were they doing together at three-thirty in the morning? I ask you that, Kate!"

"The point here is—" Kate began gently.

"The point is," Mrs. Johnson interrupted, all the lines on her forehead collapsed into one fierce frown, "that they were together at three-thirty in the morning. At that hour, decent, God-fearing people are at home asleep." She sighed. "Nothing good can come from a young girl and a young boy being together so late at night. I told Greg that, and Janice, too, time and time again. When they lived here, I insisted that they be home by eleven. And they were, too, if they knew what was good for them." She gave a short, cruel chuckle. "The hours after midnight are the Devil's hours. Those are the hours that are full of the temptations of the flesh. At that time of night we are weak. We are mortal. We fall." She seemed to savor every word.

"We must be sober. We must be watchful. We must resist him, for Satan and his helpers, like Laura, have the fires of hell waiting to catch souls and toss them like leaves into a bonfire. At every moment, the Devil prowls around like a roaring lion seeking whom he may devour."

Despite the heat, Kate shivered. Mrs. Johnson's words were so graphic, her feeling so strong, that Kate almost visualized a red-horned devil stalking the Johnsons' living room. All this hell and damnation when the woman thought the pair was just talking! Imagine what she'd say if she knew that Laura and her son were actually living together.

Kate shot Gallagher a warning look. If he mentioned it, they'd never get out of here. Her signal wasn't necessary. The expression on his face showed he wasn't about to offer any such information.

The *squeak, squeak* of the rocking chair was the only noise in the room. Mrs. Johnson, her brown eyes glazed over, had fled to some other reality. Watching her, Kate felt an overwhelming pity for the Johnson kids. Imagine growing up in this upright, judgmental, unforgiving home! No wonder they were so eager to leave it.

Down the block, Kate had grown up with her parents. They, too, were practicing Catholics. Good, loving people whom she always considered strict. Now, beside Mrs. Johnson, they looked like a pair of libertines, and she thanked God for it!

A thud from the heater snapped Kate out of her reverie. "I don't want to take up too much more of your time, Mrs. Johnson," she said, sounding all business.

Marva Johnson blinked as though trying to remember who these people sitting in her living room were.

"I do want to ask you a couple of questions," Kate said, smiling, "if I could."

"Ask your questions, then." Mrs. Johnson crushed the already dead cigarette, lit a fresh one, and put it in the ashtray. Rather than smoking them, she seemed to burn her cigarettes like incense.

"According to Laura, your son received a phone call saying that you were ill and in the emergency room."

Mrs. Johnson looked astonished. "Ill? Me?"

"Yes. And that is apparently why Greg left the house. To go to the hospital."

Quick tears flooded Marva Johnson's eyes. She swallowed, but said nothing.

"I take it you were not ill." Kate studied the woman's face.

Still unable to speak, Marva shook her head.

"And so, you did not ask anyone to call Greg for you?"

Mrs. Johnson pressed her lips together. Tears ran down her pale cheeks and splashed onto her cardigan.

"Do you have any idea who would have called your son?"

"No," she whispered hoarsely. "I don't even know Greg's phone number."

That made sense, Kate thought. Why would he take the chance that she'd call and get Laura on the line?

Mrs. Johnson dug into her sweater pocket for a tissue. "I wasn't sick," she said, "and even if I was and had Greg's number, I wouldn't call him, and I wouldn't call Janice either."

Kate was taken aback. "Why is that, Mrs. Johnson?" she asked.

The woman took a deep breath and let it out slowly. It was as if she were summoning up the courage to put her reason into words.

"Because," she said, all the life gone out of her flat eyes, "I would be afraid that neither one of my children cares enough about me to come."

❖❖❖   ❖❖❖   ❖❖❖

"Trip two to the mother from hell," Gallagher said when they were outside. After the sweltering living room the crisp, wet fog felt wonderful. "I can hardly wait until one of my kids gripes about how tough I was." Gallagher turned the key in the ignition and, without waiting, flipped on the car heater. The sudden cold blast turned Kate's legs to gooseflesh.

"Can't you wait until the motor warms up?" she asked, already knowing the answer. This heater business was an ongoing argument between them.

"By the time we get to the corner, it'll be hot," Gallagher said.

Kate gave an exaggerated shiver. That was what he always said. "This is the kind of thing that leads to murder," she snapped.

Much to her surprise, Gallagher turned the fan down a notch.

"You sick?" she asked.

He shrugged. "That goofball of a lady got to me, I guess."

"In what way?" Kate wondered if he'd picked up something in the conversation that she'd missed.

"I just can't help feeling real sorry for those two kids of hers. They are damn lucky they turned out as good as they did. Must have been a hell of a father figure somewhere," Gallagher needled and waited for Kate to react.

She smiled halfheartedly.

"Imagine living your whole life with a mother whose elevator doesn't go all the way up." Gallagher gave a friendly honk to a white-haired lady who looked as if she had fallen asleep at the stop sign. She gave him the finger.

Or parents whose elevator gets stuck halfway up, Kate thought, feeling the hint of heated air on her frozen ankles. Like Jack and me, stuck on this moving business.

Before long their car was warm and cozy. The tires from passing vehicles shot up tiny fountains while their heater fan gave off a steady hum. The two partners fell into a comfortable silence.

All kids are affected by their home life, Kate thought, staring absently at a window washer who seemed totally oblivious of the fog. Little John must be affected by their arguing, although Jack and she tried never to discuss the move while he was present. Kate knew by the way his big, serious baby eyes studied them that he sensed something. Well, tonight, one way or the other, it would stop. She would see to that. After all, home was where the three of them were, together and loving one another. What did a house or a neighborhood or a city matter?

"Do you see what I see?" Gallagher, stopped at a traffic light, pointed.

A gaggle of tiny youngsters bundled up to their eyes in sweaters and knitted caps were being shepherded across Geary Boulevard by a slender woman pushing a stroller. One slightly larger child carried a brown paper sack.

Immediately Kate recognized the group. It was Sheila Atkinson, John's baby-sitter, and her charges. The precious woolen bundle in the stroller was her John. All she could see was his button nose, red with cold. Happily he banged his rattle on the tray.

Gallagher tooted. Sheila, rounding up her little brood safely on the curb, paused from wiping runny noses to wave.

Little John, recognizing his mother, stood up in the seat, waved his baby rattle at her. "Ma, Ma, Ma," she heard him call before he went back to his banging. "Qwa, qwa, qwa." He was on his way to feed the ducks.

For a moment, Kate didn't know whether to feel happy or sad. Mama versus ducks. Ducks, one; mother, zip. Could a toddler be too well adjusted? Feeling her stomach drop, she forced herself to be realistic. Gallagher and she were on their way to do a door-to-door interrogation of Mrs. Rosen's neighbors. What would she do if John wailed and begged to be taken along?

"Want to stop?" Gallagher asked.

Of course she did, but she knew better. Sheila was on her morning walk and had her hands full without a stray parent disturbing her schedule. She shook her head.

"Where are they going?" Gallagher asked as the tiny band disappeared down the hill.

"Spreckels Lake. To feed the ducks," Kate said.

"Looks more like they're going to the Klondike to feed the penguins." Gallagher turned the heater up a notch. "Are you warm enough?" he asked after the fact.

"Fine," Kate mumbled, only half aware of the heat. Gallagher had struck a chord. It was the middle of June, summer for God's sake, and her baby was bundled up like an Eskimo's child. A few miles away, he'd be out on a soft green lawn, brown as a berry, running and picking dandelions and chasing butterflies, instead of dripping wet. Maybe Jack was right. Maybe they should move to Cordero where there was sunshine and safety. Tonight she'd tell him that she'd changed her mind. Tonight at dinner, she'd tell him that she was willing, no, happy! to make the move.

His mother would feel betrayed, but that was Jack's problem. Let him deal with her. Her concern was with her husband and with her son. After what she'd just witnessed at the Johnsons', she'd do everything she could to surround them both with love.

For the first time, the idea seemed palatable. Even as her head was congratulating her on the common sense, the wisdom, of her decision, she felt the pain in her stomach grow and expand like yeast in warm dough until it threatened to completely smother her heart.

+I+ +I+ +I+

After breakfast, Bob Little was surprised to find Sergeant Eric Loody no longer guarding the entrance to the retreat center. He was even more surprised when he passed the kitchen. The door was flung open, and through the screen he spotted the sergeant settled at a table with Beverly Benton.

Beverly's broad back was to him and her hips hung over the chair seat like a couple of polyester saddlebags. Across from her, Loody's large frame bent forward, a cup of coffee cradled in his thick hands.

Their combined bulk somehow made Little think of *Gulliver's Travels*. It must be the rarefied air on this hill. He hadn't thought about Gulliver for years, if ever, after he escaped Sister Immaculata's English Lit class. It took him a minute to remember the name of the giants' land. Brobdingnag! He smiled to himself. Brobdingnag! Those two were a Brobdingnagian sight. Sister Immaculata and her *Word Smart Vocabulary* drills would be proud!

From the posture, Little knew that Sergeant Loody was absorbed in what the cook was saying. He strained to hear, but the large ceiling fan whirring above the pair served as an automatic scrambler.

Loody must have sensed his presence. All at once, he raised his head. Their eyes met and Loody's smile twisted into the beginnings of a smirk. Or so it seemed to Little. Unless that annoyingly complacent expression was because the guy's schnozzola was set high on his face, making him perpetually look down his nose at you.

He can't help that, Little thought, feeling a surge of sympathy. He smiled and waved.

Loody lumbered to his feet. All the leather on his uniform creaked to attention. He pushed back the screen door. "You need me for something, Bob?" he asked, all spit-and-polish politeness. Yet Little sensed something taunting in those narrow agate eyes.

"No . . . no, thanks, Eric," Little heard himself stumble. What was it about this man that made him so uncomfortable? "Finish your coffee break," he said. "Today's going to be another scorcher. You'll need all the breaks you can get." For some reason, his words sounded sarcastic, even to him.

Loody's face darkened, but he bit back any reply.

Turning slowly in her chair, Beverly viewed Little with a bright metallic stare like a volcano ready to erupt.

That lady is the one who ought to make me squirm, Little thought, giving her his friendliest smile.

Beverly continued to stare. Where had he seen her before? She looked so familiar. Maybe if he interviewed her again, she'd say something to spark his memory.

Loody cleared his throat. "Sergeant, I've been doing some nosing around, asking some questions." His voice was deep and swollen with importance. "I need to talk to you later. Alone. I feel that what I've uncovered will prove helpful."

The pomposity of his stance and the macho arrogance of his tone needled Little. He felt the prickle of sweat on his forehead. It was already too hot to put up with this know-it-all, although he guessed he'd have to sooner or later. With any luck at all, tomorrow Loody would receive another assignment!

Little mopped his face and tried to regain his good humor. "Great, Eric," he forced himself to say, "but right now I want to talk to the guys from Crime Scene before they get called away. To see if they've come up with any admissible evidence." As soon as the words left his mouth, Little regretted them. He really hadn't meant them to sound like such a put-down. After all, they were all on the same side.

Loody studied him. His eyes blazed, but he said nothing. The perfect police officer, always in control. "Right!" With an expressionless face, Loody checked his wristwatch. "After lunch, then?"

With a feeling of reprieve, Little agreed to a one-thirty meeting in St. Colette's gift shop.

"And Miss Benton." He met her stare.

"Ms.," she corrected, ice dripping from the capital M.

"Excuse me. Ms. Benton, I need to talk to you, too, before you leave today."

"I'm not staying past three o'clock." She swiped at her face with a soiled paper napkin. "It's too damn hot to fix a big dinner. As far as I'm concerned they're too pampered anyway. Tonight they can all fend for themselves."

Little wasn't sure if she meant the priests, the nuns, the Sheriff's Department, or all three, nor did he want to know. "Two-thirty, then," he said pleasantly, "in the gift shop."

"I told you I was leaving at three," she said, her fleshy face glowing.

Little gave her his "kill 'em with kindness" smile. "I only have a few questions," he said, although at the moment he'd be damned if he had any idea what they were.

What the hell is the attraction? Little wondered, watching Sergeant Loody stride across the kitchen and once again take his place opposite an eager Beverly. Whatever she was telling him, Loody was impatient to hear. Would he be privy to it at one-thirty? Would he have to listen to that oversized blowhard recount everything Beverly should be telling him? He caught himself. After all, they were on the same team. Weren't they?

Little was glad to see Dave Kemp waiting for him outside St. Philomena's Hall. He was curious to know how Dave felt about Loody. Was this strong aversion strictly his problem? He wanted to ask, but it sounded too much like gossip. He hoped that one of these days, while they were having a beer after work, Kemp would bring it up on his own.

At the far end of the parking lot, the three-member crime scene team stood in a tight group, waiting for them.

"Where the hell have you been?" one of them called out, "we're melting here."

"Who'd have thought you guys would work fast?" Kemp quipped. "Find anything?"

Much to Little's disappointment, the trunks of the priests' cars revealed very little that the team thought criminal. They had, however, collected bits of hair and fiber, dirt and and leaf samples, small fragments of whatever they hoped might turn up anything. Now they were ready to go.

"No sign of blood from the guy's head, huh?" Little asked, although he really hadn't expected there to be. Any perp with an ounce of sense would wrap the victim in a tarp or plastic— anything that could safely be destroyed or disposed of.

Just once, he'd like a nice easy case with a dumb murderer; one where he opened the trunk of a suspect's vehicle and found the victim's bloodstains and the murder weapon thrown in for good measure. That only happened on television, and even there, much less often than it once had.

"Find anything else? Something that might be cause for suspicion?" At this point, he'd take any lead.

One of the team laughed. "The only thing I found that could remotely be called suspicious was in"—he consulted his notebook for the name—"in Father Tom Harrington's trunk."

Little's blood quickened. That guy Harrington was awful slick. "Yeah?" He tried not to sound too eager.

"The padre is carrying nearly a case of booze in his trunk. Funny thing, it's in a box marked 'Will and Baumer Sanctuary Lamps.' Hell, he'd be lit up all right!"

Bob Little tried to laugh at the joke, but he was disappointed. The priest could have liquor in his trunk for any number of reasons. And even if he was planning to drink it all himself during retreat, that made him an alcoholic maybe, but not a murderer.

Something had to break soon. He and Terry were planning a few days in the mountains. Terry had promised not to bring work and he wanted this case solved and off his mind so that they could concentrate on each other.

He took off his jacket. Rings of sweat had already formed

at his armpits. The blacktop burned right through the soles of his shoes and he felt its heat on the balls of his feet.

One of the deputies shaded his eyes from the full, hot sun. "If you let us go so we can get this stuff analyzed, then we will all have some answers!" He sounded irritable. Little chalked it up to the persistent heat.

✦I✦   ✦I✦   ✦I✦

"They sure got out of here in a hurry." Kemp watched the crime scene car round the corner, slow down, then merge onto the road back to their air-conditioned headquarters in Santa Cruz.

For some reason, the fiery red taillights reminded Little of Beverly's angry stare. Beverly! He shut his eyes in exasperation. He should have asked the team to search her car while they were here. That was stupid! When he'd put in the request, he hadn't expected her to be at St. Colette's.

He ran across the parking lot shouting, but their car was already well out of earshot. He'd wait until they got back to headquarters to call. They'd have to come back and, three o'clock or no, Beverly wasn't going anywhere until he said so.

I'll deal with Loody first, he thought, wondering if he was still with Beverly. What was it she was telling him? The thought of that pompous stuffed shirt looking down his nose and filling him in on his murder case. This is my case! Loody should stay the hell out of it. The more Little thought of it, the madder it made him; mad enough to question and requestion everyone connected with this case until he found a motive.

He'd save that for the afternoon. Before it got any hotter, he'd take the whole hillside apart, board by tree if necessary, in search of something, anything that might give him a lead.

"Take off your jacket, Dave," Little said more roughly

than he intended. "And for God's sake, get rid of that damn
bow tie!"

◆•I•◆   ◆•I•◆   ◆•I•◆

After breakfast Sister Mary Helen settled herself on the wide
sundeck that wrapped around the buildings. By scooting her
chair back under the eaves, she was able to enjoy the panorama of the valley beyond—and stay out of the direct sun.

The view was full of surprises. She supposed that no matter how many times you took in a view this vast, you'd always
discover something new. Like that English holly stretching up
between two orange trees. And the bench hidden around the
corner, built entirely of black enameled horseshoes. Or those
three yellow rosebushes. She hadn't noticed them before.

She shaded her eyes. In the distance row after row of fir
trees shimmered with heat against a cloudless blue sky. At her
feet, the cherry-red dahlias planted in redwood tubs along the
porch rail had burned and faded since yesterday. Even the
sweet William was wilted. No wonder. No one watered them.
Undoubtedly, no one even thought about them. Everyone,
especially Felicita, who was the most logical waterer, was too
involved with death to think of such small bits of life.

"How about a morning trot around the property?" Eileen's question startled her.

"Trot?" she stared in disbelief. "Have you any notion how
long it's been since I trotted around anything?" Good night
nurse! Today she felt as if she could barely stroll. Let alone
trot!

"I remember way back when you were the best turkey
trotter in the Order," Eileen said with a mischievous glint.
Raising her toes and rocking on her heel, she hummed something between "If You Knew Susie" and "Don't Bring Lulu."

Despite herself, Mary Helen laughed. Usually she hated

Eileen's "remember way back when" stories. "Living in the past is a sure sign of aging," she contended time and time again. But at the moment, the past seemed comforting. Much easier surely than dealing with the present.

Encouraged, Eileen sat down beside her. "Come on along, old dear," she coaxed. "A walk will do us both good."

Mary Helen's stomach pitched at the thought of her last walk around St. Colette's: the angry insects buzzing, the dogs, stiff and staring. She closed her own eyes, trying to block out the memory. "You go on," she said, forcing herself to picture only the ageless redwoods and the tranquil horizon. "I'll just sit here and think."

"Suit yourself." Eileen sighed. Without another word, she left Mary Helen alone on the sundeck.

Sister Mary Helen felt the sun warming the tips of her walking shoes. Studying them, she noticed that they were covered with soft, fine dirt and small dried bits and pieces of needles and twigs, and crushed pinecones much like the cone stuck in Greg Johnson's tennis shoe.

She wiggled her toes, trying to blot the gruesome scene out of her mind. Before long the sun would creep across the entire porch, making it impossible to sit there without melting. She tucked in her feet and gazed out over the vista. There was such peace, such quiet, it seemed impossible that a brutal murder—actually three murders if you counted the animals—had taken place here.

Who was responsible for them? And why? That was what she had better think about while she had time. With supreme effort, Mary Helen focused her mind on the situation and called up her mental list of those most unlikely to be guilty.

Laura. She had talked with Laura and determined, once again, to her own satisfaction that the girl was telling the truth. Laura Purcell was dramatic surely, but the girl had no reason and no heart to murder Greg Johnson. Mary Helen supposed that she'd be hard-pressed to convince Sergeant Little of this since she had no positive proof whatsoever. But there was just something in the way the girl acted and reacted, in the way she spoke . . . Just a "gut feeling."

Sister Mary Helen knew well how poorly policemen—oops, policepersons—reacted to gut feelings as a reason to pronounce a suspect innocent—or guilty, for that matter. She strongly suspected, however, that they had gut feelings of their own.

Her best bet was to uncover Greg's murderer herself. That way she wouldn't need to prove anyone's innocence.

Sister Felicita was in the clear too. Mary Helen had never considered her a serious suspect. Too nervous! And again, what motive? She barely knew Greg Johnson, or so it appeared.

The next least likely on her list was the monsignor. Although she had fully intended to question him at breakfast, she never had the chance. She was about to go in search of him now when she smelled the faint, familiar vanilla fragrance of his pipe tobacco.

Feeling lucky, she waited for Monsignor McHugh to round the corner of the porch, but nearly groaned aloud when she saw what he was doing. The good monsignor was reciting the Divine Office! Not at all the ideal time to launch into a casual conversation, or any other kind of conversation either. He seemed intent on pacing up and down the sundeck reading his breviary. Her questions would have to wait. "And the smoke it encircled his head like a wreath," she thought, watching him approach.

Wasn't there some canon law against smoking while you said the Office? she wondered peevishly. Or had he figured out a theological loophole, like saying the Office while you smoked? Whichever, this was clearly not the time to interrupt him to ask if he was innocent of murder.

As he passed, the monsignor raised one long, thin finger in recognition and continued on his way, moving his lips around the pipe. Frustrated, Mary Helen watched him go. Who was next on her list?

"Hi, Sister." Mike Denski's voice cut through the stillness. Why not? she thought, greeting him with a wide, welcoming smile.

The young priest gave her a toothy grin that must have paid the orthodontist's rent for several months.

"Can I join you?" he asked.

Mary Helen nodded. Come into my parlor, said the spider to the fly. "You may if you can find a chair," she said, unable even in these circumstances to resist a grammar lesson.

Giving a slightly bewildered shrug, Mike pulled over another director's chair and settled next to her. The pair sat side by side like two passengers on an ocean cruise. It took only a few seconds for the young priest to begin to fidget. First, he crossed and uncrossed his legs, then he wiggled his right foot. Finally, he curled the piece of hair at the end of his long sideburns.

Well, it was less annoying than drumming his fingers on the chair's arms would be, Mary Helen thought, watching him twist the hair.

"A penny for your thoughts," Mike said at last.

Mary Helen glanced over with an abstracted calmness calculated to drive him crazy. I'll bet you'd give a lot more than that, she thought, wondering what exactly was bothering him. She reckoned it wouldn't take too long to find out.

"My thoughts?" she repeated, as if she hadn't quite heard. "You're interested in my thoughts, are you? Well, to be perfectly honest, they aren't really very profound. I was just sitting here thinking about how unpredictable life is. You never know from one moment to the next what God has in store for you."

She paused for effect. A small lizard sidled its way along the edge of the porch. She pointed to it. "Did you know that lizards remain motionless about ninety percent of their lives?" Then added with a whimsical smile, "Aren't we lucky to see that one move?"

Mike Denski stared at her openmouthed.

Mary Helen congratulated herself. Keep him slightly off balance, wondering if her mind wandered or if she was just a font of little-known facts. It was a stroke of genius, affording her the perfect opportunity to ask him questions apropos of nothing.

"How did you say you knew Greg Johnson?" she asked.

It was clear from his puzzled expression that, as intended, the jump from lizard to murder victim took Mike by surprise. "We were in the same class at St. Patrick's Seminary," he blurted out.

"Did you know him well?"

"Too well." There was an acidy edge to his voice.

"Deep friendships do form when young people are thrown together in a small, intense community like a seminary," Mary Helen said, knowing full well that deep animosities can fester as easily if not easier.

Mike Denski stared straight ahead. The frozen lizard stared back. "I wouldn't call him a friend, exactly," Mike muttered.

"What would you call him?" Mary Helen's question sounded much more direct than she intended and too quick if she wanted to keep her slightly deaf act believable.

The young priest's foot began to wiggle again. "What I'd call him is a goddamn hair shirt!" Mike burst out.

"A hair shirt?" His unexpected reference to the austere ascetic practice surprised her. She hadn't thought of hair shirts for years. In the hagiographies of her youth, it seemed that almost every saint wore one as part of his or her road to sanctity. She had often wondered what they looked like. Fruit of the Loom T-shirts cut from one hundred percent horsehair?

Today in our complex world, Mary Helen thought, just living and acting with love seemed to afford enough penance and self-denial to make trumped-up penances unnecessary.

Mike Denski was waiting for her reaction. His eyes, like two topaz stones, dared her to contradict him.

"I know exactly what you mean," she said, and she did. "Believe me, after you've been in religion as long as I have you'll run across not only hair shirts, but whole suits of underwear. 'Hair long johns' to coin a phrase!" She waited for an appreciative laugh. What she got was more of a halfhearted grunt.

That's the trouble with some of the young ones today, Mary Helen thought, watching Mike's serious face. Little to no sense of humor. Everything so deadly serious. You'd think God took a coffee break and left them in charge!

"I guess I shouldn't talk that way about him," Mike said, no longer sounding defensive, just uncomfortable, "now that he's dead and everything, but at St. Pat's Greg Johnson really acted like he thought he was something. You know what I mean? Good at his studies, a big jock, and he didn't mind telling you what hot stuff he was with the girls when he went home on vacation. That's until they found out he was in the seminary. When we first went in, I thought he was great. Somebody I'd like to be like."

"The Bing Crosby model of priesthood," Mary Helen said.

Mike Denski gave her a blank stare.

"Remember in *Going My Way* and *The Bells of St. Mary's?*"

"What?" The light in his eyes merely grew dimmer.

"Never mind," Mary Helen said, somewhat ruffled. Almost as bad as no sense of humor, was no sense of history. "I didn't mean to interrupt you," she said. "He was someone you wanted to emulate. Then what happened?"

"We got into it after dinner one Visitors' Sunday. My mom had come." Mike's face flushed as if even the memory of what had happened angered him anew. "I love my mom. I even like her. She's a good, unselfish woman who's made all kinds of sacrifices for me. I guess I was talking about her too much. Anyway, whatever I said ticked Greg off. He acted like he hated his mother, although she'd seemed nice enough that day, and like he despised me for loving mine. Called me a 'mama's boy,' or something like that. He kept it up and kept it up until I finally couldn't stand it any longer. I took a swing at him."

Mary Helen cringed. The slight, sensitive seminarian would have been no match for the Johnson boy.

"I got in one sucker punch." Mike gave a crooked smile. "I guess he would have killed me if a couple of the other guys hadn't pulled him off. I don't know what the rector would have done if he'd found out, but nobody ever told him and things just went on, but they were never the same. From that day on, Johnson took every opportunity to make my life miserable. He made snide remarks about my mother and me and he rubbed my nose in the fact that I only got in one good punch."

"How long did the harassment last?"

"Until he left St. Pat's." The color began at his jaw and grew until his face blazed. Only his eyes remained cold. "And I can't say I was sorry to see him go. I came as close to hating him as I ever came to hating anyone." He gave a caustic laugh.

"Foolishly, I thought I'd be rid of him, but Greg was tenacious. Just weeks before my ordination he showed up at St. Pat's again. Said something about asking the archbishop if he wasn't afraid he'd have to ordain my mother, too, 'cause I couldn't let go. I lost it, Sister." Denski swallowed. "I don't know where I got the strength, but I beat the sh—" He stopped. "—the you-know-what-I-mean out of him. I'm not proud of myself, but I did it."

"How did Greg react?" Mary Helen asked, trying to hide her surprise.

"He swore he'd get even," Denski said miserably. "And I'm afraid he would have, too."

So that was what had been bothering the young priest. He despised and feared the victim. Wished and maybe even prayed that he could rid his life of Greg Johnson. Had he run into Greg on the grounds of St. Colette's? Was he so afraid of Greg's revenge that he had seen his chance to rid himself of his tormentor once and for all? Did he actually hate his brother seminarian enough to murder him? Mary Helen doubted it, yet she must somehow broach the subject.

"One thing puzzles me," she said gently. "You seemed so upset when we discovered the body."

As suddenly as it had come, all the color left Mike Denski's face. Mary Helen suspected he was reliving the gruesome scene.

"I'd be upset about finding anyone murdered, Sister, even a perfect stranger. I guess I don't hate anyone enough to want them killed." Mike swallowed as if he were about to make a meal of every word. "Not even Greg Johnson," he said deliberately. "Although, to tell you the truth, I didn't realize that until I saw him lying there in his own blood."

✦I✦ ✦I✦ ✦I✦

By the time Mike Denski finally excused himself, the morning sun was quickly swallowing up all the shade on the wooden deck. Before long it would be too hot to sit there. Mary Helen mentally crossed the young priest off her suspect list.

Although he had shown the first glimmer of a motive so far, she didn't consider him mean enough to be a real dyed-in-the-wool murderer. He might have killed from passion on the spur of the moment as he threw that one punch so many years before, but this murder was clearly planned and coldly orchestrated.

Mary Helen shielded her eyes and watched Mike cross the broad lawn surrounding the small, neat blue swimming pool. A figure—from this distance it looked like Ed Moreno—was furiously swimming laps. Back and forth, back and forth.

Mike approached the pool, stopped, and stared down at the swimmer, but seemed to say nothing. Seconds later, he disappeared into a grove of sycamore trees abutting the lawn.

No, the murderer was not Mike Denski. She was sure of that, although she was not quite as sure of what she thought about Ed Moreno.

Mary Helen shifted in her chair. The canvas seat was beginning to feel like a slab of granite. Her back and shoulders were stiff. She turned to let the sun warm them. Undoubtedly tension. And no wonder! The last thirty hours had been filled with nothing else. Her conversation with Mike Denski was simply icing on the cake.

Although she had eliminated three unlikely suspects, Felicita, Laura, and Mike, to her own satisfaction, the identity of the murderer was not coming at all clear. She checked her wristwatch. Perfect time for her coffee break. Whoever invented coffee breaks should be canonized! Mary Helen pushed herself up from her seat. Only a true saint could think of such a simple way to insert a few quiet minutes into our busy lives; a time when it is considered perfectly respectable to blow and sip and just daydream. Murder or no murder, she would have her coffee break!

St. Jude's dining room was empty. Or so Mary Helen

thought when she stepped in from the sun's glare. Only after she'd poured herself a large mug of coffee did she realize she was not alone.

Father Andy Carr was seated in a remote corner of the large room, far away from the windows, almost as if he were deliberately trying to stay out of sight. *Maybe he's avoiding the glare,* Mary Helen thought, smiling over at the priest.

"Care to join me?" Father Carr invited.

Although she would have preferred time with her own thoughts, Mary Helen hated to pass up the opportunity to pare down her list further. Outgoing Andy Carr would not be her pick for the murderer, but one never knew.

"What are you up to?" Father Carr asked as soon as she sat down.

His question took Mary Helen by surprise. *Did he suspect?* One look at his open, friendly face and she knew better.

"Nothing much." She fudged a little. No sense scaring him off by announcing, "I'm eliminating murder suspects from my least-likely list." She wondered crazily what the expression in his candid hazel eyes would be if she were perfectly honest.

"It's going to be a hot one," Carr remarked, taking another stab at being affable.

Mary Helen nodded, realizing that she wasn't being much help.

"Where is everybody?" he asked.

"Not very far away, that's for sure," Mary Helen said. Father Carr chuckled.

"This retreat's turned out to be one fine mess, hasn't it?" He spread his broad hands on the tabletop. "Who would ever have imagined last Sunday that you—"

"No one." Mary Helen cut him off. She didn't want to be reminded once again that she had stumbled onto the body. Something in his tone suggested guilt by discovery.

Carr must have sensed her discomfort. He studied her.

"My heart goes out to you," he said. "I didn't mean . . ."

Unexpected tears flooded her eyes and she turned her head.

"May I warm your bottom?" Carr asked.

His question shocked her until she realized he was pointing to her coffee mug.

"Dumb joke." He lumbered up from his chair. "It always works at AA meetings."

And here, too, Mary Helen thought, no longer feeling like weeping. Instead she felt like grabbing the conversation by the horns and wrestling it right down to her satisfaction.

"How did you say you knew Greg Johnson?" she asked when Father Carr had refilled their two cups.

It was Carr's turn to look surprised, but he recovered quickly. The man, obviously used to handling all types of crowds, simply rolled right into the answer.

"The reason I made the young lad's acquaintance"—Carr blew on his coffee—"is because while he was still in the seminary he managed to get himself arrested in a Gay Rights demonstration. Would have ended up in the pokey, too, if I hadn't pulled in a couple of favors."

"You got him off, then?"

Carr nodded grimly. "With just a few hours of community service."

"Why didn't you let him go to jail? That was his purpose, wasn't it?"

Carr stared at her in unconcealed admiration. "My point exactly, Sister. But you have no idea what Absolute Norm, the archbishop, is like when there's the hint of a scandal."

Mary Helen did not have to wait long to be told.

"He's like a crazy man, Sister. That kid hadn't been cooling his heels five minutes before 'himself' is on the horn insisting that I talk to somebody, anybody, and get the little smart-ass out before he"—Carr dropped his voice in a perfect imitation of the prelate—" 'does irreparable harm to the image of the Church.' As if the Church hasn't weathered its share of scandals over the years."

"And did you? Get him out, that is?"

"Yeah, I did. You can't be chaplain for the Police Department, the Fire Department, AAs, Knights of Malta, and the Port of San Francisco for as long as I've been without having a few connections."

He pulled on the corner of his scruffy beard. "But I'm telling you, Sister, I sure didn't want to. I think if those young guys want to champion a cause, we owe it to them to let them do it and take the consequences of what they choose."

From the vehemence in his usually jovial voice, Mary Helen knew that Andy Carr deeply felt what he was saying. "Why didn't you?" she asked.

His hazel eyes softened. "I've been a priest for so long," he said, almost as if he was just realizing the reason, "that when your bishop, himself, asks you to do something, if you can, you do it. You know what I mean, Sister? I guess it's an old-fashioned kind of obedience."

Mary Helen smiled sympathetically. She did know what he meant. They were both members of a vanishing breed.

"Besides," he added with a chuckle, "when the archbishop called me he sounded so upset, I was afraid that if I didn't do something, he'd go into cardiac arrest. And the Norm you know," he said sheepishly, "to put it quite brutally, Sister, is better than the Norm you don't!"

Mary Helen was tempted to cross Carr off her list right then, but she wanted to make absolutely certain. "You sound angry that Greg Johnson put you in an awkward position," she said flatly.

"And you sound like a Perry Mason rerun." For the first time, Andy Carr's chuckle had a hollow ring.

Mary Helen felt her face flush. "I guess I do," she admitted. "I'm just inquisitive."

"No, Sister, not just inquisitive." His eyes bored into hers. "If I remember correctly, you have an extraordinary talent not only for discovering dead bodies, but for stumbling on perps who did them in."

Mary Helen wondered how to respond and was relieved when there was no need.

"But I tell you, Sister, in my case you are barking up the wrong cleric. You're absolutely right that I was mad, hopping mad, at that kid for putting me in a very awkward position. But he's not the first person, nor will he be the last, unfortunately, who's done that."

Mary Helen thought with abhorrence of all the stories that had surfaced recently in the *Chronicle* about priests. One had to work hard to discover God's presence in the midst of all the scandal. Her dismay must have shown in her face.

"Fortunately, Sister, the guys I've pulled out of the fire are small potatoes compared to the ones you're thinking about. Thank God!" He cleared his throat. "It's hard to reconcile, isn't it? Until you remember that there are no perfect people. Priest or no, we're all sinful human beings. What is it that good old St. Paul says? That God chose what is foolish and what is weak in this world to confound the strong?

"And, while we're on the subject, I don't kill my fellow priests, or anybody else for that matter, because they are weak or sinful or because they get themselves into situations which I neither understand nor condone.

"Actually, I try my best to deal with each one of them with compassion. I hope with the same compassion that Christ showed in dealing with the publicans and the sinners of his day. I hope with the same compassion that Christ will one day show to me."

Mary Helen caught the flash of innate benevolence in his

intelligent eyes and knew that no one could doubt his innocence.

"Most of the guys are penitent and grateful," he continued. "No, I take it back. All of them are penitent and grateful. Some of them are more vocal about it than others. But
this Johnson kid? This guy was a whole different kettle of fish.
He wouldn't even admit that what he did might possibly have
been imprudent. If anything, he acted as if my pulling strings
somehow tainted his integrity, which in a way, I guess, it did.
If it was up to me, I'd have let him have a taste of jail. It
would put some teeth into his commitment, if you know what
I mean."

Carr gave a grudging chuckle. "He told the archbishop in
front of me that it was his right to go to jail 'for justice's sake.'
Which is easy to say when there's no chance of your staying
there. I thought Norm was going to come unglued." Carr
shook his head.

"No, Sister, I wouldn't kill anyone for his imprudence or
even for his sinfulness. If I had killed that kid, which by the
way I didn't, it would have had nothing to do with the causes
he supported or even for the sins he committed. If you'll
excuse my language, Sister, it would have been because the
pompous little bastard was nothing more than a gosh darn
grandstander! Half the people he met probably wanted to
wring his neck."

Father Carr gave an embarrassed little grin. "In answer to
your original question, however, I did not kill Greg Johnson
and I can't imagine who did! Anything else you want to
know?"

His question hung on the silent air waiting for Mary
Helen to answer. For once, she was relieved to see Beverly
and her cart slam through the swinging door with the mak-
ings of a cold buffet lunch.

‣‣ ‣‣ ‣‣

"How about a picnic?" Mary Helen asked, thrusting a hastily made bologna sandwich toward Sister Eileen.

Eileen wrinkled her short nose. Her face was flushed and she was still puffing from her walk around the property. "I never eat bologna without potato chips," she said.

"Well then, hurry up!" Mary Helen whispered although no one was in sight. "I want to get away before the rest arrive."

"Get away from what?"

"Meet me at the picnic table next to the sycamore grove."

"Is it in the shade?" Eileen asked, but Mary Helen pretended not to hear. This partial-deafness business was really quite handy.

‣‣ ‣‣ ‣‣

"Now, what or who is it that we want to avoid?" Eileen straddled the attached bench. "Back there you were beginning to sound suspiciously like a James Bond movie."

She set down chips, napkins, paper plates, and two cans of diet cola that she'd somehow managed to juggle all the way from the dining room. "I'm a regular Houdini," she said, surveying her cache.

"I want to avoid them all." Mary Helen watched Eileen pile chips on her bologna, add the top slice of bread, and then push. Although she had witnessed the ritual hundreds of times before, it always fascinated her.

"Delicious," Eileen said, taking a crunchy bite.

"That walk surely did relax you," Mary Helen snapped. "It's as if you've completely forgotten our list."

"Of course I haven't." Eileen broke off a crust for the blue jay perched at the end of the table, eyeing them. "Tell me what more you've found out."

With a noisy flutter of wings, the bird scooped up the bread as if he were afraid that Eileen would change her mind. They watched him dart away.

"We agree that Laura is innocent, right?"

"Right. If she really did kill Greg, she'd have made up a much better alibi. Besides, under all that drama I think she is genuinely heartbroken by his death," Mary Helen said.

"And Felicita?"

"No apparent motive. Besides, she's too high-strung."

"The mother?"

"I'll have to call Kate and ask what she found out." Mary Helen checked her wristwatch. "I'll do it this evening when she gets home from work."

"What about young Father Mike? Did you have a chance to talk with him?"

Mary Helen was relieved. Obviously the list was on Eileen's mind. In fact she had it down pat. "No love lost between Greg and him, but he's not mean enough," she said, wasting no time on explanation.

Surely soon someone would spot the two of them on the secluded bench and join them. If not for their company, then for the fresh air and shade.

"Andy Carr?" Eileen was doctoring the second half of her bologna sandwich.

"He hasn't the heart for murder," Mary Helen said. "And no real motive."

"Who's left, then?" Eileen's gray eyes were worried. "The monsignor, Ed Moreno, and Tom Harrington. I can't imagine any of them killing that young man."

"I can't either." Mary Helen hated to admit it, but absolutely nothing was becoming clearer.

"Could it be someone we've yet to meet?" Eileen offered hopefully. "An acquaintance? Someone from school or work? Someone from his protesting past?"

"Laura said Greg never gave out their phone number, remember?" Mary Helen felt like the proverbial wet blanket. "How long do you think the Sheriff's Department can keep us sequestered at St. Colette's? Three or four more days?"

The prospect of more days at the retreat center gave Mary Helen renewed impetus. "What about Beverly?" she said.

"Good choice," Eileen agreed, "except that she wasn't here when it happened."

"Just because she went home that night, doesn't mean she didn't come back."

Eileen frowned. "As far as we know, she hardly knew Greg Johnson. What would be her motive?"

"What is anyone's motive?" Mary Helen snapped, then instantly regretted it. She felt frustrated, but Eileen must too. It wasn't fair to be short with her.

"Sorry," said sheepishly.

"Forgiven, old dear." Eileen fed the jay another crust of bread. "You've heard of cabin fever, I know."

Mary Helen nodded, wondering where this was going.

"I think we're getting its cousin, mountaintop pyrexia." Eileen popped a stray potato chip into her mouth. "Even poor Felicita. You haven't forgotten her outburst in the dining room this morning?"

Mary Helen hadn't forgotten it. Neither, she suspected, had Ed Moreno. It was extraordinary for the outgoing priest to be silenced at all by anyone, let alone by meek, accommodating Felicita.

"Beware the fury of the patient man. In this case, woman," Mary Helen corrected herself. "Although I think she felt more frustration than fury."

"My point, exactly! Mountaintop pyrexia! And the only way out is to discover the murderer, the quicker the better!"

"Maybe we are being a bit foolhardy," Mary Helen said, more for form than from actual reluctance. Eileen winked. "When in the name of all that's good and holy has that ever stopped either one of us?" She began to gather up the empty cans and plates. "How shall we approach the remainder of the list? Each take a priest? Then whoever's finished first tackle the final one?"

"Let's not overlook Beverly."

Eileen's gray eyebrows shot up. "I think Beverly is a two-woman job."

Without further discussion they decided to question the cook together.

"Which priest do you want?" Eileen asked.

"Good afternoon, Sisters." A deep, sonorous voice floated out from the sycamore grove, cutting off Mary Helen's answer. "Monsignor! Good afternoon to you." She hoped she didn't sound as caught as she felt.

"Dibs," Eileen said under her breath.

The old man smiled down benignly. "Ah, both a bench and shade. May I join you?"

Eileen slid over to make room.

"I'll just take these things to the trash can." Mary Helen gathered up Eileen's neat pile. "Bees and bugs, you know." She swatted at an imaginary insect.

The monsignor made a halfhearted but gentleman-like stab at helping, which Mary Helen deftly declined. "I'm sure you and Sister Eileen will find plenty to talk about until I get back," she said.

"Yes indeed." Eileen smiled her cat-in-the-cream smile.

The monsignor lowered his tall, stately frame onto the wooden bench, looking a little bewildered, but pleasant enough.

Poor devil, Mary Helen thought, wishing she were a bird on the bench. He has no idea what he's in for. But neither do I, she reflected, wondering about whom she'd bump into first, Father Moreno or Father Harrington.

She was picking her way across the lawn when an unsuspecting Ed Moreno climbed out of the swimming pool and stood, dripping wet, in her path.

◆I◆   ◆I◆   ◆I◆

Searching through the piles of junk in St. Colette's sheds and storage areas for anything that might provide a clue was a much bigger job than Bob Little had anticipated. Straightening up, he checked his watch. Soon it would be time for his meeting with Loody.

Unfortunately, Kemp and he had uncovered nothing more than rusty tools, broken boards, stacks of torn window screens, and at least one hundred varieties of bugs. Nothing that could in any way point to the murderer. A couple more days and the case would be cold.

Anyone seeing Kemp would guess that he'd been crawling through caves. Dirt encrusted his flaxen hair, and his face and shirt were smeared with sweat and who knew what else.

Little imagined that he looked about the same. His stomach growled. Great! Not only was he hot, tired, and dirty, but now he was hungry too! He kicked at a stack of clay flowerpots partially covered with an old black plastic bag. They clattered to the ground.

"Find something?" Kemp asked hopefully.

"Not a damn thing. Only more junk!" Little surveyed the reddish-brown shards. "Hell, you wouldn't need that many pots if you were replanting the Garden of Eden!"

He rubbed his forearm over his sweaty brow. He could feel the grime. "God," he said, "I need a vacation."

"How about a lunch break?" Kemp asked, obviously try-ing to sound upbeat.

Little dusted off his filthy hands. "Sounds good. I'll wash up and call the office."

Kemp looked puzzled.

"I need Crime Scene to examine Beverly Benton's trunk. I'll meet you in the dining room after I talk to them."

✦I✦   ✦I✦   ✦I✦

When Little arrived, Kemp, too, had made an attempt to clean up. Only one or two cobwebs still clung to the back of his shirt. He was seated next to Loody, whose tan and green uniform was fresh and crisp. For some reason the contrast between the two men infuriated Little.

"Hi, Bob." Loody glanced up from a mountainous turkey sandwich. "Find anything the other guys didn't?"

The smirk on his sunburned face stoked Little's rage. "No luck," he said, fighting down the urge to punch Loody in the nose.

"Don't forget we need to talk." Loody bit into his sand-wich.

Was Little reading it wrong or was Eric Loody gloating? What the hell had he uncovered?

✦I✦   ✦I✦   ✦I✦

At one-thirty sharp Bob Little stood outside St. Jude's dining room. His hastily eaten sandwich formed a cold lump in his stomach.

"What do you have, Eric?" he asked when finally Loody appeared. He hoped he sounded open and receptive. Why was it so easy to forget that they were on the same side?

Deliberately, Loody pulled himself up to his full height so that he topped Little by three or four inches. The narrow agate eyes shone with a foxlike sharpness that made Little think of Red Riding Hood.

What is this all about? he wondered, moving back.

"I've been talking to Beverly. The cook," Loody added unnecessarily. "She's been telling me some very interesting things. Apparently you don't remember her."

He waited while Little scoured his memory. Beverly, actually her bulk, was familiar, but to save his life he couldn't remember where he had seen her before. Was it a murder case? He'd investigated so many over the years that sometimes witnesses tended to blur.

The smirk on Loody's face made his memory search more frantic. What does he know that I should know? Little wondered uncomfortably.

"I can't remember where I've seen her," Little admitted finally. "What did she tell you?"

Eric Loody eyed him maliciously. "I bet you'd remember if you tried," he taunted.

Unexpectedly, Little felt the anger swell until his head throbbed with it. "God damn it, Eric! I'm telling you, I don't remember the woman and I haven't got time for guessing games. Now, what the hell did she tell you? If you have anything, let me hear it!"

Loody's face darkened and his lips grew pale and tight. For a split second, Little thought that he might stomp away. But obviously the disclosure gave him too much pleasure. "She told me she is sure that little Miss Laura is the one that stabbed Greg Johnson."

Could Beverly be right? Little wondered. In his mind he had ruled out Laura Purcell. Was he so far off? "Motive?" he managed to ask. "What was her motive?"

"Jealousy—according to Beverly. She claims that Laura went ballistic if Greg even looked at another girl and he did, or so says Beverly. She can cite chapter and verse." He gave a hard, cruel bark.

"Has she any proof? Hell, she's only known Laura a few weeks. And did she know Greg at all?"

"Once you talk to her you'll discover she's a very keen observer of human nature." Loody gave a knowing smile.

Little studied him skeptically. "I did talk to her," he said. He had been with the woman for almost an hour. Usually people opened up to him, even those who had things to hide. Why not Beverly? Why hadn't she told him about her suspicions?

"You've got to win her confidence." Loody's obnoxious grin was back in place. "Yes, sir, Bob, she sees plenty. Told me a lot of interesting things."

Bob Little could feel Loody's hard eyes on him. "Yes sirree, Bob, the lady knows puh-lenty."

Little's mind raced. What was Loody hinting at? Where had he seen Beverly?

A quick, sharp laugh rang out from the dining room. Something about it was familiar. He heard a door open. Turning, he locked eyes with Beverly. All at once it returned to him like a heavyweight punch in the stomach. The air left him. He steadied himself against the building. His ears were ringing.

"You know what I mean?" Loody's words sounded far, far away.

He did know what Eric Loody meant. Sure! He knew Beverly Benton. He also knew who had killed Greg Johnson. And with absolute certainty he knew exactly what he must do about it.

+>I+   +>I+   +>I+

Father Ed Moreno stood on the lawn beside the swimming pool facing Sister Mary Helen. Without warning, he shook himself like a dog after a bath.

If he thinks a few drops of water will put me off, he's got another think coming. She sniffed and gave him her friendliest smile. "How-do?" she called.

Moreno buried his face in his towel. Water ran in rivulets from his deafening Hawaiian print trunks down his hairy legs. Despite the heat, he shivered. "Hi, Sister," he said finally.

Mary Helen watched him dig the towel into his ears, then run his fingers through his thinning hair.

"What are you up to?" he asked with just a hint of suspicion in his voice.

"Me?" She feigned surprise. "Just trying to keep cool." She glanced up at the cloudless blue sky.

"Is that so?" His lips twitched the way they did when he was about to make a joke.

Well, the joke wouldn't be at her expense! She put on her most businesslike face. "I was on my way to the trash." She lifted both hands, still full, and hurried off, hoping he'd stay put.

When she returned, she was relieved to see the towel spread out and Ed Moreno lying on it, facedown. His muscular shoulders and the balding spot on his crown were both beginning to redden. If she didn't hurry, he'd be burned to a crisp before she was half through questioning him.

The problem, of course, was how to settle down casually next to him. There were no movable chairs around, and squatting on the soft grass seemed impractical. Getting down would be fine. Getting up was the trick!

Father Moreno must have sensed her presence. He lifted

his head and squinted against the sun. "Can I do something for you?" he asked, rolling over and up into a sitting position. It wasn't the perfect setting for a quiet conversation, but it beat talking to his back.

"I was curious about your relationship with Greg Johnson," Mary Helen blurted out, unable at the moment to think of a more tactful way to put it.

Ed Moreno gave a surprised laugh, "Anyone ever accuse you of being coy?" he asked.

Mary Helen's face warmed. "Not too often," she admitted.

Moreno struggled to his feet. "Let's sit," he said, and pointed toward a bench half hidden under a towering sycamore. A shrine to St. Francis hung from the tree's trunk. The gentle saint's hand was raised in blessing. A good omen, Mary Helen thought, settling herself beside the damp priest.

"You want to know about my relationship with the Johnson kid," he said, his eyes not meeting hers. "Well, there wasn't any. Next question?"

After years of teaching eighth-graders Mary Helen was immune to flip answers. "Why not?" she shot back.

Moreno's head jerked up. "Why not what?" Obviously he was stalling.

"If the boy worked with you, why didn't you have some sort of relationship with him?"

"When you say 'work' with Greg Johnson, you are using the term *work* lightly, Sister. Very lightly," he replied, avoiding her question entirely.

Mary Helen perked up. "He was lazy, then?"

"That guy had lazy down to a science." Father Moreno draped one leg over an arm of the bench and wriggled his bare toes in the sunshine. "When he first came to help out at Juvenile Hall, I thought he was just warming up. But then when he never really did start to perk, I got concerned. He talked a lot, but never really did anything. You know the kind of guy I mean?" He raised his hand like an old-fashioned cigar store Indian. "Heap big smoke. Very little fire."

Mary Helen nodded. Indeed she did. Over the years she'd run into quite a few people who fit the description.

"Then, I thought he was just one of those guys that liked to hear himself talk, and it was harmless. You know—just a lot of gab. And most of the kids in Juvie have plenty of time. They aren't going anywhere, so to sit and listen to a guy B.S. was, I thought, just a different way to pass the time.

"He was a clean-cut, open-looking guy and as I say, he was just talking, right?"

"What did he talk about?"

"Anything, everything. What kinds of programs he was going to start. What he was going to do for the kids. He was everybody's pal. Knew most of the kids by name. So far, so good. Right, Sister?"

Mary Helen nodded, waiting for the *but*. It wasn't long in coming.

"But he didn't deliver." Ed Moreno's face hardened like a fist. "That was the thing about him. It was almost diabolical. He'd promise the kids things, get them all revved up, give them a taste of hope and friendship. And then he wouldn't come through. These kids are experts on adult betrayal. The last thing they need is another adult letting them down, especially one who represents the Church."

Moreno's mouth took on a bitter twist. "And that ain't all," he said in an attempt to sound lighthearted. "When Greg started to make innuendos about what I did with those young boys in my office, I went nuts. It's absolutely untrue, of course, but it would end up my word against his. You know what even any hint of impropriety would do to my work with the kids. And he had no right. That bastard . . ." He caught himself. "Excuse my language"—he gave a short, cold laugh

—"but when I think of Johnson and the harm he did in just six short weeks, I could kill him.

"But I didn't," he added quickly. "Not that I didn't want to. And the feeling was mutual."

Mary Helen raised her eyebrows.

"That's right, Sister. I think the kid wanted to kill me as much as I wanted to ace him. Maybe more so."

"Why's that, Ed?"

Moreno turned toward her and with one big hand gripped the back of the bench. "I called his bluff, that's why. I was counting on the kids at Juvie and the arch to back me up. They did, too. So, I'm the one who finally had the guts to tell him that I didn't think he had a vocation to the priesthood. Maybe to politics, but not priesthood. The dedication, the responsibility, the call. It's hard to put your finger on, Sister, but something was missing. Something necessary. So, I figured I'd do us all a favor—the Church, his fellow priests, God knows, his future parishioners."

He pushed back a strand of wet hair from his forehead. "It's not as if he had a sterling seminary career. Stories get around. When I said something to him, he looked as if he'd just bitten down on something sweet with an exposed nerve. You know what I mean?"

Mary Helen winced.

"At first, I thought he was going to cry," Ed continued. "Then I caught a flicker of what looked like relief in his eyes. But, by the end of the week when he left to return to the seminary, those same innocent blue eyes had hardened. He gave me a look when he said good-bye that burned with such hatred, such absolute loathing, it gave me gooseflesh."

And it still does, Mary Helen thought, noticing that, right now, despite the heat, Ed Moreno's bare legs were covered with bumps!

"So, Sister." Ed stood and pulled down the legs of his

trunks. "If anybody was to kill anybody in this relationship, as you call it, I think Greg Johnson would kill me. Not the other way around. Does that answer the question to your satisfaction?"

"I guess it does," Mary Helen said. "Thank you."

The short, wiry man strode toward St. Philomena's Hall, and the sun moving through the leaves cast delicate shadows across the damp spot where he had sat.

Near Mary Helen, a metallic hummingbird whirred and darted in and out of an enormous snowball hydrangea blossom. Such a peaceful place, she thought, watching Ed Moreno disappear into the building. The perfect spot for contemplation. It seemed so out of place to be contemplating only betrayal and murder!

"So there you are, old dear."

Mary Helen's heart jolted. She hadn't heard anyone approaching. She made a conscious effort to calm herself. After all, it was only Eileen, but it could have been anyone.

"I'm so sorry." Eileen studied her. "I must have startled you. Your face is the color of cold Cream of Wheat. Look." She pointed to Mary Helen's hands. "Even your knuckles are white. You didn't hear me coming, did you?"

Mary Helen knew where this conversation was leading.

"My mind was a hundred miles away, thank you," she said. "I would have heard you if I had been paying attention."

"I swear, old dear, you should get those ears of yours checked."

"My hearing is just fine, if you please, Eileen. If some people only spoke distinctly instead of mumbling through a mouthful of mush."

Eileen said something that Mary Helen didn't have the humility to admit she missed. "How did you do with the monsignor?" she asked brightly.

Eileen sat down, avoiding the print of Ed Moreno's wet

trunks. "He really is a lovely gentleman," she began, "and everything about him shouts 'innocent,' I'm sure, but we've an old saying back home." She rolled her eyes knowingly. "'A saint in the face may be a fiend in the heart.'"

Mary Helen's mouth went dry. Had Eileen stumbled onto the murderer? "Are you suggesting—"

"Of course not." Eileen cut her off. "Not for a minute. I was just reminding us that appearances can be deceiving."

"Did you suppose we didn't know that?" Mary Helen grouched.

After a short but dangerous silence, Eileen gave a long-suffering smile. Mary Helen felt ashamed. This murder on what should be her retreat was affecting her nerves and she was taking it out on Eileen.

Waving aside Mary Helen's attempt at apology, Eileen hurried on with the account of her meeting with Monsignor McHugh. His connection to Greg Johnson hinged chiefly on his long-standing friendship with Greg's mother.

"He's known her for years," Eileen said, swatting at an insect buzzing close to her face. "Since both children were little. And to tell the truth, I don't think the monsignor had much contact with either Greg or his sister. Certainly, he has no motive for killing Greg, or at least no motive that I uncovered."

Mary Helen's heart dropped. Not that she actually suspected the monsignor of murder. It was just that they were nearly through the list of unlikely suspects, and so far they were stumped. Soon Sergeant Little would have to let them go home.

She sighed, knowing she'd have to let go. After all, solving murders was not her job. It was the job of the police. In this case, the Sheriff's Department. It's important to know— how had that popular song put it?—when to hold, know when to fold. She'd just have to fold. Although unfinished business rubbed at her like sand in a bathing suit.

"The monsignor did admit that over the years Mrs. Johnson has become a bit obsessive about religion." Eileen was still talking.

"So, you think the monsignor is innocent?" Mary Helen asked, wondering what she'd missed. The look on Eileen's face told her.

"Does he think that Marva Johnson may have killed her own son?"

Eileen frowned. "I really am getting concerned about your hearing," she muttered, and Mary Helen chose not to hear that remark.

"A mother killing her son seems so unnatural, although we both know such things do happen."

"I told you." By now, Eileen's voice had an edge on it that Mary Helen did not much like, although, she reminded herself, Eileen's nerves were frayed too. Turnabout is fair play. If the whole business wasn't solved soon, they'd both have the screaming meemies!

"I told you," Eileen repeated, "that the monsignor said he tried to counsel Marva several times, especially about her disproportionate disappointment when Greg left the seminary. But he's a busy man and she was a difficult woman, especially as she became older.

"None of us gets any easier, I guess." Eileen gave Mary Helen a knowing glance.

Mrs. Johnson was probably no piece of cake when she was young, Mary Helen thought, knowing full well that old age doesn't bring on eccentricities, it simply accentuates them.

"And to tell you the truth," Eileen said, narrowing her eyes, "the monsignor's fuse isn't getting any longer in his old age either."

"Did you get the rough edge of his tongue?" Mary Helen

asked, concerned. She needn't have bothered. One look at Eileen and she knew better.

"Even a monsignor is smart enough not to cross an Irishwoman!" Eileen winked. "To be perfectly honest, I was as sweet as sugar. As we say at home, 'soft words butter no parsnips, but they won't harden the heart of the cabbage either.' "

"Are you calling the monsignor a cabbage?" Mary Helen couldn't resist.

"Whatever he is, he is convinced, and he convinced me," Eileen said, "that both he and Mrs. Johnson are innocent of any part in Greg's death. In fact, the monsignor ended our conversation by stating, quite emphatically, that Marva Johnson is—how did he put it?—'nothing less than the salt of the earth!' "

Mary Helen leaned her head back against the wooden bench. The sun, inching its way west, left one end of the swimming pool dark with shadows.

The salt of the earth, is she? Mary Helen thought, listening to the soft *pee-ur* of a tiny phoebe. And we all know what happens when the salt loses its flavor. It is good for nothing, but to be thrown out and trampled underfoot!

Next to her, Eileen was checking off names on her fingers. "Do you figure Ed Moreno is innocent?" she asked, two remaining fingers still sticking up in the air like a victory sign.

Mary Helen nodded. Eileen folded down her middle finger. "Then, there's only one priest left." Her face wrinkled. "I can hardly imagine that handsome, charming Tom Harrington is our murderer, Mary Helen. We must be missing something."

"Murderers come in all shapes and sizes," Mary Helen said, bolstering her own resolve, as well as Eileen's. "Nobody ever said they must be ugly and boorish, now, did they? And who said it was one of the priests? We haven't even considered Beverly yet."

From the expression on Eileen's face, Mary Helen knew she was not looking forward to a confrontation with the cook.

◆I◆ ◆I◆ ◆I◆

The two nuns spotted Father Tom Harrington by the ice ma-chine on St. Philomena's porch. The frozen-eyed statue of the saint, standing amid rocks and cactus, blandly watched the priest fill a plastic bucket.

"How-do, Father Tom?" Mary Helen called.

The priest made a slow, almost sleepy, turn toward them.

"Hi, Sisters." He treated them to his famous crooked grin. His curly hair was so tousled that Mary Helen wondered if he'd just rolled out from a nap.

"I'm about to fix myself a drink." The liquid brown eyes focused on them. "Won't you join me for a little happy hour? It's four o'clock somewhere, you know."

Mary Helen glanced at her wristwatch. They still had an hour to go in Santa Cruz. From the odor of his breath and the swimming look in his eye, Mary Helen suspected that Father Harrington was clocking his happy hour on New York time.

"Won't you join me," he invited with a deep, theatrical bow.

If that's what it takes to get this job done, Mary Helen thought.

"We'd be delighted." Eileen must be thinking the same thing. She accepted for them both.

Tom's leather traveling bar was set up on the bureau top. He had moved a small picture of Our Lady of Perpetual Help to make room for the case, which seemed terribly out of place in the bare, almost monastic room.

"What will it be, Sisters?" he asked with largesse.

One look at the bureau top betrayed their limited choice. A bottle of bourbon, a bottle of Scotch, and a bottle of vodka stood in front of the mirror like three musketeers awaiting battle. Spying tonic water, Mary Helen chose the vodka. Eileen followed suit. Besides, Mary Helen thought, taking the first sip, vodka is supposedly odorless.

Perfectly at ease, Tom sank into the room's one easy chair. Mary Helen took the straight-backed desk chair and, good sport that she was, Eileen perched on the edge of the bed.

"*Sláinte!*" Tom cried out in Gaelic, raising his glass. The two returned his toast.

"Nasty business this." Tom examined the shiny toes of his Gucci loafers. "What do you two make of it?"

"That's what we wanted to ask you." Mary Helen smiled her kindest smile. "Who do you think had reason to kill Greg Johnson?"

Father Tom's eyes came into sharp focus. He was not nearly as "iffy" as she'd first thought. "Do you mean who among those of us who were at St. Colette's the night he died?"

"Well, yes." Mary Helen nodded.

The priest's face flushed and his lips pressed into an angry cut. "Are you suggesting that one of us did it?"

"Not really. What I'm actually trying to do is to prove that one of us did not."

"Isn't that a little bassackwards?" he asked with a disdain that made Mary Helen bristle.

"Perhaps," she said, struggling to keep her tone even, "but I thought that if I proved to Sergeant Little's satisfaction that none of us was guilty, we'd be able to go home."

"So, Sister, you aren't perfectly content to be sequestered in this idyllic spot where you can contemplate God in nature and in your fellowman?" He drained his glass.

"Sarcasm doesn't become you, Father," she said stiffly,

and watched him struggle before the arrogance slowly faded from the handsome face.

"You're right," he said softly. "Some would say it's the booze talking, but anyone who really knows will tell you it's me talking, uninhibited by this." He rattled the ice cubes in his glass, then rose and refilled it.

"What was your question? Who had a reason to kill Greg Johnson?" He gave Mary Helen that crooked smile, then blew back a curly lock that had fallen across his forehead. "And, of course, you don't mean 'who,' you mean 'did you' kill him? Right?"

"Not entirely." Mary Helen wanted her options kept open.

With a grunt Tom positioned himself back in the easy chair and stared pensively out the small bedroom window. Just beyond it a clump of periwinkle shimmered in the sun. The heat in the room was stifling.

"I can't speak for the others, naturally," Tom said, taking a long swallow from his glass, "but as for me, I had no reason to kill the kid. Not that I knew him all that well. He only worked for me for a couple of weeks. The archbishop thought communications might be his bag. He communicated all right! With everything in a skirt. It got so that none of the secretaries felt comfortable around him.

"I took him out for a drink a couple of times after work and tried to tell him, man to man, to knock it off." Harrington's face flushed. "You know what that little twit—who, by the way, could match me drink for drink—had the nerve to tell me?" He stared, enraged by the very remembrance. "That I was nothing but an aging souse. He threatened to write a letter to the *San Francisco Catholic* denouncing me as nothing but a glib-tongued alcoholic. Wouldn't Absolute Norm love that? And I think he would have done it, too, except that one of the secretaries threatened a sexual harassment suit.

"So I canned the kid. He wasn't pleased, naturally. Nor was the archbishop. Not to mention Ed Moreno when Greg landed at Juvie. Actually, the only ones thrilled were the women in my department, and me, of course. It was a little chilly down at the Chancery Office for a while, but we all survived. No, I can't think of any reason I'd have for killing him, now."

"Because he threatened you?" Even as she said it, Mary Helen knew she was reaching, and she wasn't surprised when Tom Harrington objected.

"That's a little far-fetched, even for you, Sister," he said, haughtiness creeping back into his voice. "He never actually carried out his threat."

"Well, it's impossible to predict what anyone will do under stress." She was determined that he was not going to have the last word.

Tom Harrington stared sullenly into his glass. "Under stress! Under stress!" he repeated, almost as if he were mocking her. "Some guys thrive on it, you know, Sister. Some of the guys grapple with stress and become saints. Some guys, too many guys, crack under stress. Some fool around with their secretaries, some with the altar boys. I know that it's no excuse, but at least it's a reason. And some, like me, go for the sauce." He raised his eyes, trying hard to focus. "I started out drinking socially. In my line of work, I'm invited to so many parties. When I got home, I'd be wound up and I'd take a little nip to put me to sleep. Now, I'm afraid, it's starting to take me over. Do you have any idea how often I wake up in the morning with the 'Irish flu'?"

Mary Helen didn't nor did she really want to. She had discovered what she came for. Tom Harrington might be arrogant and an alcoholic, but in all probability he was not a murderer.

+I+   +I+   +I+

"Another fallen idol," Eileen mumbled as they crossed the sweltering parking lot.

"Weren't you the one who was reminding us, not an hour ago, that people are most often not what they seem?"

Eileen sighed. "You're right. But this one looks so charming and handsome on the television! And that crooked grin is so beguiling."

"I'm sure Tom does a lot of good with his particular brand of charm," Mary Helen said, trying to cheer up her friend. "And remember we're talking about God here who can write straight with the crookedest lines." She shrugged and added logically, "God has to if He wants His message out. All He has to write with is a lot of us sinners. Nobody knows better than you and me that we are only earthen vessels."

Eileen's gray eyes looked sad. "You're right, old dear," she said, her brogue thickening a bit, "but somehow I didn't expect this particular pot to have so many large, ugly cracks."

+I+   +I+   +I+

On the pretext of taking an afternoon coffee break, the two nuns entered St. Jude's dining room. Their real objective was a chat with Beverly. From the absolute silence in the kitchen, they surmised that Beverly had left. When Felicita, scapular askew, burst through the kitchen door, they knew for sure.

"She's left without preparing one single thing!" Felicita's round apple face blazed and she looked near tears. "I have eight people to feed—and more if the policemen stay, and then the bug man is coming tomorrow. I need to get things ready for him. Someone has to see to Laura, bring her a tray, and that blasted phone is ringing off the hook.

"If it isn't Mother Superior, it's someone wanting to make a retreat here. We've never had so many requests as since this murder hit the morning papers." She shuddered. "It's positively ghoulish!"

"It made the morning papers?" Mary Helen asked, wondering how long before Sister Cecilia called.

Apparently Eileen was having the same thought. "Let's be unavailable," she whispered.

Felicita rushed on. "That's the least of my troubles right now," she said, her pale blue eyes sparking. "What will I serve for dinner?"

"Let us give you a hand," Mary Helen offered, knowing Eileen was a whiz with leftovers. Besides, thinking about something completely different cleared the mind. When her mind was clear, the answer that she was groping for sometimes just popped right up.

Felicita stared at her as if she'd just suggested that the tooth fairy cook supper. In the end and without much coaxing she capitulated gratefully.

Before long the refrigerator door was opening and slamming. Plastic containers were emptied and the most delicious aromas floated up from the enormous gas stove and filled the entire kitchen.

◆I◆   ◆I◆   ◆I◆

Sergeant Bob Little spent the better part of the afternoon walking the extensive grounds of St. Colette's on the pretense of checking evidence. What he was really doing was mulling over his decision. He'd stopped now and again at small, hidden grottos to pray to whatever saint—and to be honest he wasn't sure—for some guidance.

Yet all the while he knew exactly what he must do. He had known since the moment he realized where he'd seen

Beverly. He knew it from the smirk on Eric Loody's pugnacious face.

Fighting down his repugnance, Little decided to act.
What else could he do? And the sooner the better! He
checked his watch. It was nearly quitting time. If he played
his cards right, he'd arrest the suspect and beat it off this hill
without running into anyone else. He wouldn't have to look
anyone in the eye, or justify his decision.

Not that it was anyone's business. This was a police matter. Still, he hoped like hell to avoid everybody, particularly
the nuns. There was something about them that made him
feel like a kid again.

Little drew in a long, deep breath and pulled himself up
to his full height. He was a grown man, for chrissake! A
homicide detective, not some scared kid.

Despite his protestations, he felt the flesh beneath his
mustache tingle at the thought of telling the nuns his decision. He tried to ignore it. What could possibly happen?
Would some sudden thunderbolt strike him? He glanced up.
The sky was absolutely cloudless. The feeling was nothing
more than a hangover from Sister Immaculata, who, he'd
sworn as a kid, had absolute control over all the elements.

Little sat on the end of a fallen log. Even under a roof of
redwoods, the afternoon heat was stifling. He mopped his
forehead and was surprised at all the dirt that came off on his
white handkerchief. He must have kicked up the dust as he
walked along. No matter how I cut it, he thought, staring at
the dark smudge on his handkerchief, I have to make the
arrest.

The evidence, he knew, was largely circumstantial, but
that was the district attorney's problem. The suspect had motive. She had opportunity and she had means. And since
recognizing Beverly, Little had the incentive to make them
stick.

He pushed himself off the log, brushing the specks of dirt and moss from his hands. "What you are going to do, do quickly!" Where had that come from? Sister Immaculata's religion class. He stopped, stunned, realizing those were the words of Jesus to the traitor Judas. Maybe the nun's thunderbolts were becoming more subtle.

Once again, standing in the scorching parking lot, Bob Little hesitated, but not for long. He needed to wrap up this case, get back to headquarters, finish the paperwork, and go home to Terry.

Tonight he could really use a drink and maybe a rubdown. He smiled and felt a ripple of delight at the prospect of talking Terry into giving him a complete full-body massage. But before he'd allow himself even to imagine the pleasure, he'd have to make the arrest. What he needed was moral support. Where the hell was Kemp?

Dave Kemp's legs jutted from the open door of the unmarked car. He was talking on the radio. Little reached him just as he signed off.

"What's up?" Little asked, hoping that someone had stumbled on a solution to his dilemma.

Kemp stood up and slammed the car door. The bang reverberated over the silent hillside. "The boss sent a message. He wants to know if we're about finished up here. Seems some big noise from San Francisco called and wants the group released. To hear him, you'd think we were holding them in solitary confinement." Kemp's cobalt eyes had a hurt expression. "One of these bozos must have called out to somebody with connections."

"Don't sweat the small stuff," Little said, realizing that he was trying to sound nonchalant. Another of Sister Immaculata's *Word Smart Vocabulary* words. Why was she torturing him this afternoon?

"And another thing, Bob. Inspector Kate Murphy from SFPD left you a message."

Little's heart leapt. Had she found something?

"Murphy says Johnson's mother is fine. She knows nothing about any phone call. Another blind alley?" Kemp asked.

"Quite the contrary." Little put his hand on Kemp's shoulder. He hoped his partner wouldn't feel it shaking. At least Kate Murphy's information wouldn't hinder his plan. "I'm about ready to make an arrest," he said.

Kemp frowned. "What?"

"An arrest."

"Who?" The word came out like a jab.

Little cleared his throat and said with as much conviction as he could muster, "I'm going to arrest Laura Purcell."

The expression on Kemp's face told him that his partner did not concur. How much convincing was this going to take? Jeez, he wanted to get it over and done and get home. Maybe at this moment, a thunderbolt wouldn't be too bad.

As if on cue, Sister Felicita emerged from the kitchen door carrying a covered tray. Her flushed face glowed in the late afternoon sun. Through the open doorway, Little noticed some activity: Sister Eileen at the enormous stove. And was that Sister Mary Helen pushing the stainless-steel cart? He didn't know why it surprised him. It shouldn't have. Obviously Beverly was gone. He should have known it would be the nuns who pitched in and got the job done. He figured it had been that way from time immemorial.

"Are you almost done for the day, officers?" Felicita asked "Or are you staying for supper?" Even her deep-seated habit of hospitality couldn't conceal her hope that she'd guessed right the first time.

"Can we get room service?" Little couldn't resist a little jibe.

Flustered, Felicita glanced down at the tray. "Oh, this. It's

for Laura. Poor girl has eaten nothing all day but some soup.
A little nourishment never hurt anyone."

The two men watched Sister Felicita, black scapular
swinging behind her, bustle into St. Philomena's Hall. "Are
you going to wait until she's done eating?" Kemp asked. "Or
do we go in right now?"

"Even the condemned get a last meal, right?" Little answered, feeling sapped of the energy and satisfaction he usually felt when he was about to arrest a murderer.

Kemp's mirthless laugh was cut short by a splintering
crash and the hollow ricochet of jagged screams.

"What the hell . . . ?" Little bolted toward the building,
the slap of Kemp's shoes behind him.

The steady shrieks drew them to the room where Laura
Purcell was resting. Felicita, surrounded by cracked dishes,
spilled water, and clumps of steaming goulash, sagged against
the doorjamb. She groaned when she saw the two officers and
waved a limp hand toward the bed. "She's dead," she whispered hoarsely, then hunched over and began to weep.

Bracing himself, Little moved toward the body. Laura
Purcell was sprawled across the bed, almost as if she had tried
to get up but had been pulled back. Her hair hung over the
edge like a flaming waterfall. Her green, glassy eyes stared
flatly at Little and her mouth yawned open.

Fighting down a sickening sensation, Little touched her
cold, waxy neck, then her bluish wrist, feeling for a pulse.
There was none. Nor were there any apparent signs of a struggle. In fact, there were no visible signs of the cause of Laura's
death.

Little, moving his ankle, kicked against the leg of the
nightstand. A sticky soup spoon clattered to the ground. Sister Felicita groaned. Despite the unbearable heat in the room,
her teeth were chattering.

"Get her out of here," Little mouthed to Kemp. Or soon we'll have two corpses, he thought.

The spoon had fallen from an empty soup bowl. Bending over the table Little sniffed the contents. Tomato soup. Beside it, a small, empty brown pill bottle lay on its side. The prescription label was torn off, but a powdery film still adhered to the inside. It would be a piece of cake for the forensic team to discover what the bottle had contained.

"What do you make of it, Bob?" Kemp reentered the room.

"Looks like she may have overdosed." He pointed to the empty bottle. "Time and forensics will tell."

Kemp put his hands in his pockets and stared down at Laura's body. "Such a waste." He shook his head sadly and Little saw his bow tie bounce when he swallowed. "Why would someone so young and so beautiful kill herself? Unless you were right after all, Bob, and she did murder the boyfriend. That's the only way it makes sense." Kemp looked up at him with a kind of grudging admiration. "You've done it again, fellow, but this time I'll be damned if I can figure out exactly what made you come to that conclusion."

And I hope you never do, Little thought, leaving the sweltering bedroom to make all the necessary phone calls.

◆·I·◆   ◆·I·◆   ◆·I·◆

Inspectors Kate Murphy and Dennis Gallagher arrived back at the Hall of Justice at about four o'clock. Kate was tired and discouraged. Their door-to-door interviews with Mrs. Rosen's neighbors had yielded nothing more than sore feet and a slight headache. She sank back in her swivel chair and closed her eyes.

"Coffee?" Gallagher asked.

Kate shook her head. "By this time of day it tastes like battery fluid," she said.

"When's the last time you tasted battery fluid?" Gallagher muttered crankily, and without waiting for an answer, crossed the room toward the pot.

What a do-nothing day! Kate thought, conscious of the hum of traffic on the freeway outside the Hall. She hadn't even been able to talk to that Santa Cruz detective. She'd left a message. Now she wondered if he got it. She hoped this morning's meeting with Mrs. Johnson had done him some good. The day wouldn't seem quite so completely wasted if at least one case, somewhere, benefited from her efforts.

The sudden ring of her phone startled her. It took a few words before she recognized Bob Little's deep, friendly voice.

Yes, he had received Kate's message. Yes, their visit was helpful. He had been about to arrest the Johnson boy's girl-friend, Laura Purcell, when she was discovered dead. Suicide, which he took as an admission of guilt.

So Mrs. Johnson was right about Laura after all. Kate felt saddened rather than happy at the outcome. Something in her wanted Greg's mother to be as wrong about his choice as Kate thought she was about almost everything else. But life was never that simple.

"The others, of course, will be free to leave," Little said.

"Will be?" Kate asked, wondering how her two nun friends were faring.

"Yes, when I tell them," Little said, "which I plan to do the moment I get off this phone. So, case closed and thank you, Inspector, for your help. If there's ever anything I can do, I owe you one. And, if you're ever in Santa Cruz, stop by and let me buy you a drink."

Kate felt her face flush. Was that a come-on or did that deep, throaty voice just make it sound like one?

"Thanks, Sergeant," she said, and hung up quickly. No

sense even trying to figure it out. Jack was all the come-on she needed and she'd tell him so as soon as she saw him tonight. She missed their easy intimacy more than she'd ever imagined she would, and she hungered to have him back. No "place" was worth the toll it was taking on their lives. Tonight, even if it killed her, she'd make up.

The phone rang again. "Hi, hon." Jack sounded frustrated. "I'm going to be late," he said. "My case is breaking and—"

"I understand," Kate interrupted, trying not to let her annoyance show. "I'll be waiting for you when you get there," she said, hoping she sounded like a doting wife and not like a half-wit.

⁘ ⁘ ⁘

The digital clock on the bedstand read 2:32 when Kate finally heard Jack's key in the front door. She leaned over and switched on the bed lamp. Quickly, she ran a comb through her short red hair and put a drop of the Per Donna cologne on each wrist and on the nape of her neck. The delicate aroma of honeysuckle and jasmine floated on the air. Tonight, she was determined to make up, no matter what it took.

"Are you still awake, hon?" Jack sounded surprised. His jacket was off and he had unbuttoned most of his shirt on his way up the stairs.

"I'm waiting for you, pal," she said, hoping she sounded like Lauren Bacall.

"Are you getting a cold?" Jack yawned.

Kate felt her temper fizz. Deliberately, she calmed herself, threw the covers back, and patted the space beside her invitingly.

Jack let out a deep breath. "I'm beat." Giving her a perfunctory peck on the cheek, he climbed in. "Sleep tight," he said, turning off the light.

In the shadows, his back rose in a giant hump beside her. Fighting down the urge to punch him, Kate ran one finger down his spine. "Jack," she whispered, "don't go to sleep yet. I have something I want to tell you."

"Can't it wait, hon, I'm really zonked."

"It's important." Kate brought her lips close to his ear.

Jack rolled over. "Are you okay?" he asked.

Kate bit back her impatience. "Yes, pal, I'm just fine, but there's something I want to talk about."

Jack moaned. "At two-thirty in the morning?"

Leaning over him, Kate flipped the light back on. Subtlety and Per Donna were getting her nowhere. Tonight Jack required the direct approach. "I've made a decision about Cordero," she said, biting off each word.

Jack raised himself up on his elbow and stared. "Which is?" he asked, his face white with fatigue.

"I'll move," she said flatly.

"What?" Jack ran his fingers through his dark curly hair.

Kate loved it when he did that. She slipped her hand onto his thigh. "I'll move," she repeated.

"Why?"

"Because I've been thinking about it. Maybe you're right about raising little John outside the city . . . the weather, the safety . . ." Kate glanced over. To her surprise, her husband didn't look nearly as pleased as she expected him to. In fact, he was frowning. Maybe breaking the news to his mother was bothering him.

"Admittedly, your mother will have plenty to say." Kate's words tumbled out. She wanted so badly to put all the weeks of coldness behind them. "I'll try to defend you when you break the news, Jack, but you are the one who will have to do it. Much as I love you, pal, and I do love you, I am not going to tell Loretta Bassetti that her 'little family' is moving across a bridge! For all I know, she still believes in killing the messenger."

Jack let out a long breath. "I hadn't even thought about her reaction."

Kate shifted. "Then what the heck is bothering you? I thought you'd be ecstatic."

"What happened to 'whitebread'?" Jack asked.

"We'll deal with that when the time comes."

"And moving because everyone else is moving?"

"I didn't say that, your mother did," Kate snapped. If she was going to have to deal with every objection that was ever made to this move, it was going to be a very long night.

"What is it, Jack?" she asked. "What is bothering you?"

Jack's eyes avoided hers. "Since you were so opposed to the moving, I've been thinking about it, that's all. Maybe you have a point. Maybe we should just stay put."

Kate felt an unexpected flutter of relief. "So now you're the one who doesn't want to move?"

"No, that's not it, exactly." Jack put his arm around her shoulder. Swallowing her sudden roller coaster of disappointment, she snuggled into his familiar nooks and crannies.

"It's just that I hope we're not making a mistake," Jack said.

"If we are, it probably won't be our last." She reached over her husband to turn off the bed lamp.

"You know what else, pal?" she whispered, her mouth close to his. "What I really want to do tonight is make up. I've missed you so much, Jack. I need you." She felt his hands on her shoulders.

"What's that smell?" he asked sleepily.

"You mean the Per Donna?" Kate sighed and, lifting her head, brushed his nose. Maybe it was worth thirty-seven dollars an ounce after all.

"No, not that one."

It took several sniffs before Kate realized what smell he was talking about. Irate, she sat up. "You mean the baby powder on my hands?"

"I just love that smell," Jack said, reaching up to her and with both hands, slowly and tenderly, pulling her down to him.

◆I◆   ◆I◆   ◆I◆

Detective Sergeant Bob Little's announcement hit the dining room like a bomb. Even now, several hours later, Sister Mary Helen was still stunned.

It was amazing how quickly the five priests had left the mountaintop. In fact, by now, even with traffic, they should all be back in their respective rectories, wading through mail and messages in an effort to put the gruesome murder and suicide behind them.

To his credit, the monsignor had stopped long enough to offer Eileen and herself a ride back to Mount St. Francis College, but they refused. Felicita would be alone. Too tired to answer a lot of questions, she had decided to wait until morning to notify her Sisters.

But Mary Helen had an even more compelling reason for staying the night at St. Colette's. She did not want to face her own Sisters at the college—not until she had had time to sort out things for herself.

After tidying up the kitchen, the three nuns settled on director's chairs along the sundeck outside St. Jude's. Above the treetops the sky was flushed with peach, a sign that the sun was finally setting. Mary Helen checked her wristwatch. It was eight o'clock. Too late to begin a long walk in the woods. Too early to go to bed. The only thing to do was sit and mull over the happenings of the past few days.

"I'll never be the same," Felicita said.

She was right, of course. None of them would ever be quite the same after their retreat experience. And Felicita sounded amazingly cheerful about it. Mary Helen glanced over at the plump little nun. Felicita, who on Sunday had appeared as meek and mild as milk toast, now wore a crusty expression.

"I'll tell the world!" Felicita said with an unexpected fierceness in her pale blue eyes. Mary Helen suspected she would.

Without warning, Felicita yawned. "I'm going to call it a night," she announced, all reserve gone. "Tomorrow the D-Pest Control man comes early. And then I have to call Mother Superior and tell her that the nuns can come back. And I am going to insist that Sister Timothy get that blasted car fixed once and for all. And . . ." For a moment her voice faltered, but she caught herself. "And then, I am going to demand that, lawsuit or no lawsuit, we terminate Beverly Benton."

Her eyes shone and Mary Helen was tempted to sing, "Wimp No More My Lady." Under the circumstances, she thought better of it!

"Will you two be all right alone?" Felicita asked, finally remembering her role as hostess.

"We're fine, thanks." Mary Helen hoped Eileen wouldn't mind her speaking for both of them.

With a quick wave, Felicita disappeared into the shadows of St. Agnes' Hall. "The mouse roars," Eileen whispered with a grin.

Mary Helen laughed, glad finally to be alone with her friend. Since Sergeant Little's announcement, she'd been dying to ask Eileen what she thought, but she hadn't had an opportunity.

Clearly, Eileen was feeling the same. "What do you make of it all?" she asked the moment Felicita was out of earshot.

"I don't know what to think." Mary Helen was frankly baffled. "I would have bet my life on Laura Purcell's innocence." She paused to watch a curious blue jay land on the porch rail and eye them both.

Eileen nodded in agreement. "But Laura's suicide seems as good as an admission," she said gravely. "At least that's what Sergeant Little said. What do you think we missed?"

"I don't know." Mary Helen felt unsettled. "Something is not fitting together. The motive and the murderer should fit into a perfect whole. It's as if our thoughts lost their way, somewhere." She struggled to calm the mental maelstrom of uncertainty.

"Perhaps we're just losing our touch." Eileen studied her thumbnail. "Things like that do happen when you start to grow old."

"We've more than started," Mary Helen snapped, "and we've never been so far off."

Eileen squirmed in her chair. "What shall we do, then?" she asked.

Mary Helen shrugged, her eyes suddenly heavy. "What can we do? The girl is dead, the police are gone, and the case is closed." She drew in a deep breath and let it out slowly. "Maybe you are right, my friend, maybe we are losing our touch."

Bending forward, Eileen patted her hand. "Nonsense, old dear"—she had clearly jumped in on the other side—"after all, we can't win them all."

"I feel so sad about that girl." Mary Helen's words strained around the growing lump in her throat. "Sergeant Little assumes she killed herself because she was guilty and couldn't face the consequences. She just as easily could have been despondent. You saw how inconsolable she was today. If we'd only been able to discover Greg's murderer." She swatted at a mosquito diving dangerously close to her bifocals. "I am so sorry."

"What is it that St. Thomas Aquinas says?"

"About what?" Mary Helen was too tired to keep up.

"About sorrow?" Eileen thought for a moment. "It can be alleviated by a good sleep, a bath, and a glass of wine." She paused. "The wine went home with Father Tom, but two out of three should be good for something."

✦I✦   ✦I✦   ✦I✦

Unfortunately Mary Helen had to settle for a shower. And sleep still eluded her. She bounced on the mattress, punched the pillow, and flung out her feet, wrestling with the events of the last three days. No matter how hard she tried, she could not peacefully accept Sergeant Little's decision that Laura's suicide was a proof of her guilt. And why hadn't he bothered to toy with the idea that her death might not be suicide at all? Beyond her open window, the night was still and black. In the distance, she heard the short high trill of a screech owl. Closer to her, trees and bushes rustled in the warm breeze and scratched against the porch rail. An insect *ping*ed against her screen. Her sheet felt as cloying as a winding sheet, grabbing and binding her. She kicked it back, turned on the lamp, and reached for the Office book on her bedstand.

Paging through it, she looked for Compline, the last canonical hour of the day. "God commands you to pray, but forbids you to worry," some wise saint had said, and she knew it to be true.

Slowly, calmly, she began the prayers for the feast of Saints John Fisher and Thomas More.

"The saints endured many torments to gain the martyr's crown," the antiphon began. They surely did, Mary Helen thought. Both men were beheaded about two weeks apart because they stood up for what they believed was true against the powerful King Henry the Eighth.

Even when all of England accepted Henry as head of the Church, these two men refused. They followed their consciences and lost their heads for their trouble.

Nothing so drastic would happen to her if she refused to believe that Laura Purcell was a murderer, would it? Bob Little was no Henry the Eighth. She wouldn't lose her head, but she knew instinctively that it would not be easy to convince the sergeant that Laura was innocent or even that her death might not have been a suicide. But she, too, would follow her conscience.

Tomorrow, she thought drowsily, trying to focus on the psalm, she'd contact him. She'd tell him that she refused to accept his conclusion. The words on the page swam before her eyes. She'd insist he look further into Laura's death. For heaven's sake, no one even questioned Beverly's whereabouts. No matter how it came out, she knew she'd never rest until she had at least tried.

Mary Helen didn't even feel the Office book slip from her hands. Nor did she hear the soft thud as the book slid off the bed and sprawled open on the bedroom floor.

WEDNESDAY, JUNE 23

— ⚔ —

VIGIL OF THE BIRTH OF
ST. JOHN THE BAPTIST

— ⚔ —

DAY FOUR

Despite the trouble she had falling asleep, or maybe because of it, Mary Helen did not awake until the morning sun streamed into the room, making warm, thick strips across her bed. She was shocked when she checked her wristwatch. It was nearly nine o'clock.

If she didn't get up, the D-Pest Control man would be spraying around her in her nightgown. Not a pretty sight, she thought, dressing quickly.

She slipped on her windbreaker, just in case, and picked up the book on coastal plants and trees that Sister Blanche had insisted she bring. Mary Helen guessed that this morning was her last chance to explore the breathtaking mountaintop. Moreover, she suspected that she might never return to St. Colette's. The supposition made her sad.

After breakfast, she'd telephone Sister Anne, who, she presumed, would hurry right down. Not only was Anne accommodating, but she was desperately curious. If the nuns had wind of the murder, and Mary Helen couldn't imagine that they didn't, Anne would be dying to find out all about it.

Mary Helen listened. No sound came from the adjoining bedroom. Eileen was either up and out, or still sound asleep. She peeked in and was surprised to see that the bed was neatly remade and the used sheets, stuffed into a soiled pillowcase, were lumped in the corner. How in the world had she slept through all that?

Her head ached. She needed a cup of coffee quickly. She'd take care of her own bed later.

Fortunately, the small electric pot in the vestibule of St. Agnes' Hall was still half full and the coffee hot. Beside it, someone, presumably Felicita, had set a plate of bran muffins.

Mary Helen filled a styrofoam cup. Juggling her book and the muffin, she walked out into the morning. The sun was already warm and the air sticky. It was going to be another scorcher. The cool, wet June fog swirling around Mount St. Francis College would be a welcome sight.

Mary Helen blew on her coffee, then sipped. St. Colette's was still. Not a soul, not even a breeze, stirred. After all the activity and confusion of the last four days, it was suddenly a ghost center. Mary Helen was glad. She didn't feel up to company quite yet, even if it was only Eileen and Felicita. What she wanted was a little quiet, a little time to strengthen her resolve of last night.

A wooden bench had been built around the tall, thick sycamore tree behind St. Agnes'. Next to it was an old oaken tub full of Johnny-jump-ups blooming out of season. Perfect, Mary Helen thought, slipping off her jacket and leaning against the smooth white trunk.

She closed her eyes, breathing in the fragrant air. Suddenly she was aware that it was filled with trills, high-pitched pips, raspy *quees*, and tiny-tin-horn sounds as sparrows and crespin and cinnamon-colored towhees foraged for their breakfast.

A strong, high whistle rang out above the rest. The tune

was familiar. Something from a Broadway musical, if Mary Helen wasn't mistaken. Her eyes shot open. What species of bird whistles show tunes? she wondered, and laughed aloud when the D-Pest Control man rounded the corner with a cylinder of insecticide slung over one shoulder. In his hand he held a long pipe, which he guided along the building's foundation.

Actually, on closer examination, he was a she. The D-Pest Control man was the D-Pest Control woman. Or perhaps the D-Pest Control person was the politically correct term.

As she was dressed in a uniform of dark blue twill pants, a blue-and-white-striped shirt, and a blue baseball cap, at first glance it was difficult to tell which sex the controller was—especially since her blond hair was pulled back in a ponytail and she wore heavy brown hiking boots. At one time the earrings would have been a dead giveaway, but no more.

"Oh, hi!" The young woman sounded startled.

"I hope I didn't scare you," Mary Helen said.

The girl's face broke into a wide, friendly smile. "The whole place is so quiet," she said, "I just wasn't expecting to run into anyone." She balanced her cylinder against the edge of the bench. "Is that coffee I smell?"

"There's plenty right inside the front door. Help yourself," Mary Helen invited, and the young woman did.

"Whew!" she said, settling down on the bench. "It's sweltering already!" She removed her hat and studied the logo. A forlorn-looking nondescript bug in an Eton jacket had a stick and sack slung over his shoulder. "Makes you feel kind of sorry for him, doesn't it?" she said, and wiped her forehead with a clean, white handkerchief.

Before long, chatty Candy had introduced herself, announced that her father owned the company, and given Mary Helen more information than she needed or wanted.

Candy was a junior at the university; hated her nickname, would rather be called Candice; did not know either Greg Johnson or Laura Purcell, although she had read about their deaths in the *Santa Cruz Sentinel,* and she only worked for Daddy during the summer, since she did not really approve of killing living things.

Candy's true love was botany. She hoped someday to be a botanist. Her eyes gleamed when she noticed Mary Helen's plant book. She paged through it, pointing to the trees around them. Deftly, she explained the differences between a Douglas fir and a grand fir, the live oak and the scrub oak, the madrone and the California Bay.

"You won't find any of these trees around here," Candy stated. She pointed to a picture of the Santa Cruz cypress with a close-up of its tightly shut cones clinging to the tip of a branch.

"Why not?" Mary Helen studied the thick green twisted tree.

"Because they are found only in a few locations in the Santa Cruz Mountains. The place has to be dry." Candy batted at a mosquito. "And the tree only grows inland on marine soil deposits."

Candy sounded like a textbook. "In places like . . ." She let the sentence trail while she tried to remember. "Like Bonny Doon," she said finally.

In Bonny Doon? Mary Helen stared at the colored photo of the tight green cone. She had never been to Bonny Doon, but she had seen that cone before, somewhere. Caught somewhere. Where? She shuddered. Caught in the sole of Greg Johnson's tennis shoe!

All at once her own tight, caught thoughts exploded like a cypress cone in time-lapse photography, scattering tiny, brown-winged seeds into the air. Her thoughts floated freely, winging to the only conclusion possible.

Of course! She knew exactly who Greg's murderer was. It was the only person who made any sense. Surely Sergeant Little had seen the cone too. Then why hadn't he come to the same conclusion? She would call him and ask.

•┼• •┼• •┼•

Inspector Kate Murphy arrived at the Hall of Justice ten minutes late, which was a miracle of sorts. After making up last night, both she and Jack had slept through the alarm. The rush when John's hungry cry woke them was like something from an old Mack Sennett movie.

They barely spoke, knocking into one another in their haste to feed and dress the baby and themselves. Little John stared at them, fascinated at their antics, and clapped his hands and giggled happily when they bumped heads reaching for the same baby shoe.

"You go, hon," Jack said finally. "I'll finish dressing him and drop him by Sheila's. I worked late last night. No one expects me in on time."

Hearing the wail of the foghorns blowing in from the Golden Gate, Kate grabbed for her heavy coat and opened the front door. The wall of dripping fog made her shiver.

"Shall we both call in sick and go back to bed?" she asked, and could tell by his hesitation that Jack was tempted.

"On second thought, let's save it for a long weekend," she suggested, realizing they'd need all the time off they could accumulate for their move to Cordero. Even the thought of cleaning out this old house full of three generations of treasures from basement to attic exhausted her, but anything was worth it to be a happy family again.

Pumping gas into the cold engine, Kate compared the idea of moving from San Francisco to removing adhesive tape from a wound. The first pull hurts like hell. You stop. Pull

again. Stop. It still hurts, but not as much. Pull again. Finally
the whole thing comes off, and you look at the wound and
discover it's healing.

Kate flipped on the windshield wipers and shivered in the
icy car. She glanced up at the baby's bedroom where the thick
fog formed a halo around the lighted windows. Jack was right
about one thing—the weather! Sunshine in summer would be
good for them all.

"You're late," Dennis Gallagher growled when he saw
her. "I thought you were maybe sick, but one look at that
Irish mug of yours and I know you're not. In fact," he said,
studying her as if she were a bug in a bottle, "the bloom is
back in your cheeks, Kathleen! Things better?"

She nodded, although the details were none of his business. Not that that ever stopped Denny! What actually did
stop him was the loud entrance of Inspector O'Connor. For
once, Kate was glad to see him.

"You're late!" Gallagher turned on him. "Have trouble
leaving paradise?"

"It's that goddamn traffic on the way to the bridge.
Bumper to bumper and already it's sweltering, so cars are
overheating! Then, the bridge!" He did a theatrical swoon
into his desk chair. "Its name should be changed to the goddamn Golden Gate parking lot!"

"He exaggerates," Huegle called over from his desk. "I
heard Frank and Mike on the radio on my way to work and
they said that the bridge was moving at twenty miles per
hour. The whole thing isn't even two miles long. You must
have stopped off for breakfast."

Kate laughed, but she felt a flurry of dread in the pit of
her stomach. She knew what Jack and she were giving up.
Had she any idea what they were taking on?

She had just accepted a mug of coffee from Gallagher
when her husband slammed through the Detail door waving

the *Chronicle*. During their morning rush neither of them had even glanced at the headlines, let alone read the front page.

Jack pointed to the bottom left-hand corner. "Maybe I was right after all," he said. CORDERO POLICE BREAK UP KID ROBBERY RING, the headline shouted.

Scanning the article, Kate was shocked at the thieves' ages—some as young as nine—and at the extent and sophistication of their operation.

Finally, Jack's words sank in. "What do you mean, you were right?" She could feel her back get rigid. She squared her jaw. He was the one who'd initiated the idea of moving, who'd kept at it until their discussions became battles. It was he who had needled her about the crime in the city, about the weather, even about a place for little John to play, until she felt guilty.

He it was whose infuriating calm and patience finally convinced her that she was only being stubborn about leaving her home. It was he who had made her afraid that their baby was suffering from their difference of opinion. It was Jack who finally had made her give in and make up and agree to move. She turned on him cold with fury.

"Gotcha!" he said, his old playfulness returned.

The only thing that saved him from grave bodily harm was the insistent ringing of Kate's phone. She was surprised to hear her mother-in-law's voice, but not a bit surprised when Loretta Bassetti asked to speak to Jack. The woman had radar!

"Is everything all right?" Kate asked.

"Just fine," her mother-in-law huffed, "unless you consider having a nincompoop for a son a problem. Can I talk to him?"

"With pleasure!" Kate covered the receiver with her hand. "There is a God," she said, handing the phone to her husband. "It's your mother. I think she just read the paper."

"Hello, Ma," Jack said reluctantly.

Eager to eavesdrop without actually looking like it, Kate thumbed through the rest of the front section of the paper. On the next-to-last page, her eye caught a brief article about Greg Johnson's murder. The Santa Cruz Sheriff's Department was declaring Laura Purcell guilty and the case closed. She wondered what Sister Mary Helen thought of the outcome. She'd probably know soon enough.

"Yes, Ma, I read it. No, Ma, of course not . . ." Jack lowered his voice to a whisper in hopes of not being overheard. Kate moved closer.

"What do you mean irresponsible . . . You have to speak English, Ma. I don't know what those words mean. . . . Not that I want to."

Trying not to gloat, Kate glanced at her husband's frowning face. She could imagine the other side of the conversation.

"No, Ma. We are not moving. . . . We did discuss it. . . . Yeah, I know what I told you. But Kate and I talked about it . . . I know, Ma . . . We did decide not to . . ." He winked at Kate, who glared back at him.

"Ma, stop! I'm a grown man. . . . I swear if you bring up that motor scooter—I'm not raising my voice. . . . Yes, I love you, too. And Kate and John . . . Speaking of which . . . Sorry, Ma, I meant whom . . . I know he's a person. Listen, Ma, will you? Are you busy this weekend? I'd like to take Kate away for a romantic weekend."

Kate felt her anger start to thaw and with it came a sense of relief. She'd never have to look at the wound again. There wouldn't be one. Jack reached for her hand and she let him take it. The old familiar ease was back in their touch.

"You're right, Ma. I owe her one. Thanks. We'll drop the baby off late Friday afternoon. . . . Sure, if you want to, you can come to our house instead. If that's easier."

Kate's stomach pitched forward. What was he thinking? He'd given them just two nights to straighten up the house.

Jack squeezed her hand. Kate scowled at him. "Okay, Ma, thanks," he said. "I'll tell her."

"Tell me what?" she asked when he'd hung up.

"That I gotcha again! She hung up right after I said 'Friday afternoon.' "

"One of these days, Jack, I swear I'm going to murder you and even a hostile jury won't convict me." She tried to sound angry, but she didn't fool anyone, especially herself.

✦I✦ ✦I✦ ✦I✦

Sister Mary Helen was surprised at how quickly Sergeant Bob Little responded to her call. She'd scarcely had time to plan her strategy when she heard the squeal of tires in the parking lot.

The moment she laid eyes on him, she knew no strategy was necessary. His face had paled beneath the deep tan and his brown eyes were red-rimmed and haunted, as if he had spent all night escaping demons.

As he approached her his tall frame stooped a little and he ran his knuckles over his mustache as if it itched.

To the unpracticed eye, he might look ill, but Sister Mary Helen knew that what ailed him was beyond the scope of the most skilled physician. When an ancient Greek, Polybius, said, "There is no witness so dreadful, no accuser so terrible as the conscience that dwells in the heart of every man," he could have been looking at Little's face. Clearly the sergeant was a man with something on his conscience and he wanted to get it off.

Without meeting her eyes, Bob Little led Mary Helen to the gift shop off the main lounge. The room was as cramped and airless as she remembered. For the first time, it struck her that there was a "confessional" feeling about it: small, dark, enclosed, secret.

Little motioned her to a chair, and quickly sat down beside her. With a hollow, mirthless laugh, he pointed to the large poster on the wall. " 'Truth will rise above falsehood, as oil above water,' " he read aloud. "I guess that's what this is all about. Right, Sister?"

Mary Helen nodded, but said nothing.

Little gave a weary sigh. "Where do I begin?" He was having trouble getting his tongue around the words, as if his mouth were dry and parched. He rubbed at his mustache.

"Tell me about Laura," Mary Helen prodded gently.

"Laura!" The large man stretched back in his chair searching the ceiling for his words. He cleared his throat. "That poor kid was innocent, but you know that. More than likely, she was murdered herself, although the coroner's report will never be conclusive." His voice cracked. "The girl was distraught, stole or found sleeping pills, and took too many. Who's to prove otherwise?"

"And the cypress cone caught in the sole of Greg Johnson's shoe. How will the forensic team explain that?"

Little's anxious eyes searched her face. "Oh, you know about the cone, too. Then you must know that around here it grows in the Bonny Doon area. You're something." He shook his head in grudging amazement. "I suppose you figured out why a smart cop like me didn't remember that Beverly lived in that area and that she had access to a kitchenful of knives besides? I supposed you've figured out why it is that I didn't arrest Beverly Benton for murder?"

"No, Bob," she said honestly. "I didn't figure that out. To tell you the truth, that is what has me stumped." Her palms were wet and the muscles in her neck and shoulders cramped with tension as she watched him wrestle with the truth.

"Because I'm gay!" he blurted out. His eyes blazed, daring

her to say something, anything, that would let him vent his anger.

A swirl of disbelief washed over her. Only the buzz of a horsefly broke the quiet of the small room. She hoped her surprise didn't show on her face. Still, that was no answer. Why would he allow an innocent girl to take the blame for a murder she didn't commit just to cover up his sexual preference. It made no sense to her.

"What does that have to do with anything?" she asked as evenly as she could.

"Didn't you hear me? I said, I'm gay!"

"I heard you and I'm asking you again, what does that have to do with anything?"

"You really don't know, do you?" he said, his brown eyes hawk-sharp. "I'm gay and Beverly knows it."

"How would she know that?"

Little gave a nervous laugh. "She saw me a couple of weeks ago at the Gay Pride Week celebration here in Santa Cruz. It was a risk going, I guess, but it was a lot of fun. Terry and I went to the Blue Lagoon and Beverly must have seen us there. Over the weekend we went for salsa lessons at the Methodist Church hall, and that's where I remember noticing her.

"When I first saw her at the retreat center, I realized that I knew her from somewhere. You know how you do?" He was almost talking to himself. "It really bugged me, but when someone is out of context . . ."

Mary Helen sympathized. She had that trouble all the time.

"Then when I heard her laugh while I was with Loody, it all came back to me. I guess I recognized that laugh from the dancing lessons. I couldn't believe it."

"That still doesn't explain why you didn't arrest her if you suspected that she was guilty."

"You really don't get it, do you, Sister?" His tone begged her to understand, but she didn't. He sat forward with a thud that startled Mary Helen. "If I made the arrest, Beverly had threatened to blow open my secret. 'To explode your queer ass right out of the closet,' as she sweetly put it! Already she's dropped subtle hints to Loody that she has something on me, although he's not sure exactly what. I can tell by the insolent way he looks at me. That guy is an obnoxious, bigoted bastard on his best day. I wouldn't want to give him any ammunition. I just couldn't risk him knowing that I'm a gay cop. At first, I thought I'd do anything to keep it from him."

Maybe twenty years ago, but still? Mary Helen wanted to ask, but the misery on Little's face stopped her.

"Do you have any idea what it means if it gets out that I'm gay, Sister?" Little's question reverberated through the small room. "It means that I'll be the butt of hundreds of jokes, the object of thousands of double-meaning witticisms. I will be looked upon with disgust and hatred and suspicion. My judgment will be questioned. No one will want to have a beer with me in case they get contaminated by association. I will be distrusted, snubbed, humiliated, debased, disenfranchised, and we are not even talking about anyone thinking I have AIDS. Then, someday, I may even get a bullet in my back, a friendly bullet, of course, by accident!"

Despite the heat in the room, Mary Helen shivered. "But you are a very successful homicide detective," she said softly, trying to reason with his terror. "I can tell that you are well liked by the other officers. It's obvious that Deputy Kemp tries to emulate you. You are a good, kind person and an insightful detective. Wouldn't that count for something?"

Little's face contorted in anguish. He stared at her. His eyes narrowed. "That wouldn't count for shit, Sister!" he shouted. "Not for shit!"

Unexpectedly his bottom lip quivered. "What am I going

to do?" he pleaded. "I haven't been able to sleep and when I do, I dream of that innocent girl being murdered with me watching it happen. I can't let Beverly go free." He smiled wryly. "I guess I absorbed too much of that Catholic guilt at Holy Cross. And I can't arrest her." His eyes searched Mary Helen's face for help, but she couldn't give any. There was really only one thing for him to do.

"What will I do? What? What?" he chanted, slumping forward in his chair. Suddenly, he covered his face and wept.

Sister Mary Helen reached over and touched his thick brown hair. She ached for this lovely young man and wished she could think of something to say to console him. . . . Some way she could make doing the right thing, the just thing, easy for him. Even as she wished that she could remove this suffering, she knew that it was part of life, everyone's life.

It belonged to the mystery of the Cross. Jesus' own suffering raised questions about all the suffering in our world. Why must innocent people be hurt? Why do the young die? How can a loving God permit so much prejudice and violence and abuse?

And the Cross would always remain a mystery, as does God's plan for each of us. The only thing we can do is embrace it with courage and with faith.

"Do what you know is right, Bob," she whispered around the lump in her own throat. "Just do what you know is right!"

I *I* *I*

Sergeant Bob Little hadn't been gone five minutes when Mary Helen ran into Sister Eileen.

"I've been looking all over for you! I was beginning to worry, although I don't know what could possibly have happened to you, unless you fell or something. Which you obviously didn't." Eileen was dithering. "When I couldn't find you, I went ahead and called Sister Anne, God love her, and she says she'll start right now and be here to pick us up in about an hour. I was on my way to fix us some lunch. I met Felicita, who'd just finished with the bug man—woman— person. . . ." She corrected herself. "And Felicita looks as if she could use a pick-me-up."

"Do you want some help?" Mary Helen offered halfheartedly. "Not that you need any."

For the first time since they'd run into each other, Eileen actually looked at her. "You're exhausted," she said. "I thought you slept in. Where have you been?"

Sister Mary Helen was still too shaken to explain. There'd be plenty of time once they got back to the college. She'd tell Eileen all about her conversation with both the bug person and Sergeant Little, but not before she'd digested it all herself.

Fortunately Eileen was too preoccupied to insist on an answer. Instead, she rushed on. "Maybe it's the heat, but whatever it is, you look as if you need a rest. And I'd suggest getting all the rest you can. According to Anne, everyone at home is anxious for us to get there. No one wants to believe the rumors that are flying around the hill."

Mary Helen felt her stomach drop. "Which are?"

"That we actually stumbled on another murder."

"And how are we going to answer that?" Mary Helen asked, hoping Eileen would pull a good offense from somewhere.

"I say let's not shake hands with the Devil till we meet her." She rolled her gray eyes heavenward. "And we've got at least two hours' grace before we have to, so let's enjoy. Why don't you find a nice cool place and I'll be with you in no time flat. Will tuna salad be okay?" Eileen threw the words over her shoulder like spilled salt.

"Anything at all," Mary Helen called, watching her friend bustle toward the kitchen.

Mary Helen pulled open the door of the deserted chapel, genuflected, and slid into the cool back pew. The late morning sun struck the flame in the stained-glass window and shot fiery reds and blues across the sanctuary and over the front pews. The enormous dove leapt from the core of the flame like Hopkins's ". . . Holy Ghost over the bent / World broods with warm breast and with ah! bright wings."

She repeated the words over and over. It brought her comfort to remember that God's love hovers over us all, embraces us all.

Silently, she prayed for Bob Little, for the strength to do what he knew he should. She wished there were something more she could do for him, but she knew it was best to place him in God's loving care.

She prayed to St. John the Baptist, whose vigil was being celebrated today, and asked him to touch Bob Little with his own lionhearted courage. If what the young man says is true, she thought sadly, he'll need every bit of it.

She gazed through the glass chapel wall, contemplating the trees beyond. Although the panorama was breathtaking, Mary Helen was even more certain than she'd been earlier this morning that she'd never come back to St. Colette's. Disturbing memories lurked at every turn. In fact, she'd probably never make another annual retreat without being haunted by this one.

Mary Helen was so absorbed in her own thoughts that she jumped when Felicita tapped her on the shoulder.

"The telephone for you. Take it in the office," Felicita whispered. "It's Sergeant Little."

With a feeling of dread, Mary Helen picked up the receiver. "Yes, Bob?" she said.

"I did it." His voice was low with emotion. "I arrested Beverly. When I realized she was at the rally, well, that put me on the right track. I was able to figure that she might have a motive. . . ." His words were stop and go. "I don't know who was more surprised when I arrested her, she or I."

Relief made Mary Helen's knees melt and she buckled into the desk chair. "For Greg's murder and Laura's death, too?"

"Affirmative," he said, all at once more businesslike. "When I first read her her rights, she raged like a madwoman, which she well may be, accusing Monsignor McHugh of the crime."

Mary Helen was stunned. "Why the monsignor?"

"Seems she had a bad experience with his temper as a child in San Francisco. Something about losing his temper in the confessional and it made her hate all priests. The monsignor, of course, didn't have a clue who she was.

"When the first heat was over and she knew I wasn't going to change my mind, she broke. I think even she was shocked by what she had done, especially, if you can believe it, about killing the dogs."

"Did she tell you why she murdered them?"

"She didn't mean to. She only wanted to sedate them because she knew they would bark and chase her car when she drove away."

"No." Mary Helen dismissed the answer impatiently. "Greg and Laura! Did she tell you why she killed them?"

"With Greg it was flat-out jealousy. As I think I indicated earlier, Beverly is a lesbian. She wanted all of Laura's attention and affection. She thought that if she did away with Greg . . ." He let the sentence dangle.

Each of Little's answers raised another question in Mary Helen's mind. "How did Beverly persuade Greg to go to the grotto without making any commotion?" she asked. "If any one of us had heard him . . ."

"Let me tell you what she told me." He sounded eager to get through with her questions. "Beverly called Laura's number, which she, of course, knew. She pretended to be from Dominican Hospital and told Greg his mother was in Emergency."

"Why would he believe her?" Mary Helen wondered.

"I don't know, Sister, but when they are awakened in the middle of the night, most people aren't thinking too clearly. Remember, this guy was also full of bubbly, which didn't help make him any more logical. Anyway, by the time he arrived, he was probably beginning to have some doubts and when he saw Beverly, they struggled."

Little cleared his throat. "Beverly's a strong woman and he fell and hit his head against the car door. She shoved him into the car and drove him to the entrance. When he came to, he didn't have any idea how long he'd been out. Anyway, she took advantage of that. Beverly had the knife at his throat and told him that she had Laura at the grotto and if he made any sound she'd kill him first and then kill Laura.

"You can imagine how quickly and how quietly the guy got up there. When he saw the place was empty, he turned, but she was on him. You saw the results."

Mary Helen's stomach roiled. "Why did she murder Laura?" she asked softly.

"Because Laura wanted no part of her. Their meeting in the bedroom must have been brutal. Enraged that she had killed for no reason, Beverly dissolved sleeping pills in Laura's soup and sent an unsuspecting Sister Felicita over with it on a tray. Later she slipped into the room, put the overturned vial on the bedstand, and figured I'd call it suicide!"

"How do you account for Greg getting the acorn stuck in

the sole of his shoe?" she asked quickly, sensing Little's growing impatience to get off the phone. "Did she take him to
Bonny Doon?"

Little gave a dry cough. "The acorn that gave you the
break, you mean? As far as I can figure, Beverly never went
near Bonny Doon, but the carpet of her car was full of stuff
from living in the country. You know what I mean?"

Mary Helen did. Sister Therese was always complaining
about the twigs and leaves that appeared on the carpet of the
convent's Nova from just getting in and out at the Mount.

"Somehow, he must have stepped on it when he was
getting out," Little said.

An awkward silence filled the line while Mary Helen
searched for a way to frame the next question tactfully. There
was none. "Did Beverly threaten to expose you?" Mary Helen
asked, dreading the answer.

"Yeah, she did. But don't worry." Little's voice was thick.
"I talked to Terry and regardless of what happens, he'll stick
by me. With him I'll get through this. I'm a survivor!" The
old good humor was slowly returning.

"And you know what, Sister?"

Mary Helen could not imagine what else.

"The two dogs were drugged with the same pills as Laura.
Beverly crushed them into their water. Like I said, she had no
intention of killing them. She just wanted them out for a
while. Beverly really loved those dogs and was distraught
when she went looking for them on Monday and found them
dead."

Mary Helen imagined Little shaking his head in amazement.

"I guess nobody's all bad!" he said.

"Nobody is all bad!" Little's words haunted Mary Helen
as she slipped back into the chapel pew. And nobody is all
good either, she thought. We are all just human beings.

She thought of the five priests, back in their own parishes by now. And who, she was sure, after this retreat experience would never be the same. The renowned monsignor, a dedicated, faithful man who still struggled to conquer the quick temper that had planted the seeds of hate in a young child. Ed Moreno ministering compassionately to the lost children in God's flock, without ever being able to own his own feelings. The extremely talented Tom Harrington with a drinking problem. Zealous, good-hearted Andy Carr unaware of his own goodness. Young, sensitive Mike Denski, yet to find meaning in his commitment.

Maybe that was what this retreat was all about—facing our shortcomings, acknowledging our strengths, and allowing God to love both. For she knew with certainty that God does love each of us individually—the priests, Greg and Laura, Bob Little and Terry, Sisters Felicita, Eileen, and herself, Eric Loody, and Beverly Benton!

God looks on us and the mess we have made of the graces He gives us, yet He continues to love us gently, deeply. There is nothing we can ever do that will change it.

In this quiet, beatific spot, she was suddenly overwhelmed by the reality of God's unconditional love. Maybe that was the fruit of any retreat: realizing that great love and then spending our lifetime trying to extend the same unconditional love to one another.

The chapel door swung open. Eileen stuck her head in. "Tuna salad is ready when you are," she whispered.

Slowly Mary Helen rose to join her.

"You will never guess what Sister Felicita asked me." Eileen's wrinkled face glowed with amusement.

Mary Helen bit. "What?"

"She asked me if I would consider staying on and being the cook here at St. Colette's. And . . ." She paused. Mary Helen waited for the punch line.

"And . . ." Eileen's bushy eyebrows rose. "She wanted to know if I thought you, old dear, would like to stay on and be my assistant!"

"Me? The cook's assistant?" Mary Helen repeated incredulously. All at once, facing the music at Mount St. Francis College didn't seem like such a bad prospect after all!